Off the Beaten Path

TALES OF ADVENTURE
ALONG THE WAY

STACY MONSON * ELEANOR BERTIN
SARA DAVISON * DEB ELKINK
JOHNNIE ALEXANDER

Welcome To
The Mosaic Collection

We are sisters, a beautiful mosaic united by the love of God through the blood of Christ.

Several times a year, The Mosaic Collection releases faith-based novels and anthologies in a variety of genres. Our stories range from romance and suspense to literary and women's fiction.

Join our Mosaic reader family and discover soul-affirming stories of truth and hope at www.mosaiccollectionbooks.com

Join our Reader Community, too!

Find us at www.facebook.com/groups/TheMosaicCollection

To read more about The Mosaic Collection authors and all our books, scan the QR code below.

Jesus answered, "I am the way and the truth and the life ..."

~ John 14:6a (NIV)

CONTENTS

THE COPPER HART
COFFEE
Cafe
The
POETIC
BAKER
— THE MONTANA SERIES —
STACY MONSON

THE POETIC BAKER

A Small Town Romance About Faith, Baking, and Starting Over
(Hartwell Mountain Romance #1)

Stacy Monson

After an unexpected layoff shatters her carefully planned life, Delaney Hutchins retreats to the only things that bring her joy: writing poetry and baking. But passion doesn't pay the bills, and practicality is pulling her back toward the safety of corporate life. Everything changes when she sets out on vacation and meets Patrick Finch, Montana's handsome architect—a man whose structured blueprints couldn't be more different from her flourish of words and flour. As he challenges her to build a life that's truly her own design, Delaney must decide: Will she play it safe or risk everything to create something beautiful?

Trust in the Lord with all your heart and lean not on your own understanding; in all your ways submit to him, and he will make your paths straight.
~ Proverbs 3:5–6 (NIV)

In their hearts humans plan their course,
but the Lord establishes their steps.
~ Proverbs 16:9 (NIV)

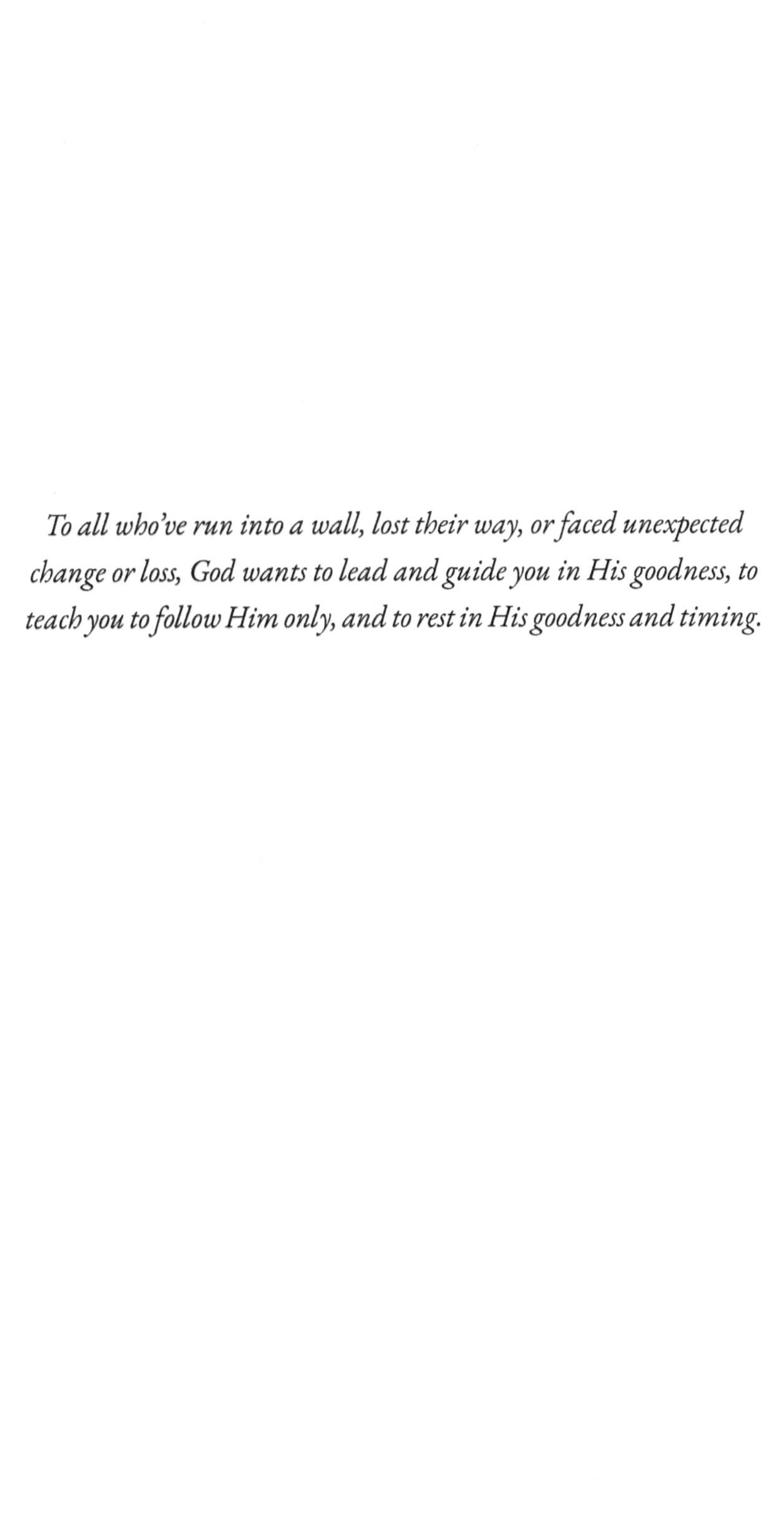

To all who've run into a wall, lost their way, or faced unexpected change or loss, God wants to lead and guide you in His goodness, to teach you to follow Him only, and to rest in His goodness and timing.

CHAPTER 1

TGIF. It had become Delaney Hutchins's mantra the past few months. She'd started living for Fridays. She pulled open the glass door of the downtown Minneapolis office building, still startled to see the new company name, and stepped into the cool air. Greeting Jeff, the security guard, with a wave, she called, "How's your wife?"

"Much better." His smile widened. "Thanks for the prayers."

She offered a thumbs-up as she passed between the security panels. When he'd confided about his wife's illness, she'd prayed with him then and continued to inquire about her. He'd been one of the first people she met when she started at POST ten years ago and was still one of her favorites.

Exiting the elevator on the tenth floor that housed part of her accounting team, she greeted Jillian, her assistant, before going into her office. She set her computer bag and purse beside her desk and dropped into her chair.

Jillian joined her with two cups of coffee and settled into a chair in front of the desk. "So what's on the calendar for this weekend?"

Delaney accepted the cup with a quick thanks and shrugged. "Not much. Cleaning. Laundry."

"Bryan doesn't have a hot date planned?"

"He's working all weekend because of the merger." Jillian was more excited about Delaney dating Bryan Johnson, the handsome Human Resources Manager, than she was. "Dating" was a loose term for their two-year relationship. "I live vicariously through you, so what do *you* have planned?"

Jillian launched into a weekend itinerary that exhausted Delaney just listening to it. While Jill was petite, blonde, and outgoing, Delaney was the opposite—tall, dark, reserved. She'd been so focused on making sure her parents were cared for these past few years that she wasn't sure she'd know fun if it came up and introduced itself. But, strangely, she'd felt restless lately, struggling to stay focused at work, which had never been a problem. Yearning for . . . something. It had started before the company was bought out several months ago, intensifying since then. She was off-balance, which was annoying. She liked balance.

As their morning chat ended, Jillian moved to the door, then paused and looked back. "Del, are you okay?"

"Sure. Why?"

"You've just seemed"—Jillian lifted her shoulders—"a bit off lately. Distracted or something. Just not yourself. Hey, wait." Frowning, she stepped back into the office. "Are you quitting?"

"No! But . . ." She leaned her forearms on the desk, lips pursed. "I guess I have been a little off. I don't know why. Early menopause?"

Jillian laughed. "I don't think that can happen, since you aren't even thirty yet."

"I will be in three months." She couldn't discuss something she didn't understand herself. "I guess I'm getting antsy for summer, so being outside this weekend will be great."

"When was the last time you took a vacation? A real one, not just helping your parents."

Delaney shrugged.

"You need one." Tapping her chin, she studied Delaney. Then her eyes lit. "I know! My parents have a cabin in Montana. Nothing fancy, but it's peaceful and has a beautiful view."

"Sounds lovely." More than lovely. A refuge. "I don't have time."

"To get out of here and focus on baking and poetry? Yes, you do. Now, I'll call my mom to find out what their schedule looks like this summer. You need to make time for a couple weeks away to get recharged."

A quiet space to write. Some down time to bake. She held back a sigh. "Thanks, Jill, but with this merger, I've got tons of paperwork, and—"

Jillian held up a hand as she turned away. "You're welcome," she said in a singsong voice. "I'll shoot you some dates."

Delaney looked at the closed door, a sudden war under her ribs. To have uninterrupted time to write, in the mountains, away from her boring life . . . Nope. Not now, when they were barely into the merger. Vacation could come later, after things around here were settled. But it gave her something to look forward to.

An hour later, Jillian stepped into her office just as Delaney's phone rang. She held up a finger and answered the call from Maureen's assistant. "Hi, Jeanie."

"Hi, Delaney. Maureen would like to see you in her office for a few minutes. Are you able to come up?"

"Right now?"

"Yes. She said it won't take long."

"I'll be right up." Delaney replaced the receiver, lips pursed. That was unusual.

"A summons from the Queen Bee?" Jillian asked.

With a snort at the nickname, Delaney pushed to her feet. "Maybe some new projects for the team. Hard to tell with all the merger changes. Be prepared for whatever she throws at us."

"Yes, ma'am," Jillian said with a grin and returned to her desk.

Delaney gathered her phone and the neon yellow "Maureen" folder. As she passed Jillian's immaculate desk, she winked. "You rock," she said.

"I know."

Still smiling as she exited the elevator on the hushed top floor, she approached Jeanie, fighting the urge to tiptoe. "How was your weekend?" she asked the older woman.

"Fine, thank you. Go right in."

The smile faded at the woman's abrupt response. Rounding the corner to Maureen's office, she knocked and entered at the summons. The spacious office was eerily quiet as she stepped in and faced four people seated around the meeting table.

Nerves on alert, she approached the open chair, greeting first Maureen and then the executive VP beside her. Having an EVP in the meeting was disconcerting. Completing the circle was Bryan and . . . Jeff from Security?

"Have a seat," Maureen said. She added, "Thank you for being so prompt this morning."

Delaney nodded, keeping her gaze away from Bryan, and breathed slowly as her heart rate ramped up.

"Delaney," Maureen said, hands clasped on the table, "you've been with the company for ten years and, from what I've read, been an excellent employee. Your management style has been exemplary. I've certainly enjoyed getting to know you since the merger. You are highly regarded here, and you should be proud of your tenure."

A promotion? She smiled politely. "Thank you."

"That makes this an especially difficult conversation to have."

Her breath caught. Not a promotion. "Are you firing me?"

"This isn't a performance issue, Delaney. It's simply part of a layoff as the reorganization takes shape. Sadly, there are numerous middle management positions like yours being eliminated. There's far too much overlap in accounting, not to mention that automation is becoming more the norm."

Simply part of a layoff? Being "eliminated" wasn't simple to her. "I'd be happy to move to a different position, even a different area." She'd miss her teams like crazy.

"There isn't a position that matches your pay grade or skill level. Placing you in a specialist role would be a demotion for you. Some of those positions are also being phased out. Mergers are never easy. Changes must be made, exemplary employees let go as positions are terminated."

From her salt-and-pepper hair smoothed back into a bun to her red cat-eye glasses and the heavy jewelry accessorizing her tailor-made suit, she was every bit senior management. Delaney leaned back against the chair on which she'd perched and moved her gaze around the circle as she tried to absorb the words. While

Bryan shuffled papers, the other three regarded her with somber expressions. "When will this be effective?"

"Now."

She sat up straight, eyes wide. "Now? As in right now?"

Jeff's presence suddenly made sense. She was being escorted out.

CHAPTER 2

Never one to fall apart emotionally, Delaney was exhausted and confused by the crying jag that hit after the termination. She kneaded out her frustrations on bread dough and then wrote angry poetry until falling asleep on the couch.

Saturday morning she indulged in a pity party and stayed in sweats, eating every sweet she could find in the condo and watching mindless movies. A knock at the door startled her out of a doze. She straightened her sweatshirt and trudged across the room to peek through the peephole. Bryan. Drawing a slow breath, she set her shoulders and opened the door. Dressed casually in khakis and a polo shirt, he clutched a bouquet of roses.

"Hi." His smile wavered. "Can we talk?"

She stepped back and let him in, then turned away and settled in the rocker. He followed and stood awkwardly in front of her, holding out the bouquet. She set it aside on the table and motioned for him to sit on the couch.

"So." Elbows on his knees, he clasped his hands and looked at the floor for a moment. "I'm sorry for how things turned out at work."

"Mm-hmm." She adjusted her ponytail. Just another day at the office for him.

"I fought for you, Dela," he added, using the nickname she'd asked him not to use. "You have a great reputation and a strong work ethic. Everybody likes you at the company." He reached a hand toward her. "I told Maureen it would be a mistake to let you go, but it just couldn't be worked out."

She folded her arms. As the popular head of Human Resources, Bryan Johnson seemed to be everywhere and know everything and everyone. Tall, lean, blond and blue-eyed, he was the dream date of most of the women in the company. For some reason, he'd decided she was the one worthy of his attention.

He smoothed his hair and shifted on the couch. "Dela, there's something I've wanted to talk to you about. Long before yesterday happened."

It had been two years of occasional dating, and he'd no doubt come to break it off. "Bryan, if you don't want to keep dating, or whatever it is we're doing, it's okay. I won't fall apart."

"No! I want to spend *more* time with you, not less. Dela, let's get married. We've been together for almost two years, and I think it's the right next step."

Her mouth dropped open. Laid off one day, proposed to the next. What was happening to her life?

His eyes were bright, his face slightly flushed. His words came more quickly as she stared at him, unable to pull in a breath.

"Everyone thinks we're a great team," he said, then winked and added, "and we do make a pretty good-looking couple. Maybe one day we could even start our own company. I'd handle the hiring and firing, and you'd be the brains behind the scenes. We'll be great together! What do you think?"

In all her childhood dreams, getting a marriage proposal that sounded more like a business transaction had never come up. She shook her head slowly. "You think now, the day after I got laid off, is a good time for this discussion? Bryan, you sat there and had me sign forms before they booted me out onto the street!"

"It wasn't personal. I had no choice. Those were my job duties. I honestly tried to keep you out of the layoffs, but I don't have the clout. I'm going to keep campaigning to get you back. I wish I'd asked you this a week ago. It would have been much easier for both of us." He leaned toward her. "I'm hoping this will give you something to look forward to, until you get your next job."

She rubbed her face, exhausted and confused. She hadn't known he was this serious about her. But he'd known she would be laid off and never said a word. Not that he could, as the HR manager, but still . . .

And now here she sat in sweatpants and a ratty T-shirt, unemployed, having hardly slept, and he was proposing. Sort of. She looked at him through gritty eyes, the handsome young man others swooned over at the office. His name often came up at meetings as "the one to watch" for upper management. She could do a lot worse.

He abruptly knelt before her and took her hand between his. "Delaney, I would be honored if you'd be my wife."

"Bryan, this is so . . ." Bizarre. "We've never talked about a future together or what our dreams are. Maybe we aren't even headed in the same direction." She slid her hand away and stood. "I had no idea you were this serious about our relationship. I need to adjust to being laid off first and figure out what my next steps are."

He stood. "Okay. Sure. This is a tough time for you." A boyish smile grew. "If I know I have a chance, I'll wait however long it takes."

"I don't know what to think about anything. It may take a while." She went to the door, tears threatening.

He followed and stopped before her. "Got it. I messed up. How about we go out to dinner tonight and talk about our future, what we want to do together? That will cheer you up. Then I'll take a do-over on the proposal in a week or so, which will give you time to think about what to wear and who we'll tell first. How's that?"

For a man who seemed so put together, so sophisticated at work, he was astonishingly clueless. "No. I don't want to go out or even talk about this anymore. I'm just . . ." She put a hand to her pounding temple. "I'm tired." And sad, and scared.

"Okay. I'll go so you can rest. We'll talk in a few days, okay? Go lie down for a bit. You do look tired."

She closed the door and slumped against it. What just happened? Could her life get any weirder? She needed a good cry, some aspirin, and sleep.

Delaney called her parents after dinner to share the events of the last few days, from the busy week to the termination and then the proposal. As she expected, they were angry and heart-broken for her.

Finishing the story with a sigh, she said, "Maybe I should accept because it might be my only offer. I could do worse."

"Absolutely not!" her father declared. Though the stroke had slowed his speech, Dad was unafraid to speak his mind. He hadn't been shy about his opinion that Bryan wasn't the right guy for her. "You don't marry someone you aren't crazy about, and you never, ever settle for less than God's best for you."

"I'm not sure I know what His best is." She closed her eyes against the sudden burn and dropped her head back against the chair. Nearly thirty years old and whining to her father.

"You'll know. Forcing these things works against us, and against God."

She'd never felt this lost or uncertain. She preferred order, routine, and being in charge of her life.

"Laney, you have the gift of time now. Go on a trip or visit your sister. Get a fresh perspective."

Alone? That hardly sounded fun. Although getting away was tempting.

"Think about it. Your mom and I will support you in whatever you do, except if you decide to marry Bryan."

She laughed. "I just wish I knew what direction to go, what God wants me to do."

"Keep asking. We'll be praying too. Now, your mother has practically climbed onto my shoulders to get to the phone. Here you go. Love you, honey."

"Thanks, Dad. Love you too."

Delaney knew they were right. She needed a change of scenery and a new perspective. She'd been strangely at odds with her life the past six months, so what better time to reset than being unemployed?

She grabbed her purse and headed to the car. They'd eliminated her job and kept her electronics. She'd picked up a phone after the termination but, if she wanted to plan an adventure, she needed a computer and a good GPS.

CHAPTER 3

Talking about going on an adventure was easier than planning one. With the world at her fingertips, she could go on a cruise or safari, discover Europe. She could drive, fly or travel by train. Revived by a fresh cup of coffee, Delaney plopped back down at the computer and asked the cyberworld for suggestions. A list of states popped up with "Things to do while in . . ." and she half-heartedly skimmed it, then stopped. Montana. While her family had taken road trips years earlier, they'd always sped through Montana toward other locales. She'd been mesmerized by the mountains, disappointed they couldn't explore.

The vacation conversation with Jillian leaped to mind, and she straightened. She'd mentioned her parents' cabin. She could start with a small town, get a feel for something completely different. She sent a text asking where it was and how soon she could rent it, then returned to the online information with renewed energy.

A knock at the door made her glance at the clock and blink in surprise. She'd been so immersed in discovering Montana that two hours had passed. Jill had responded with the name of Hartwell, a small town in the southern part of the state. Excitement kept her scrolling and jotting notes—

Another knock, and she went to the door. "Hi, Arlene." The elderly neighboring tenant in the condo.

"Hi, dear. When I went down for my mail, this package was there, so I brought it up to you." The older woman cocked her gray head. "I didn't think you'd be home on a Monday. Are you ill?"

"No, just took the day off." And tomorrow and Wednesday and . . . She reached for the small package. "Thank you for delivering this. Have a good afternoon."

"You're welcome. You have a nice day, too, and let me know if you need anything."

Delaney nodded and closed the door, grateful to have been able to cut the conversation shorter than usual. Dear Arlene was lonely. And very nosy.

She sat at the kitchen table to open the package from Dad. The square brown box held a smaller jewelry box and a folded notecard. She opened the box and gasped. Grandpa's compass! One of his most-prized possessions, Dad had taken such care of it since Grandpa's death ten years ago. She unfolded the note.

Laney, Mom and I are praying for you at this crossroads in your life. It's a great opportunity for you to find out who you were truly created to be. I'm hoping Grandpa's compass will remind you to look to God for direction as you head out on a new journey. I know it will be in good hands. And I know it will help you find your way home.
Love, Dad (and Mom)

Tears formed. The handwriting was his with a wobble now, but his heart was as strong and faithful as ever. She brushed her fingers across its patina, the compass worn and faded after decades of use. Grandpa had received it as a child, and he'd passed it to her father when he was young.

She pressed the tiny button, and the cover eased open. The N, S, E, and W were clear, though the red paint of the arrow had faded to pinkish now. Grandpa used it growing up on the farm and took it to war with him.

"No matter how far I traveled," Grandpa had told them, "it always helped me find my way home."

She closed it gently. She'd bring it back safely when her adventure ended. Clutching it to her chest, she hurried back to the computer. The email response from Jill contained all the details she needed for her stay in Hartwell.

She might be going alone physically, but she'd be surrounded by the prayers of her friends and her parents. And she had the compass to guide her and help her find her way home.

As she packed for next week's trip to the great unknown, three headhunter emails popped into her inbox offering jobs with staggering salary potential. Stunned, she responded with her résumé that Jill had insisted she keep updated, adding that she wouldn't be available for an interview for at least three weeks. Each response was cordial and suggested dates that might work for her.

Returning to the bedroom, she giggled. Look at her being all "not now" when normally she'd be chasing down job leads. She'd never have thought even one headhunter would search her out, yet here were three, all with management jobs like what she'd been doing.

As a child, she'd dreamed of being a baker or a poet but never a manager in accounting. Did anyone? A temporary position after college had revealed she was surprisingly good with numbers. And even better at managing teams of focused, productive people. She'd enjoyed the challenge of all of it. Until the last few months. What did she want at this point in her life?

She added a T-shirt to the stuffed suitcase and zipped it closed. An adventure stretched before her. She would deal with the rest of her life once she returned. Until then, she'd focus on her first real "vacation" in ten years.

According to her research, the drive to Hartwell would take two days. She left early Saturday morning, stomach knotted with excitement and fear. Late Sunday, having visited Mount Rushmore, seen distant bison, and giggled every time the GPS lady stated "recalculating," she rolled into Hartwell, Montana. Population 2,040. It had been remarkably freeing to be on her own, navigating, driving, taking photos.

Now she followed Grandpa's compass, and the beleaguered GPS lady, to find the cabin. As dusk settled, her fingers tightened around the steering wheel. Jillian hadn't been kidding when she mentioned the cabin was a bit difficult to find.

"I must be close," Delaney muttered. "If not, I can see the headline—woman found in stalled car deep in the forest." Another turn. "There it is!"

Finally! A few more twists and bumps, and she turned into a driveway that sloped upward to a small cabin, inside lights blazing a welcome.

"Thank you, Jesus!"

The A-frame home, with its weathered brown paneling, large windows displaying warm golden light, and tuck-under garage, looked like it was made just for her. Glowing in the dark night, it beckoned her inside. After two long, adventurous days of driving, it felt like she'd come home.

CHAPTER 4

Delaney blinked against the sunshine streaming in the windows, momentarily confused by the view outside, then she smiled and stretched lazily. Through the spindly branches of pines surrounding the cabin, she could just see the silhouette of the Beartooth mountains in the distance. She'd reached Montana! Why lounge in bed when there was so much to explore?

She slid into her robe and padded down the circular staircase to the kitchen. She'd started a grocery list last night, coffee in the number one spot. Now she looked through the cupboards to see what else she would need. This cozy, two-bedroom cabin would be her home for three whole weeks! She'd drink coffee on the balcony, write on the patio by the stone fireplace, and breathe. Deeply.

But right now, she needed coffee. She changed clothes and headed into town, list in hand. Before locating a grocery store, she'd find a coffee shop for a quick boost. A tinkle of bells welcomed her into the comforting aroma of fresh coffee in The Copper Hart. She paused and drew a breath. Heavenly.

"Hello and welcome!" A woman's voice greeted her.

Delaney turned but saw no one. "Hello?"

"Oops, sorry." The woman popped up from behind the counter with a grin. "I was filling a drawer with filters. "Come on in. What can I get you?"

Delaney studied the list of drinks. Some she recognized, others sounded intriguing. "You have quite the offering."

The red-haired woman glanced over her shoulder at the menu board. "We aim to please every palate that comes in to The Copper Hart. Hot or cold?"

Delaney raised her brow.

"Do you prefer hot or cold? Iced? French pressed?"

"How about just a cup of your best medium brew. Hot please."

"Black?"

"Yes, please."

As the woman busied herself getting the drink, Delaney wandered the shop. Warm wood tones with real stone accents. Tables in a variety of shapes and sizes with padded chairs. Natural light from the large front windows. Even a gas fireplace in the center.

"Your shop is lovely," she said, returning to the counter.

"Thanks. We did a major reno a year ago, when I took over from my aunt, and people have loved it. *I* love it."

"You're the owner?"

"I am." She held her hand out. "Liz Stiller."

"Delaney Hutchins." Liz's grasp was warm and firm, her smile welcoming.

"Are you staying here in Hartwell or just passing through?" She slid the steaming cup across the counter, waving off Delaney's attempt to pay.

"Staying for a few weeks. The little I've seen so far is amazing."

They chatted about the route Delaney had taken, what sights she needed to see during her stay in Hartwell, and what they did in their spare time.

"I've worked so much the past ten years, I haven't had much down time," Delaney admitted. Now she had lots of it. "When I do, I like to bake and write poetry."

Liz's red-tinged eyebrows lifted. "I thought we'd be friends," she declared with a grin. "You like to bake and I like to eat. Your baking is good, right?"

Delaney laughed. "I'm no professional, but I've won a few awards. It's fun *and* a great stress reliever. Especially when I'm kneading dough."

A family came in and Liz went to work, chatting with the kids as she showed them how she made their hot cocoa. A bundle of smiling energy, she was slightly shorter than Delaney, with a thick braid down her back. Perhaps ten years older? And she was obviously in the right job. Owning a coffee shop couldn't be easy, but she appeared to love it.

Getting to her feet, Delaney tossed her cup into the nearby can. A year ago she might have said she loved her job, but it had become questionable right up to the layoff. She waved at Liz as she headed to the door, then jumped when it swung open from outside. "Oh! Sorry. I didn't see you."

The man held it open for her. "Happy to hold the door for a lovely lady."

"Thank you."

"You're welcome." His voice was a pleasant baritone. "Have a nice day."

Biting her lip to hold in a girlish giggle, she hurried to her car. Hopefully she'd get to meet more cowboys like him during her stay. That alone would make the drive out here worthwhile.

After the best sleep she'd had in months and a leisurely breakfast in her sweet new home, Delaney gathered her notebooks and laptop and headed back to The Copper Hart. The call in her heart to spend quiet time writing before more exploring was too strong to ignore.

Settled in one of three soft leather chairs gathered by the front window, a cup of coffee nearby, she prepared to start the writing she'd longed to have time to do. The notebooks were filled with journaling and poetry, often intermixed as she poured herself onto the paper. Working with numbers might be how she paid the rent, but her heart belonged to this.

Pen in hand, poised over the lined paper, she waited. Nothing. She sipped her coffee and told herself to be patient. Still nothing. Where was the creativity that usually flowed out of her at home late at night? Maybe she couldn't write in the daylight. The thought made her grin. The Dracula of poetry.

She watched people wander in to enjoy the drinks and the atmosphere before heading back out into the sunshine. Regulars in dusty denim and cowboy boots, visitors in souvenir T-shirts and baseball caps. All ages and sizes and personalities. So different from the corporate world she'd lived in for a decade, where everyone dressed and acted the same.

Inspired by the quaint scene, warmed by the sunshine pouring over her, and surrounded by the aroma of fresh coffee, Delaney scribbled a few lines, then stopped. Maybe she should be looking at job openings first. She should check out the listings from the headhunters in more detail. And she could do some investigating on her own for possibilities.

She paused, propping her chin on her hand as she gazed out the window. Apparently it would take time to get out of work mode. With ten months of severance, she didn't have to find a job by next week.

"Mind if I join you for a bit?" Liz plopped into the next chair and set her feet on the round coffee table. "My feet are killing me today."

"You must walk miles every single day."

"Some days it feels like it. I'm down a part-timer until next week, so that means lots of extra hours." She shrugged. "So goes the life of a shop owner."

"I can't imagine the logistics of running a place like this. The inventory, payroll, maintenance, insurance, marketing . . ."

Liz narrowed her eyes. "You certainly sound like a business owner."

"I've been in accounting for the past ten years, so I know a bit about line items, cash flow, and all the fun things businesses need to keep track of."

"You don't look like an accountant."

Delaney laughed and swiped her forehead. "Thank goodness! I'm in management, or I was, with fabulous accounting people who knew the work inside and out. I know enough to be dangerous."

"Sitting down on the job, I see." The man who approached was smiling at Liz. The same man Delaney had nearly run into yesterday.

"Oh, don't you start." Liz shook a finger at him. "I've been working since you were riding ponies."

"Right. I forget you're that much older than me."

She gave a good-natured huff and looked at Delaney. "This ill-mannered man is my cousin, Patrick. And this is my darling, well-mannered new friend, Delaney."

Delaney stood and offered her hand. "It's nice to meet you. Delaney Hutchins." She was tall but he was taller, with a refined western look in jeans, a cotton shirt, and cowboy boots.

His grasp was warm and brief. "Patrick Finch." He turned his attention to Liz. "She's well mannered because she's a city girl."

Apparently he had an issue with people from the city. Sitting back down, Delaney said, "I'll take that as a compliment."

Liz laughed. "You could learn a few things from her in the manners department." She glanced at customers entering the café and stood. "Why don't you take her on a walkabout to show her our lovely town?"

"Aside from back-to-back meetings today, I'm thinking she wouldn't last three blocks in those shoes."

Delaney stifled the urge to slide her loafered feet to the side.

"Bah," Liz said with a snort. "I suspect she's a lot tougher than she looks. I'll see you kids later." She bustled away. "Hello, folks! Welcome to The Copper Hart."

When Patrick remained standing there, Delaney lifted a smile to him. "That was kind of her to offer your tour service, but I have quite a bit of work to do here. I hope your meetings go well."

Without waiting for a reply, she opened her laptop and got to "work."

He paused. "I hope they do too. Have a nice day, Miss Delaney."

Fingers on the keyboard, she watched him leave the café and climb into a black pickup. Cranky cowboy. He and Liz must have come from totally different parts of the family tree.

Chapter 5

Delaney stayed snuggled in the soft queen bed the next morning, gazing out the window in drowsy wonder. The sunshine, clear blue sky, and occasional wildlife wandering through the woods seemed almost other worldly. Accustomed to a time-constrained life in a cement world, this new freedom in a natural setting was jarring. Her life had been scheduled, vacation time used to assist her parents however necessary. Even "dating" Bryan had rarely been spontaneous.

But now she could stay up late and sleep in. Eat when she wanted. Plan her day however it suited her. It was disorienting. When she'd called her parents yesterday, Dad had teased that she'd adjust so well she might never go back to the corporate world. Doubtful unless an amazing opportunity popped up. She climbed out of bed. For now, she would revel in the freedom of being master of her own tiny universe, and that meant getting coffee.

Each morning of her first week in Hartwell was spent writing in her favorite chair at The Copper Hart. The creative spigot had opened, and she filled a new notebook. With a nod to adventure, she tried a new flavor of coffee each day and discovered she enjoyed combinations she'd never have considered before. Today was vanilla, hazelnut, and cinnamon.

And, strangely, the Cranky Cowboy came in each morning for coffee and a visit with Liz, then he'd stop to greet Delaney and ask what flavors she'd explored so far. He even added a few of his own suggestions before strolling back out. His brief visits left her shaking her head. Odd.

After writing, she'd wander through the delightfully eclectic shops lining Main Street. A bookstore, a cigar shop, a restaurant. Stores offering gear for the adventurous, upscale clothing, pottery. Even an old-fashioned candy store and a thrift shop. She enjoyed visiting with the store owners and hearing their stories.

Afternoons she'd check off must-see items from the list Liz had provided and several Cranky Cowboy had suggested. She couldn't get enough of the vast scenery, from rolling foothills colored with sagebrush to the rise of the Beartooth mountains. Forests of various pines, meadows she longed to wander through. People hiking and biking, cattle roaming. So very different from the world she knew.

Nature's silence was also vastly different from the hush of the office building. At first, sitting on the balcony with a cup of tea, the quiet had been unsettling. She'd jumped at every noise, sure the moose or a bear lurked just off the deck in the surrounding woods.

Now, settled on a bench beside picturesque Wild Bill Lake, her favorite place just outside of town, she breathed deeply. This silence spoke life, calm, and peace into her soul, while the corporate silence had hovered, holding its breath, waiting for a misstep.

She hadn't known how dry her soul was until arriving in Hartwell, how desperately she'd needed this time away. As she seemed to do daily, she prayed with a grateful heart, "Thank you for this amazing place, and for pushing me out of Minnesota. I'm all yours, Lord. Guide me through these weeks of rest."

Liz had mentioned that Friday evenings were live music nights and invited her to stop by, promising to save a chair for her. Delaney had agreed, but that evening, nerves dancing, she debated skipping it, then scolded herself for letting fear make the decision. She tamed her dark curls, added a bit of makeup, and hoped her jeans and cotton blouse would help her blend in. Maybe she could buy some cute cowgirl boots.

Arriving at The Copper Hart just before seven, legs wobbling, she found it surprisingly crowded. Liz waved her over to a stool beside the counter, giving her a welcoming hug and a cup of coffee before returning to the line of customers. When the band, Sagebrush Run, took the stage, Delaney blinked in surprise. Patrick was the lead singer in the band of three guys and a young woman. And they were very, very good.

From her stool off to the side, Delaney swayed to the music, laughed at the silliness on stage, and reveled in people watching. Young women in tight tops, shorts, and cowgirl boots danced close to the stage, flirting with Patrick between songs. He exchanged jokes and laughter with them but didn't seem interested beyond that.

"New to Hartwell this week," Patrick said between songs, "is Delaney Hutchins from the land of lakes, Minnesota."

She nearly dumped her coffee in her lap when he called her out.

"Give a wave, Delaney. Let's give her a good ol' Hartwell welcome."

Cheers and whistles erupted, and she waved self-consciously, then turned a shaming frown at the culprit on stage. He chuckled and started a new song. Throughout the evening, people stopped to greet her, welcoming her to their town, offering to buy her a specialty coffee and inviting her to dance.

"I've never line danced," she protested as a smiling young man held out a hand. When he persisted, she agreed with a warning. "Prepare to be embarrassed."

"This is an easy one," he assured her. "You'll catch on real quick."

And she did. Only a few missteps and then she blended into the lines of people. Liz, dancing in front of her, offered a thumbs-up as the lines moved forward, back, and swung to the side. The lines again faced the front, and she met Patrick's inscrutable gaze. She was glad she hadn't let fear keep her away.

After the show, friendly young men surrounded her, telling jokes and razzing each other about who would take her out first. Then Patrick slid through the group and took her hand. "Sorry, guys. She's with me. Better luck next time."

Her eyes went wide as he tugged her through the sweaty group. They groaned good-naturedly and tried to jostle him away, but his grip only tightened around her fingers as he led her out of the shop. They shouted after her.

"Delaney! I'm a better date than him."

"I'll call you. I'm Justin."

"You don't wanna go with City Boy," a third called.

Outside, Patrick released his grip, and she welcomed the cool night air against her cheeks, her fingers still tingling from the warmth of his hand. She'd never had anyone fight for her attention before. Or come to her rescue.

"Sorry about that," he said. "I think they took the idea of welcoming you a little too far. I figured that, since I caused the ruckus, I needed to get you out safely."

"They were all very polite."

"That might've changed if I hadn't stepped in. A few too many beers."

Her brow lifted. "But it's a coffee shop."

He shrugged. "They usually visit the bars before coming to hear the band. Speaking of which, what did you think of the music?"

They ambled past the darkened stores and into the neighborhood, chatting about the band, surprised to find they enjoyed the same music, and sharing bits of their family stories.

When the conversation paused, she filled her lungs and then sighed. "I've lived in the city for so long, I'd forgotten what it's like to breathe clean air and be able to hear yourself think." The mix of pine and sap and something earthy was cleansing. And addicting.

"Do you prefer city or country living? Or something in between?"

"City life is all I've known. But being here is amazing," she said, lifting her gaze to the sky. "Look at those stars! In the city, I'm lucky to even see the moon beyond the buildings." She would miss the wide-open beauty of the mountains. She turned the question back to him.

"They called you city boy. Are you from the city originally?"

He shook his head. "Third generation Hartwell. I got the nickname as a kid because I was more interested in drawing than riding, while they were all going to rodeos and collecting trophies."

"You're an artist?" She'd never have guessed that.

"Architect."

"Huh." But then, he probably wouldn't guess she loved writing poetry.

By the time they circled back to the coffee shop, she was unable to hide her limp from the blisters that had formed. When he commented, she shrugged. "City-girl shoes. I wasn't expecting to walk much tonight."

He frowned. "Sorry about the crack about your shoes earlier. I was out of line."

She'd never have guessed he'd apologize either. "No worries. I don't have the most practical shoes for being out west, but I didn't know what to buy that would be."

"To really enjoy this area, you'd need a solid pair of hiking boots. They cost more at first but last much longer. And your feet would thank you."

She laughed. "I've never heard a peep from my feet, so it might be worth it just for that. Any specific brand?"

He was quiet a moment, eyes narrowed as he looked at her shoes. "How about I take you over to Cody tomorrow? I know a guy who runs a great store there, and I can get you a discount."

Cranky Cowboy was offering to take her shopping? "Thank you, but that's not necessary. I'm sure I can find some here."

"But not the best kind." He gave a small shrug. "I don't have meetings scheduled, and I'd like to get out of town."

"Oh. Well . . . I'd like that. Thanks."

"Let's meet at the Hart at ten."

Pulling up the driveway to the cabin a few minutes later, she glanced in the rearview mirror. She still wore the most confused, delighted grin ever on her face. The cranky cowboy was taking her on a drive.

CHAPTER 6

The drive to Cody was filled with Delaney's questions about mountain life. What was it like in the winter? Was it annoying to have his quiet town overrun by tourists? Did ranchers and town folk get along? What was it like to live where moose and bears could wander into town?

He answered patiently, chuckling as she exclaimed over the scenery. "Do you always talk this much?"

She pressed her lips together, warmth crawling up her neck. "Actually, I've been told I'm pretty quiet."

"Really."

She faced the front and vowed to be silent the remainder of the drive. He pointed out areas of interest and described what the various ranches and farms specialized in. She soaked in his descriptions to include in writing later, and made simple, polite comments.

After getting her first pair of hiking boots at an amazing discount, she insisted on buying Patrick lunch. On the return trip, they stopped at a short, simple walking trail to break in her boots, and he explained how to care for them. When she asked, he admitted that his were nearly five years old, then laughed at her wide-eyed look and assured her she could still be wearing hers in five years.

Back in Hartwell, he suggested dinner at his favorite restaurant, Pony Express Pizzeria. Stomach rumbling loudly, she agreed. He held the door open and then followed her in. As greetings came from around the busy restaurant, he acknowledged them with a nod, then put a hand to her back. The young hostess led them to a corner table.

Feeling the interest directed at her, Delaney thanked him when he slid a chair out for her. He shared several of his favorite items before encouraging her to pick whatever she wanted. His treat. He waved off her protest. "You can buy next time."

Next time? Toes curling in her boots, she turned her attention back to the menu, hiding a smile. Cranky Cowboy was an interesting tour guide. Between bites she asked about his job and life in Hartwell, mindful not to talk too much. He shared humorous observations about growing up amidst cowboys, abundant wildlife, and the varied people who lived in and visited Hartwell.

Then he asked about life in the big city and what type of job she was looking for. When she admitted she wasn't sure, his dark brow rose. "Not more of what you've been doing?"

She lifted a shoulder. "I don't know. I feel like it's time to do something different. I'm just not sure what that is. But I'm loving the time to journal and write poetry. Not," she added, cheeks warming, "that it would be interesting to most people here."

"Why not? I'm a songwriter in my down time, and that can be a lot like poetry." He winked and changed the subject. "Have you ever ridden a horse?"

She pretended offense. "I'll have you know my grandparents owned a farm."

He nodded, eyebrows lifted. "That's nice. My question stands."

She dropped her shoulders and admitted, "I was afraid of them when I was little. I did try riding a few times, but the horses weren't good for city kids, so it didn't end well." She shivered. "I can still remember the sensation of flying, followed by a hard landing."

"Ouch. Something most riders experience once or twice."

"Not you."

He chuckled. "I've had my share."

Perhaps. He looked more refined than rugged. She set her napkin aside with a sigh. "That was more than I eat in a week."

"But it was good, right?"

"Best pizza ever."

They crossed the street and walked a block to her car, parked at The Copper Hart.

"Thanks for giving up an entire day for me," she said. It had been eye opening in so many ways. Especially how much she'd enjoyed his company.

"I'm glad you have decent boots now for roaming around town."

She giggled, glancing down at her feet. "I feel like I belong here now."

His expression softened as their gazes met, then he blinked and stepped back with a brief nod. "Don't forget to keep breaking them in."

"I won't."

Starting the car, she released a long sigh. What an amazing day. And what an interesting man. An architect and a *songwriter*?

Coolly reserved much of the time, when he laughed his demeanor changed. And that change did something weird to her heart.

Morning writing at The Copper Hart now meant visiting with Liz and some of the regulars Delaney was getting to know—including Patrick. He started bringing his laptop in, sitting opposite her doing his work while making comments that made her laugh and lose focus on her writing.

She watched him work on several designs, fascinated by the program that helped him create beautiful homes. When he asked to see what she was working on, she balked.

"I showed you my unfinished work," he said.

Meeting his calm gaze, she held her breath. Heart in her throat, she handed him her current notebook, then turned to stare out the window as he read.

Finally, he closed the notebook and looked out the window, silent. His expression remained passive. Delaney closed her eyes against the sudden sting of tears. She'd shown her writing to a select few, but Patrick's reaction mattered more than she understood. If he truly was a songwriter, he'd see her poetry as amateurish.

"Laney."

The nickname brought her eyes open.

"That's songwriting material," he said. "Professional level."

She frowned. "Hardly." She'd hoped he'd be kind.

He remained relaxed, as if he'd expected that reaction. "Whatever I say right now you'll take as me being nice. What I'm being is honest." He leaned forward, holding her attention. "I know music. I know songwriting. And I know that this"—he lifted her notebook—"is what goes into writing great songs. It's not just the word choice; it's the emotion behind the words. It's painting word pictures. It's raw honesty."

He held out the notebook but kept hold of it when she grasped it. "I may be asking you for some songwriting help in the near future."

The surprised admiration in his gaze wrapped around her heart, and she smiled shyly.

His phone buzzed, and he released the book with a wink. "Patrick Finch."

More than stunned, she went to the counter to get her bearings, or a drink, or to cry in relief.

Liz finished with a customer and met her across the counter, eyebrows pinched. "You okay, hon?"

Delaney nodded, strangely breathless. "He liked it."

"Who liked what?"

"Patrick liked my poetry. I mean, I knew he'd be nice about it, but . . ." She lifted her hands in wonder. "He seemed to mean it."

Liz reached across to squeeze Delaney's arm. "Hon, my cousin is as honest as the day is long. He doesn't waste time on flattery. Sometimes he's brutally honest, but it's always done with the other person's best in mind. If he said he liked it, he did. Plain and simple."

She glanced past Delaney, then leaned forward. "I'll tell you something about him," she said quietly. "He experienced some tough times a few years back, when people close to him were dishonest. Broke his heart, actually. Ever since, he values honesty almost as much as his faith. He offers it and expects it from people."

Delaney nodded, aching at the thought of him being so wounded.

"So." Liz straightened and grinned. "Do I get to see some of your writing?"

Delaney laughed at her friend's hopeful expression. "If you promise to be as brutally honest as you say he is."

Liz made an X on her chest. "Cross my heart. Friends are honest with each other." Customers approached, and Liz tapped the counter as she turned away. "Whenever you're ready."

Returning to the chairs, Delaney's smile faded at Patrick's absence. He'd left a note on her computer. *Called into a meeting. How about a day trip to Yellowstone early Thursday?*

She dropped into her chair and folded her arms to soak in the tingling, toe-curling sensation. He'd called her Laney, like Dad always had. But it was different coming from him. She was suddenly very thankful for being laid off.

CHAPTER 7

They left Hartwell before eight the next morning with fresh coffee in hand and hiking boots on for the adventure. The trip to Yellowstone National Park, he'd warned her, would be a few hours, since they'd take Beartooth Pass. Delaney was stunned by the beauty of the drive, exclaiming at every vista, every sighting of wildlife. Driving up and over the winding pass, Patrick stopped often to let her leap out and soak in the astounding splendor of the mountains and valleys.

At one spot, a funny woodchuck-looking creature came out from under a tree, then popped back in with a high-pitched squeak. Delaney tugged Patrick from where he stood looking across a valley, keeping hold of his arm in her excitement as they waited for the critter to reappear. When it did, she gave her own squeak.

"Isn't it adorable? Is it a woodchuck?"

"It's a marmot, a type of ground squirrel."

She frowned at him. "That is not a squirrel."

He chuckled. "It's a classification. Up here it's called a yellow-bellied marmot. Lots of people call them whistlers because of the noise they make."

Still frowning, Delaney crossed her arms. "Are you making that up?"

An older man paused beside them and asked, "Did you see that marmot by the tree, young lady? Lots of people call it a woodchuck but it's a marmot, part of the squirrel family."

She looked from him to Patrick with suspicion, then threw her hands up with a laugh. "I give up. I guess I'll have to take your word for it."

Returning to the pickup, Patrick was still chuckling. "Once we get to a place with a signal, you can look it up, Miss Suspicious. You'll see."

Liz's words about his honesty popped to mind, and she gave him a sideways glance. "I will, but somehow I have a feeling you're right."

The road continued climbing up and then winding down, as did her exclamations over the stunning views. Thankful for his willingness to stop yet again, she tried to be quick, but the panorama stunned her in place. He seemed amused by her enthusiasm rather than annoyed and willingly took pictures of her. She reciprocated, and they took countless selfies together.

In Yellowstone, she was excited to see bison at the side of the road, and then black bears in trees and elk calmly grazing while people snapped photos. The bubbling paint pots were smelly and fascinating, the hills and valleys beautiful. Standing with a crowd waiting for Old Faithful to erupt, she fought the urge to lean back into Patrick's warmth as he pointed over her shoulder at items of interest. When she was jostled by nearby teens, his hands on her shoulders kept her upright. He kept them there until the geyser finished its show.

Through the long drive back to Hartwell, they listened to more of Sagebrush Run, and he shared stories about the group. It had been the most amazing day of her life, and she knew she'd relive the memories often.

"Laney." Patrick's voice was low, nearly a whisper. Something warm brushed her cheek and she sighed, letting her eyes flutter open.

The truck was stopped and he sat angled toward her, studying her with a gentle smile. They were back in Hartwell.

Mortified, she bolted upright. "Oh, my gosh. I'm sorry! I can't believe I fell asleep."

He chuckled, his arm still resting across the steering wheel as he faced her. "I'd have been surprised if you hadn't. I don't think I've seen anyone have as good a time in Yellowstone as you did."

She rubbed her eyes. "It was all amazing, and you were so patient with stopping and telling me about the different things we saw." Releasing the seatbelt, she turned toward him and shyly touched his hand. "Thank you, again, for another wonderful day. You have the unofficial title of best tour guide ever."

"It's been my pleasure." The smile in his eyes faded into an intensity that sent a shiver up her spine. "You're easy to be with, Delaney Hutchins. I appreciate that."

She bit her lip. "So are you."

They sat in silence for a moment before the usual reserve shuttered his gaze and he opened his door. "Are you awake enough to make it home?"

She drew a silent breath to steady her heart. "Definitely. It's an easy drive." She gathered her purse, jacket, and the bag of souvenirs she'd purchased, then climbed out of his truck.

He walked her to her car and, as she drove off, she glanced in the mirror. He stood watching until she turned at the corner. She sighed, enjoying the tickle under her ribs. She would never forget this day.

They listened to a different band at The Copper Hart Friday evening, where he showed off his line dancing skills and taught her a few new steps before they strolled the peaceful streets of Hartwell. After church on Sunday, he convinced her to go riding at his sister's ranch, assuring her she would get the calmest of the trail horses. Jaw clenched, she managed a jerky nod, which made him laugh.

Ashley, tall and lean like her brother with the same green eyes and wavy dark hair, and her husband, Donny, welcomed them warmly to the expansive ranch outside of town. Ashley answered Delaney's concerns and invited her to help get Fanny ready for the ride. After a few circles of the corral, Patrick, riding Ace, led Delaney and Fanny away from the ranch.

They meandered across the prairie, around sagebrush, and through rippling grasses toward the wooded area he'd pointed out. With a padded guitar case on his back that kept knocking his Stetson askew, he kept their conversation light, making her laugh. By the time they'd crossed the prairie, she felt like an actual cowgirl.

Settled on the blanket to eat the picnic lunch Ashley had packed in the saddlebags, Patrick held out his hand to pray over their meal. Her hand in his, Delaney relished the richness in his voice and words in the simple prayer. Her fingers continued to tingle even as she ate.

Tossing the last chip into her mouth, she sighed at the panorama spread before her. People got to enjoy all this beauty every day. She saw only concrete and people and corporate hallways with generic artwork.

Patrick pulled out his acoustic guitar and played simple melodies that made her heart smile. In the peaceful setting, they chatted or sat in comfortable silence, the notes surrounding them in the gentle breeze.

"Having fun?" he asked.

She rolled her eyes. "You can say it."

"Say what?" Laughter tinged the words.

"I can handle an 'I told you so.'"

The corner of his mouth twitched as he turned his attention to the view. "This place has been in Donny's family for generations, so it was a natural fit for him and Ash to move onto the property and run the trail ride part of the operation. Unlike me, she was horse crazy from birth."

"How amazing to have this be your back yard and to share it with visitors."

"She'd agree with you on that."

After a pause, he glanced sideways at her. "If you don't mind my asking, any particular reason you haven't gotten married?"

"I've been focused on work to help my parents. They lost a lot of money to a scammer about five years ago, and I helped them get back on their feet. Then my dad had a stroke, and it's taken time to adjust."

"How's he doing now?"

"Great." Their phone conversation a few days ago reaffirmed her decision to take this trip. "They both are. They moved to

Arizona last fall so they wouldn't have to deal with winter in Minnesota, and he gets stronger every day."

"Is your sister in Minnesota?"

"Florida." She shrugged. "I'm the lone holdout."

"So there's nothing holding you there."

There'd been the proposal, but that felt far from this reality. "Not really. But I have some interviews lined up for the week after next. Having a job is good for paying the rent." She looked at him, heart fluttering, and said, "So I'll ask you the same thing. Any reason you aren't married?"

His eyes narrowed as he stared across the native grasses swaying in the breeze. "I was," he said finally, setting the guitar aside. "Got married in the middle of college to my high school girlfriend. After completing our degrees, she took a job in Portland and the marriage ended."

"You didn't go with her?"

His profile revealed a momentary clench to his jaw, then it faded, and he turned a crooked smile toward her. "I wasn't invited. She had someone else in mind."

Delaney's spine straightened. "What?" Was the girl crazy? "What is wrong with people? Doesn't anyone honor their vows?"

"I tried," he said, "but she was no longer interested. Being miles apart, knowing she had moved in with the new boyfriend, I decided to let her have the life she wanted."

"What about the life *you* wanted?"

He held her gaze for a long moment. "I have the life I want."

In the silence that followed, birds twittered overhead, a small plane droned in the distance. What life did she want? Climbing the corporate ladder with Bryan? She shuddered. No. But what options did she have? She'd been in the corporate world since college. How did she build something different?

"I'm still trying to figure mine out," she admitted. "It's been the same forever, and I'm good at what I do."

"But?"

After a long pause, she sighed. "It's comfortable." Not one she wanted anymore, but it wasn't bad. "I guess I do best with routine."

He nodded. "Then that's good," he said, gathering items to take back.

They had the area cleaned up quickly. Too quickly. Before giving her a leg up on Fanny, he paused. "Laney, sometimes comfortable keeps us from doing what we're meant to do, what God is calling us to do."

Startled, she looked up.

Standing beside her, he studied her with a serious gaze. "Don't miss out on new opportunities by playing it safe." He linked his hands together, prepared to help her mount. "Okay, I'll hoist you up."

Settling onto the saddle, she giggled. He swung up on Ace and looked at her with a quizzical lift to his brow.

"I've never had someone 'hoist me up.' Makes it sound like I need a forklift."

Eyes wide, he started to apologize, but she waved him off. "I'm kidding. It just struck me as funny."

Patrick shook his head. "You're so light that you're lucky I didn't throw you right over Fanny."

As they ambled back toward the ranch, Delaney reached for the compass in her jacket pocket. When he leaned over to see it, she explained its history. "Dad and Grandpa both said it will guide me home so, while I think I know which way is north from here, I'm going to check."

Holding it in her palm, she watched the faded red arrow wobble, then point. At Patrick. She blinked in surprise, heat rising in her cheeks, and quickly returned it to her pocket.

"Figure it out?" he asked.

"Um . . . yup." Heart fluttering strangely, she glanced at his handsome profile. *Home, Dad said. Not him. Home!* She resisted the urge to fan her face. That was just a fluke.

CHAPTER 8

Monday morning of her last week in Hartwell, Delaney arrived at The Copper Hart earlier than usual. Liz and an assistant were busy with a line of customers. Delaney didn't approach the counter until the last of the customers left with their drinks in hand.

"Wow, that's quite a morning rush," she mused.

Liz nodded, brushing several curly strands of red from her forehead. "The usuals." She leaned on the counter, plopping her chin on her hand. "But I need to do something to bring in more people. Finances are getting tight, and I need a new angle. I've been thinking for a while that offering fresh bakery items would be a good draw. They ask all the time, so I know it would be a huge boost in sales."

"Why don't you? Isn't there a bakery in town that would deliver?"

She shook her head. "We had a bakery here through several generations, but then it closed during the pandemic and never reopened."

"Ooh, that's sad. This darling town needs a bakery."

"It sure does. I know we have the best coffee," Liz said without conceit, wiping the counter, "but it's time to match the competition and offer the best breakfast treats. If I don't, I'm not sure the Hart will survive the next few years."

"It's that bad?"

"Getting there," she said with a heavy sigh. "I encouraged my aunt to diversify, but she just wouldn't, so now I have to play catchup with the competition."

"Do you have specific items in mind?"

"Cinnamon rolls are the most-requested item. Then muffins. Lots of flavors. Some gluten-free options. Start simple. Then maybe someday I can hire a full-time baker." She straightened abruptly, eyes wide. "Wait. You said you love to bake!"

Delaney stared at her a moment, then broke into laughter. A good, solid belly laugh. "Oh, Liz. Loving to bake as a hobby is completely different from what you're looking for."

"Didn't you say you've won awards?"

"Well, yes, but that's not—"

"What's your favorite thing to bake?"

Delaney held up a hand, shaking her head. "We're not having this discussion. You need to be focused on finding an actual baker."

"Well, this conversation looks pretty serious." Patrick approached from the doorway.

"Liz is a bit desperate."

He looked at his cousin. "For?"

"A start to my pastry offerings. You know we need to do something to increase business. And Delaney has won awards for her baking, so I asked what she likes baking most."

He looked at Delaney. "And the answer is . . ."

She folded her arms, frowning. This was ridiculous. Wasn't it?

Patrick and Liz looked at each other, and a smile bloomed on Liz. She bounced on her toes, clapping her hands together lightly.

"It's cinnamon rolls, isn't it? It is! That's why you won't tell us. You've won awards for baking the very thing people are asking for!"

"Even if you're right, you can't offer a treat for a week and then nothing after that. And I don't live here, remember? You need someone permanent that you can count on."

"You could be permanent," Liz countered. "You need a job, and I have one."

The debate continued until Patrick lifted a hand. "I have a suggestion, ladies."

Their heads swiveled toward him in unison.

"How about a challenge? I'll write a song using some of Laney's poetry, she'll bake cinnamon rolls, and we'll share them on Friday during the show. People will get a sweet treat and hopefully enjoy whatever I come up with. Just for fun."

"I love that idea!" Liz exclaimed. "Delaney?"

Her private words made into a song for all to hear? Her heart rate jumped. And her simple baking offered as a treat? "Both of those involve putting me on display."

Patrick frowned, then understanding relaxed his brow, and he nodded. "I get it. We won't tell anyone about your poetry. It will just be performed as a new song from the band. Better?"

Slightly. The thumping in her chest churned her stomach. Maybe she hadn't come out here to bake for strangers, but she did come for new experiences. And if it would help Liz at least start her dream . . .

Patrick lifted an eyebrow when she looked at him.

"Why not?" she said. "But don't get your hopes up. I'm just a hobby baker, not some world-famous patisserie chef."

Liz's energy lit the room as she assured her, "We're not expecting perfection."

"That's good. Okay, how many should I make?"

A smile formed slowly on Patrick's handsome face, and he nodded as if in approval. "Let the contest begin."

Delaney experimented, making sample rolls through the rest of the day—her favorite recipe and other batches with a few twists. Patrick stopped by that evening to taste test what she'd done, providing honest feedback although, he reminded her, he was hardly a food critic. They sat on the deck late into the night chatting, discussing ideas for Liz to try, and admiring the stars.

Tuesday, she baked and tasted, went online for recipes, and baked more. She'd never had so much fun in the kitchen. Patrick brought pizza and wine that night, along with Ashley and Donny. They sampled her baking and shared feedback, then played board games until Delaney was yawning.

Each night as she turned off the light and crawled into bed, she thanked God for bringing her to this amazing place. And she fell asleep thinking of the handsome architect who made her laugh, challenged her to try new things, and sent a tingle through her with a simple glance.

Wednesday morning, Delaney settled into her favorite chair by The Copper Hart front window, enjoying a cup of her newest favorite coffee—caramel coconut. She opened her Bible and read through several psalms, then closed her eyes to imagine her own words expressing the wide range of emotions.

He refreshes my soul. He guides me along the right paths for His name's sake. Psalms 23:3

She smiled. Her heart and soul were refreshed daily as she breathed in life and joy, friendship and even adventure. He was guiding her, not only for her benefit but also for His. Whatever was in her future, she wanted it to please Him. Gratitude welled in her heart, and she bent over the page to write her thanks.

When she lifted her head, she jumped. Patrick stood behind his chair, dressed in a suit, coffee in hand. The warmth in his gaze wrapped around her heart, and she smiled. "Well, good morning, Mr. Finch."

"Good morning, Miss Delaney. I didn't want to interrupt."

She set the Bible and notebook aside and stood to admire his suit with a nod. "Looking very handsome this morning."

His laugh tickled under her ribs. "I have a meeting with new clients."

"Definitely impressive." She motioned for him to follow her to the counter so she could get a refill. "High end clients, I'm guessing?"

"I always do the suit for new clients, high end or not."

Liz emerged from the back room and greeted them with a wide smile. "Well, two of my favorite people. Looking mighty spiffy, cuz."

Delaney giggled. "Spiffy. Great word."

He rolled his eyes and then turned the conversation to her. "How's the baking? Think you'll win the contest?"

"I know I will," she declared.

"I for one can't wait," Liz said, refilling Delaney's cup.

"Because it will be good for business," Patrick said wryly.

"Of course," she replied, "but also because I enjoy fresh-baked treats and good music. How's the song coming along?"

"Done. However, I got the easier part of the challenge because Laney's storytelling is so good."

Warmth seeped up her neck at the admiration in his eyes. "Thank you, but I suspect you've had to do some major tweaks to turn my ramblings into a decent song. Probably a lot of woo-woos to fill in."

Liz hooted and slapped her thigh, her face turning pink. "Oh, that's Patrick. His woo-woos always get me." She wiped her eyes.

He chuckled. "Maybe I'll add a woo-woo just for my songwriter."

Still snickering, Liz stepped away to greet a customer, and Patrick leaned against the counter, his smile fading. "You really have no idea how good your writing is, do you?"

Delaney shrugged. "It's just a way for me to get stuff out of my head."

"Well, people are now going to have those words in their heads." He brushed gently at her bangs. "You're pretty amazing, Miss Delaney."

The intensity in his gaze made it hard to breathe. "As are you, Mr. Finch."

They wandered back toward the windows. "I know we're in a fierce competition," he said, "but how about dinner tomorrow before Friday's big contest? To celebrate stepping out of our comfort zone?"

"Hmm." She placed her coffee on the table and settled into her chair. "I'd like to but, since what you're doing is hardly out of your comfort zone, we'd only be celebrating me."

"I'm good with that." He perched on the arm of the next chair. Mischief lit his green eyes. "And since you owe me dinner after I bought pizza, *you* can buy."

"What?" Laughter bubbled up at his wink. "Is this how cowboys ask city girls out for dinner?"

"I'm not a cowboy," he reminded her, "and I think you've discovered you're not a city girl. This is just the Hartwell architect asking the Hartwell poetic baker to spend an evening with him."

"Ah." She met his raised brow with a shy smile, sure her heart would dance right out of her chest. "And this is the poetic baker telling the architect she would love to."

"Great." He released a breath as if in relief. "I'll pick you up at six?"

"Perfect. If you'll excuse me for a moment, I need to freshen up." She hurried to the ladies' room on wobbling legs. His chuckle followed her.

Once she had her heart rate under control, and most of the blush more pink than red, she headed back as calmly as she could. She had an actual date with Patrick!

Turning the corner, she saw another man in a suit talking to Patrick and Liz near the counter. He looked fam— Her heart dropped. "Bryan?"

CHAPTER 9

He turned and held out his arms. "Surprise!"

Stunned, she approached slowly, glancing at Patrick before turning a frown toward the visitor. "What are you doing here?"

"You haven't responded to my emails, so I wanted to make sure you were safe. Plus I've got some great news that will make you pack up and race back to Minnesota with me."

Patrick's voice slid between them. "I have a meeting to get to." He gave Bryan a stiff nod. "Nice to meet you."

He turned and walked away without looking at Delaney. Liz gave her a quizzical frown and excused herself. Before she could stop him, Bryan wrapped his arms around her.

"Dela, you look amazing. This break has obviously been good for you, although I've been super lonely. But I'm glad you're safe."

Arms still at her side, she stepped back. "Why would you think I wasn't? I'm not a child wandering in the wilderness." Not anymore.

"Of course not, but can't a guy be concerned for his fiancée when she disappears for weeks on end?"

"I am not your fiancée, and I didn't disappear." Her tone rose. "I went on vacation. *My* vacation. Alone."

The silence that met her angry words made her glance around. Tony, Gus, and Halston, the weathered old cowboys who gathered each morning, were turned in their chairs watching, as were people at two other tables and Liz at the counter.

"Need any help there, Miss Delaney?" Halston inquired.

She released a short breath and shook her head. "Thanks, but it's okay, Halston." She took Bryan's arm and steered him around the fireplace to her chair by the window.

He raised his eyebrows as she faced him. "Wow. You even know the old guys by name. You've really tried to fit in."

"I have not tried to fit in," she said, teeth clenched. "I've enjoyed meeting people."

"Good. Well," he continued, "are you ready to hear the news? Maureen plans to hire you back! She realized she laid off a gem, so she's creating a new management training position in HR. Just for you. You'll get to design the program." He rubbed his fingers together. "Big pay raise."

Delaney stared at him. "Seriously?"

"Seriously." He rolled his eyes, chuckling. "I wouldn't come all the way out here and make that up. You should be getting an email from her any day with the details. Dela, the pay raise alone is amazing. And to get to design the program yourself?" Hands on his hips, he shook his head, smiling in admiration. "So many people spoke up for you and sent emails."

A big raise would mean more money to set aside for Mom and Dad. Designing a program to train managers? She'd love to do that. But go back to the corporate world? Her heart sank. The freedom she'd tasted here was life changing. Life giving.

"So? What do you think?"

"I . . . I don't know." She shook her head. "It sounds amazing. I guess I'll have to see what the details are."

His eyes narrowed. "I thought you'd be more excited than this."

She would have been a few weeks ago, when she thought the corporate world was her future. "I guess I'm more surprised than anything."

"You're on your way to an office in upper management," he stated, "hopefully right by mine."

"Did you get a new position?"

"Not yet, but I don't think it's far off." He took her hands. "See what I mean about being a great couple? There's so much we can do together."

She looked at the excitement shining in his eyes and waited to feel some of it. Find out who you are, Dad had said. Don't miss out by playing it safe, Patrick had warned. She drew her hands from his. "I'll take it into consideration along with the other jobs I'll be interviewing for next week." Next week. The words stabbed her heart.

He blinked. "You have interviews set up?"

"I got laid off, Bryan. I have bills to pay."

"Well, that makes sense, of course. Look, we can talk about this later," he said, "over dinner. I'm staying at the Larkspur place. Any decent food around here?"

Pizza. Saddlebag lunches. Coffee drinks.

She'd planned to do more baking tonight, hoping Patrick would stop over again. They'd have laughed and teased—

"Delaney?" Bryan's voice brought her to the present with a crash.

"Um. Dinner. Well, there's an Italian place I haven't tried yet."

"Great. I need to get checked in and do some work. How about six?"

Patrick had suggested six for tomorrow evening. Maybe they'd have gone to the Italian place. Or had pizza again. Not now. Bryan's appearance had quashed the date. Probably the relationship.

"Dela, are you okay?"

"Sorry. Yes. Six would be fine. It's just down Main about two blocks. I'll meet you there."

"Where are you staying?"

She waved vaguely toward the window. "In a little cabin just outside of town."

"I could pick—"

"No." His brow lifted at her swift response, so she added, "It's a little hard to find, so it would be easier if I just meet you at the restaurant."

"Okay. We'll do that." He put a finger under her chin and smiled. "I'm excited for our future. It feels like everything's falling into place."

She nodded and stepped back. "Things are certainly changing. Well, I have some writing to do, so you go get settled, and I'll see you at six."

"Sounds good." He wrapped his arms around her and pressed a kiss to her temple. "I'm so glad I came."

When he released her, she asked, "By the way, how did you find me?"

"Jillian." He chuckled. "I overheard her at lunch telling someone you were here at her parents' place. And she mentioned that your favorite coffee shop was also hers." He lifted his shoulders with a pleased expression. "And here we are."

"Here we are," she echoed quietly.

She watched him climb into his rental car and drive off, then sank into the chair, eyes filling with burning tears. A moment later, a hand rested warmly on her shoulder.

"You okay, hon?" Liz perched on the arm of the next chair, as Patrick had done.

Unable to breathe over the lump in her throat, she shook her head.

"Is he your fiancé?"

"No, but he wants to be. He came out here to tell me they're offering me a new job with a lot more money."

"Wow." Liz was quiet for a moment. "You've got some big decisions to make."

Delaney sat still, staring blindly out the window, then drew a short breath and stiffened her spine. "I need to go talk to God," she said.

"You do that. I will too."

Looking up at her sweet red-haired friend, she offered a trembling smile. "I'd appreciate that."

She made her way to the cabin she called home and parked. Folding her arms across the steering wheel, she dropped her head and sobbed. Patrick's stoic expression hadn't hidden the hurt in his eyes when he turned away from her. She should have told him about Bryan, about the proposal. Now she was in the same category as his ex.

"Lord, I'm not ready to go home."

Her baking attempts flopped that afternoon. The more she prayed, the more it seemed each prayer bounced off the vaulted ceiling, got caught in the fan and tossed right out the window. Giving up, she sat on the balcony with Grandpa's compass in hand, as if it might give her spoken direction. It didn't. She prayed but felt no response, no clear answer. Her thoughts were a tangled mess. It should be a no-brainer to take the new job.

Bryan was seated and waiting for her at the restaurant. As the hostess led her to their table by the window, he stood and offered a red rose, pressing a kiss to her cheek. Barely touching her food, she spent most of their dinner looking over her shoulder or out at the street. When he asked what had her distracted, she gave a vague answer and changed the subject. As he paid the bill, she pleaded a headache, afraid he would drop to a knee and propose in front of everyone. Patrick would hear about it within an hour.

Back at the cabin, she wrapped herself in a blanket and returned to the balcony to look up at the breathtaking display of stars and ask God, yet again, for guidance. Why was she struggling? It only made sense to take the new job. That kind of money would make sure her parents were taken care of and perhaps help her buy a house. Something small like this one. In a neighborhood filled with people and cars and noise.

Maybe working with Bryan would allow her to see him in a different light. Her sigh was long and deep, fading into the darkness. No. Two years was plenty of time to know if she wanted to spend a lifetime with him. Working more closely wouldn't produce stronger feelings. The question wasn't if she would marry Bryan; it was if she wanted to go back to the corporate world.

The old longing for substance in her life flared. It had dissipated when she arrived in Hartwell, as if it had been resolved. Now it was back, stronger than before. She'd come to life here. Would that life be snuffed out if she went back to the uniformity of the corporate world? But if she stayed, where would she live? Would she grow bored of the freedom she'd thrived in since arriving here? Was it all, including Patrick, just a novelty that would wear off?

When she finally crawled into bed, her head truly ached, as did her heart. She loved Hartwell and the people she'd come to know, but the smart move would be to go back to Minnesota and throw herself into the new job. There was nothing tangible keeping her here.

CHAPTER 10

Delaney met Bryan at a different coffee shop in the morning, then offered to drive him around to see some of her favorite sights. He enjoyed the tour for the first hour, then wondered where the nearest "actual city" was and if they could find a restaurant for lunch.

He thought the mountains were spectacular but admitted he preferred being at the lake. He didn't have good shoes for even a short hike, so they stayed near the car when she stopped to show him a few different views.

They had lunch in Cody, then returned to Hartwell so he could "get in a few hours of work before dinner." While Delaney explained she already had plans for dinner, her heart cracked a little more knowing Patrick wouldn't pick her up.

Bryan reluctantly agreed to spend a quiet evening at Larkspur when she didn't provide details of her plans and left her at her car with a quick kiss. She gave a longing glance at The Copper Hart, then drove to the grocery store for the supplies she'd need tomorrow.

Her writing that evening lacked the lightness that had colored her work since arriving in Hartwell. It took more energy than she had to put thoughts to the page. Instead, she doodled and covered the paper with memories. Dancing. Boots. Life. Old Faithful.

Coffee. Patrick. Then she added words about the job offer. Money. Stability. Parents. Satisfaction. Corporate ladder. Cement city. Lifeless hallways. Bryan.

Patrick didn't call or stop by. The flash of anger at his silence faded when she considered how it had looked to him. She'd said she had nothing holding her to Minnesota—except for a quasi-fiancé who showed up with big news. For a man who valued honesty, she came up short.

Sitting on the deck, she searched the sky for light, answers, a message of some sort. Clouds blocked the stars, making it seem God had closed the door to heaven. After tomorrow night, she had no reason to stay in Hartwell.

Friday morning, after a restless night of confused dreams, she headed to the kitchen to make the cinnamon rolls, much later than she'd planned. When Bryan texted, then called, she told him about the contest and that the day would be spent baking. When he offered to help, she said she needed to concentrate. He took that as a compliment and promised he'd see her at The Copper Hart that night, despite her downplaying the event.

Great. Both men would be there—one who wanted to marry her and the other who wanted to see her taillights as she headed out of his town.

She mixed and kneaded and proved as she always did, but the dough didn't rise normally. Dread festered as she slid the rolls into the oven. Something was wrong with this batch, so now she'd leave Hartwell in humiliation, having embarrassed Liz and disappointed Patrick.

The timer confirmed her fear. They were flat and misshapen, slightly burned on the edges. She set the pan on the stovetop, then scraped the rest of the dough into the garbage. If she needed a sign that she wasn't meant to stay here, this was it.

Sinking onto a stool at the island, she dropped her head onto her arms and released a wobbling sigh. She could bake for herself, and even do well for a contest, but baking for others was obviously not her thing. She'd wanted so badly to succeed.

A knock at the door startled her and she sat up, seeing Ashley holding a basket. Delaney welcomed her in with a wan smile.

Ashley glanced at the rolls on the counter. "This batch was a flop?"

Nodding, Delaney dropped back onto the stool, her spine as wilted as her spirit. "And there isn't enough time to get more batches mixed, proved, baked, and iced before they need to be at the café."

Poking at the rolls, Ashley wrestled one out of the pan. "Well, they smell great. You know, my dad once said that a life lived without passion is called existence. To pursue something new, your heart needs to be fully invested. Without passion, the desire and the dream die. I hold onto that whenever things go sideways." She chewed a bite of the roll. "Mm. With a little icing, this would be really yummy. Love the light cinnamon taste."

Retrieving the basket, Ashley set it in front of Delaney on the island and gave her a quick hug. "I figured you'd be busy baking and, if you're like me, forget to eat, so I brought lunch."

In the silence after the door closed behind Ashley, Delaney stared at the failed rolls. She'd been existing the past ten years. Her only passion was for the things she'd done in Hartwell. Her gaze jumped to the clock, and she calculated how fast she could get a batch of twenty-four done.

She couldn't get all of them done by seven, but she could get the first group finished shortly before then. She could run those to The Copper Hart while the next batch was baking. If she didn't quit, if she stayed focused, she could pull it off.

A moment later she was trashing the burned rolls and throwing pans in the sink. She wouldn't have known she had passion if she hadn't been laid off and come to Hartwell. A smile grew as she measured out the first ingredients.

She knew it now. And it was worth pursuing.

Liz sent one of her sons to retrieve the first batch while Delaney focused on the next. Sad that she would miss Patrick's song, she was also relieved not to see the disdain in his eyes. She'd prayed over the initial two dozen rolls, then released the tension and focused on the next. It was all in God's hands. She just wanted to be proud that she'd done her best.

Returning the second time, the young man said, "Good thing you planned on three batches, Miss Delaney, because they're going fast. Mom is so happy that she's singing in the kitchen."

Delaney nodded at the announcement, swiped her arm across her forehead, and concentrated on the icing. This third batch would make a total twice what Liz had suggested. What a thrill it would be if the people were truly enjoying them. Either way, she'd held up her part of the challenge.

With the last of the rolls in hand, she let herself into The Copper Hart kitchen through the back door and sighed wistfully at the sound of Patrick's familiar voice filling the café. Already she missed his smile, his teasing. The calm his presence gave her. Knowing Bryan was also out there increased the ache in her heart. If only he hadn't come . . .

The song ended, and applause followed. Liz rounded the corner into the kitchen and stopped with a squeal. "You're here! Come on."

"I'll just stay back here." She couldn't face Patrick.

"Oh, no, you won't." Liz grasped her wrist and tugged. "You need to take a bow."

"What? No—"

As Liz dragged her from the kitchen, a roar of approval swelled, and Delaney smiled in confusion as people patted her back and applauded. Liz handed her over to Patrick at the stage. With a passive expression, he held out his hand and helped her up, then quickly released his grip.

"Okay, okay," he told the crowd. "Settle down. Hey, Bobby! Chill out back there. No, she doesn't want a date with you." He waved his hand to quiet the noise, and the room finally hushed. "As most of you seem to know, this is Delaney Hutchins, tonight's talented baker. You can thank her for the world's best cinnamon rolls."

The cheers and whistles made Delaney laugh in bewilderment. All she'd done was bake some rolls, yet they were treating her like a rock star.

"This is ridiculous," she said to Patrick.

"No, it's appreciation."

From behind the counter, Liz rang a bell, and the room quieted again. "With this one last batch of rolls being served, we'll have enjoyed the first offering of the two you'll be voting on," she announced. "Now, Patrick and the band have a brand-new song, so calm down and listen up."

While she was speaking, Patrick had Delaney step down and stand in front of the band. "New song coming up," he whispered.

His breath, warm against her cheek, made her thankful the lights were low. She was no doubt an unattractive blazing red at this point. Then the embarrassment faded as the song began.

The gentle melody wove around her heart, bringing her simple words to life. Her eyes widened. He'd played some of it while they had lunch on the trail ride! She glanced back at the quiet crowd, touched to see smiles, eyes closed, people swaying.

The last notes faded and, after a hushed beat, the café filled with applause. Patrick looked down at her, a dark eyebrow raised. She pressed a hand over her swelling heart and managed a tearful nod.

Liz rang the bell again. "Okay, everyone. Quiet down. Now, here's the deal. As most of you know, this was a friendly contest between Hartwell's favorite band and Minnesota's sweet baker. We're gonna vote with applause, and the winner gets bragging rights until we do this again. Okay, ready? Let's hear your vote for Sagebrush Run's new song."

A loud ovation with whistles, cheers, and boots stomping on the wood floor. Delaney clapped and whistled along with them, sharing a grin with Patrick.

"Wow. Okay then," Liz said. "Delaney, you get up there on the stage so people can see you. Go on now. Patrick, get her up there, please."

He held out his hand and helped her back up to the stage as Liz continued.

"Now let's hear it for Delaney's cinnamon rolls."

An equal amount of noise erupted and she covered her face, laughing as Patrick hugged her amidst the racket. "We did it," he whispered.

"I'd say that's a tie, wouldn't you?" Liz asked, and the boisterous crowd agreed.

Patrick's voice quieted the room. "Well, I for one am pretty darn pleased with the results. How about you, Miss Delaney?"

She nodded, grateful for the arm he'd kept around her as her legs wobbled.

"But I do like to win," he added, "so how about a rematch?"

The crowd roared their approval and she nodded again. She wanted a rematch. She wanted to keep baking. She wanted—

"Delaney!" A beaming Bryan stood beside the stage.

CHAPTER 11

Patrick released her and turned away as Bryan helped her step down. "We'll consider that, folks. Okay, we've got one more song to close out the night. I want to see everybody dancing!"

"That was amazing," Bryan exclaimed as he led her away from the stage. Away from Patrick. They went into the kitchen, where he hugged her. "They loved your baking!"

"They did!" She was still reeling from the reaction. It was only a cinnamon roll, but it was *her* cinnamon roll. Her accomplishment. They'd loved the song as well. *Their* accomplishment.

"You can leave here proud of what you did tonight."

The words threw cold water on her excitement. Leave here. She couldn't. Even if Patrick didn't have feelings for her, this was where she wanted to be.

Bryan was still talking. "How fast will you be ready to go? Should we head out tomorrow, or do you need another day?" His grin was wide. "I'm so proud of you."

Calm filled her heart, replacing the angst of the last few days. She'd read the answer in the psalm. God had refreshed her soul and led her here, to Hartwell.

"Thank you. I'm so glad I didn't quit."

"You are no quitter. So, when should we head home?"

"Bryan, I'm not going home."

His smile faltered. "We don't have to leave right away. Whenever you're ready."

"I'm going to stay here."

"Stay here?" His frown showed genuine confusion. "In this out-of-the-way place? You've got a great new job waiting for you at home. Your friends are there. I'm there. We're getting married, right?"

"No. We're not. I should have been clear when you first asked, but I was too surprised to speak."

"Dela—"

She held up a hand. "We aren't in love, Bryan. We're friends, we've enjoyed spending time together, but we aren't in love. I'm done letting the world tell me what to do and how to feel. I want more than just existing." *Thank you, Ashley.* "I want to try new things, and push myself, and get scared, and maybe even fail. And I want to do that here, where the sky is open and the mountains are big."

Liz had bustled into the kitchen and bustled right back out. Delaney bit back a giggle at her wide-eyed expression.

"You're going to pass up this opportunity? They've created a whole new position just for you! Think of the money you'll make, the people you can mentor. You've done great work at the company. Don't throw it all away."

"I'm not," she said. "All that work has brought me to this point. But it's time to try something new, and I'm going to do it here."

He spread his arms, disbelief in his eyes. "Where are you going to live? How will you make money? What if you hate it here?"

"God will help me figure all that out. And if I hate it here?" She lifted her shoulders. "Then I'll go somewhere else. I want the freedom to try, and to fail, and I can't do that in the corporate world."

"What if your parents need help again?"

While the question pinged her heart, it no longer scared her. "Then God will help me figure that out as well." She knew that as clearly as she knew she was meant to stay in Hartwell. "I'm sorry I didn't speak up before you came out here. Honestly, I'm impressed that you did, but it doesn't change anything for me."

"But . . . I don't . . ." He stared at her like she'd gone crazy. "You're going to miss out on a fantastic opportunity, Dela. You'd have continued climbing the ladder. We'd have done it together."

"That's just it, Bryan. I don't want to climb the ladder. I want to explore my options down here. But I know you'll be at the top someday, and you'll do great work."

As the noise dwindled out in the café, they stood in stilted silence.

"You're serious," he said, brow furrowed.

"I am."

"I can't change your mind?"

She shook her head. "No."

He released a long breath and deflated. "Wow. Okay. I sure didn't see this coming. If things don't work out here, you can always come back home. You have lots of people who care about you. Starting with me."

"Thank you."

"Okay. Well, I'm just . . ." He shook his head, stunned defeat on his pale face. He started toward the back door, then paused. "You might not love me, but I do love you, Dela. Take care."

She nodded. When the door closed behind him, she wobbled in relief.

Liz reappeared and immediately wrapped Delaney in a warm hug. Leaning back, she asked, "Does this mean you'll do some baking for me? I can only bring you on part-time at first."

Fear-tinged excitement raced up from her toes. "If you're game, I am too."

With a delighted laugh, Liz hugged her again. "This is so exciting! I've wanted to do this for so long, but the timing was never right. Now I know why! *You* are the answer to my prayers, Delaney Hutchins. The Copper Hart will live on. Okay, I need to check something in the café. I'll be right back. Don't you dare leave."

"I won't." Delaney piled the empty pans to take back to the cabin and straightened the stainless counter, humming the melody of Patrick's song. Their song.

"So you're staying in Hartwell?"

She spun around at the voice, a hand at her chest. "You scared me!"

"Sorry." Patrick didn't look it as he moved into the room. "My question stands."

Her heart pounded a rhythm of hope and fear. She was staying regardless of how he felt about her. "Yes."

"Why?"

For so many reasons. "Because I want to."

With an enigmatic expression, he studied her as he stepped closer. "You do know that winters can occasionally be brutal around here, and it can get pretty isolating?"

"I grew up in Minnesota," she countered. "I'll bet it's a lot more brutal there in the winter."

"Hiking in summer or winter can be dangerous because of the wildlife."

"Montana isn't the only state that has wildlife." She shrugged. "I'll buy cases of bear spray."

"When the economy tanks, small towns like this are hit especially hard because travel is one of the first things people give up."

"That must be hard," she acknowledged. "But I'll bet the locals still need their coffee."

He crossed his arms. "Lots of tourists are charmed by happy little towns like this and think they want to live there. Then reality hits, and the sheen wears off. I've seen plenty of people come and go because real life in a cowboy town is harsher than they expected."

She mimicked his stance and cocked her head. "If I didn't know better, Mr. Finch, I'd say you're trying to scare this city girl off."

He shrugged. "I'd hate to have you break my cousin's heart by bailing on her when the sun isn't shining, the temps are dropping, and you realize you're bored."

"I get that. I like to think history shows I honor my commitments; however, I can't guarantee I won't drop dead mid-bake someday."

The corners of his mouth twitched. "Is Bill or Bob or whoever gone?"

"Yes. I convinced him that we aren't now and never have been a couple, and that what I want is here."

"What *do* you want?"

"I want to live my passion, honor God through my writing and baking, and be part of this community. And I want to get to know the town architect better." There, she'd said it.

Standing in front of her, he held her gaze. "Do you want to know what I want?"

She swallowed and nodded.

"I want to write more songs like our song. I'm not exaggerating or boasting when I say that's the best song I've ever performed. Afterwards, people said the words described their own journeys and that the melody would be hard to forget."

Delaney opened her mouth, but no words emerged. Her heart banged against her ribs.

"Liz wants to partner with you, and so do I." Mischief flashed in his eyes. "Maybe a little differently in some respects but definitely on writing more songs."

She managed a wobbly smile, cheeks flaming. "I don't know if I'll be good enough at the baking thing but, if I don't try, I'll always wonder what I missed out on."

He slid his arms around her, his expression now warm, hopeful. The reserve he'd hid behind was gone. "You'd miss out on being part of taking the café to the next level. You'd miss out on getting to know Hartwell, and we'd definitely miss out on getting to know you."

He lifted his hands to cup her face, brushing his thumbs across her cheekbones. "And you'd miss out on this."

As their lips met, the world exploded with a joy she'd never dreamed existed. She slid her arms around him and pressed closer. Oh, she did not want to miss out on this. His arms wrapped her in strength and protection. And an amazing moment later, applause and whistles filled the kitchen.

Startled, she tried to pull away, but Patrick held her close. The doorway was crammed with smiling people—Liz and her son, Ashley, Donny, and the band members.

"This is a private moment," Patrick grumbled. "Do you mind?"

"Not at all!" Laughter colored Liz's response. "I've been waiting for you two to realize you had a thing going since you first met."

Delaney turned her face against Patrick and giggled.

"Okay. We figured it out," he said gruffly, making a shooing motion. "Now go away."

"No can do, cuz," Liz said. "This place needs to be cleaned so I can go home. Everybody grab a broom or a mop or a rag and get busy."

The group did so after teasing Patrick and hugging Delaney. He pulled her back into his arms and pressed a kiss to her forehead. Then he released her with a wink and whispered, "Later."

This time Delaney didn't mind the blush that filled her face. God had indeed guided her to Hartwell, to these people and this man, using the compass of her heart. She couldn't wait for the future.

A Note from the Author

Dear Reader Friend,

I'm so happy to share Delaney's story with you here! It grew out of a writing retreat I took in Montana over the summer with Johnnie Alexander. We both fell in love with the small town we stayed in and wanted to share a tiny piece of that journey with you in our stories.

The dilemma Delaney finds herself in is one many of us have faced through our lives—a door closes, and we're not sure which direction to go next. In His Word, our Mighty and Loving God has promised to never leave us. He will guide our steps, although perhaps in a direction we have never guessed. The question at that point is always: Do we follow His path, unexpected and perhaps scary but undeniably His, or blunder on with our own plans?

I don't know about you, but too often I've blundered on only to experience one roadblock after another until I finally realized His plan is what's best for me. (I'm a slow learner! And very thankful for God's patience.)

When life takes an unexpected turn, remember to turn to Him first. He should never be our backup plan.

Praying God blesses you with the direction you need,

Stacy

ABOUT THE AUTHOR

Stacy Monson is the author of the award-winning Chain of Lakes series and is a founding member of The Mosaic Collection. She lives outside the Twin Cities metro area with many chickens, an old dog, and lots of wildlife (which includes seven grandchildren).

Learn more at https://stacymonson.com

Shattered Image
Dance of Grace
The Color of Truth

Standalone

Open Circle

Let's Connect!

Stacy Monson is the author of the award-winning Chain of Lakes series and is a founding member of The Mosaic Collection. She lives outside the Twin Cities metro area with 15 chickens, an old dog, and lots of wildlife (which includes 7 grandchildren). Learn more about her writing and her passion for encouraging others to be their best God-ordained selves at www.stacymonson.com.

Facebook: https://www.facebook.com/stacymmonson/
Instagram: https://www.instagram.com/stacy_monson
Pinterest: https://www.pinterest.com/stacymonson/
Goodreads: https://www.goodreads.com/stacy_monson
Email: stacy@stacymonson.com

The Gentling of O'Dell Adrian

ELEANOR BERTIN

The Gentling of O'Dell Adrian

Eleanor Bertin

If people were food, O'Dell Adrian would be a whole new flavour of sweet-and-sour chicken—skimpy on the sweet. En route to the Pacific coast to fulfill a childhood longing, she's waylaid by a whim in a northern BC logging town. There she meets Big Pete Neufeld, who's not afraid of her spit and vinegar and matches her spicy tongue with a few zingers of his own. But a sassy, wandering chick is not Pete's type. Though he should be glad to see the last of someone like her, against his better judgment Pete spends a day sparring with O'Dell, with surprising results.

Better to dwell in the wilderness than with a contentious and angry
woman.
~ Proverbs 21:19 (NKJV)

Admonish the young women to love their husbands, to love their
children, to be discreet, chaste, homemakers, good, obedient to
their own husbands . . .
~ Titus 2:4,5 (NKJV)

*To the memory of my beloved Tante Erica, who would have laughed
her throaty chuckle at O'Dell*

THE GENTLING OF O'DELL ADRIAN

"You go, girl!" someone shouted from the other end of the low-lit pub. A sudden kerfuffle erupted above the blaring of a Shania Twain tune.

Across the pool table, Pete caught Varmint's eye and jutted his chin toward the bar. Both of them straightened, turning to the sound and leaning against the edge of the table. Pete propped his cue on the floor and crossed his arms. "This oughta be good."

All eyes watched the drama as a chick in a red top and tight jeans flung herself across the bar to grab back a set of keys that Marian, the bartender, dangled just out of reach. Drunk Chick's comical squawking and wild, sloshed gymnastics made him chuckle.

Marian had about had it. "Sorry, ma'am. That's more than enough pink gin for you. You're cut off for tonight."

Drunk Chick wailed. "How'm I gonna get home?" She swung one leg over the bar, shrieking and sending a couple of glasses crashing. "Give 'em back, witch!"

Marian raised an eyebrow at Pete and Varmint, her unofficial bouncers. Pete pushed off the pool table, laying down his cue. He nodded at Varmint, shorter than him by a head but built like a rhino with an overbite, and the two of them strode over to solve the little lady's problem.

Varmint seized her ankle and one arm, Pete took hold of the opposite one, and together they hoisted her off the bar.

She kicked and flailed, twisting her body this way and that. "Getchyer hands off me, ya big palookas! Help, somebody! Help! This is assault."

Varmint's broad face crumpled in a grimace as the heel of her boot slammed too close to his crotch. He let go of her, bellowing. Freed from his grip, she started in on Pete, scratching at his leather vest, reaching up to yank his beard, screaming like a bobcat.

"Whoa now! Easy there!" Pete hooted, grasped a tight hold of her loose arm, and squeezed both her hands behind her back with his right hand. With his other arm, he bent her in half under the knees and swung her onto a barstool.

"You gonna stay put?"

"Pah!" was all she said. But she sat still enough.

He expected her to leap back across the bar any second, so he kept a slack grip on her arm. Varmint stood by, recovering from the blow.

Scowling deeply, she eyed the two of them with fierce resentment. She was compact and curvy, with a tousled mass of glossy dark curls and big brown eyes, though by now her makeup was a tad worse for wear.

Pete nodded at his buddy. "She'd be cute if we could get her to smile."

She responded with an ear-splitting roar, drumming her boots on the stool crossbar before kicking out at him and nearly losing her balance. Stepping out of reach of those lethal boots, Pete clutched her by the shoulders to steady her.

Varmint chucked her under the chin. "Aw, ain't the kitty-cat gonna give us a smile?"

She jerked away, hissing. "Let me go or I'll call the cops. This is finible conforcement."

At this, Pete and Varmint broke into guffaws. But a headshake from Marian prompted Pete to let go his hold on the young woman. "Listen," Pete said, sidestepping another swing of her boots, "you need a ride home?"

She leaped to her feet but wobbled enough that both men steadied her by grasping her arms again. She shrugged them off. "'M gonna call a cab."

Pete and Varmint exchanged grins. "'Fraid not in this little town. Up here in Telkwa, we're a bit off the beaten track."

"What am I s'posed to do? She stole my car keys!" Apparently, this girl only had one volume setting—max. She shook a manicured talon at Marian and looked, for a second, like she would charge the bar again. Then her shoulders dropped, and the corners of her mouth pulled down in a big pout.

Nodding to Varmint to let him know he'd take care of this, Pete got a firm grip on her elbow. "Tell you what. I can get you to wherever you're staying. You got a purse or anything?" He steered her past the spot where she'd been sitting. Marian produced a large red bag and passed it across the bar. Pete handed it to Drunk Chick, who yanked it out of his hand.

"Fresh air'll do you good." Pete guided his charge out into the cool, pine-scented darkness of a June mountain night. The woman started to move toward a dark Nissan. He steered her instead to his Harley Low Rider S/ST, its blacked-out frame and shotgun muffler velvety under the front lights of the pub entrance. "Here's my ride. Grab the red helmet. It should fit. And it matches your shirt." He chuckled to himself.

When he released his hold on her to fasten his own helmet, however, the woman missed a step and staggered into the bike, flopping over its seat like a rubber chicken.

"Easy there." Pete stood her up again. One glimpse at the pallor of her lips warned him to turn her away from the Harley. He hustled her over to the edge of the parking lot. Sure enough, she puked a huge splash onto the packed gravel. Pete jumped back to save his boots from overspray, then fished in his vest pocket for a crumpled napkin and handed it to her.

She wiped her mouth, handing it back.

"Uh, no thanks. You can keep it. Or chuck it in the trash can." He pointed, and she tottered toward it while he hovered behind her as though over a toddler, ready in case she stumbled again.

"You got a name?"

She muttered something unintelligible.

"What's that?"

"O'Dell."

"Okay, Miss O'Dell, let's see if—"

"That's my first name, you idiot," she hollered.

Pete winced at the piercing pitch. "Alright, O'Dell, don't get your knickers in a twist. Where are you staying?"

Mumble, mumble. Then, "Drove straight up from Prince George today."

Pete hesitated before cranking the engine. Now what? What was he supposed to do with this chick? He could see the motel's No Vacancy sign from here, unsurprising at this hour on a Friday night. A guy couldn't just leave a woman out on the street, even if it was summer. No telling what unsavoury characters might be out here, up to no good. He knew a few of them himself, guys that surfaced from out of the bush on a summer weekend. But Varmint would never let Pete hear the end of it if he brought her home. Not to mention Pete's own conscience. And there was no telling what this volatile chick might charge him with once she woke up sober.

Nope. Couldn't leave her on her own. He made up his mind. "I know a place you can crash."

She didn't resist when he helped her onto the rear seat, then swung his own leg over the bike. He hoped she had emptied the contents of her stomach completely by now. He had no wish to feel anything wet slithering down his back at this time of night. Turning the key, he revved the motor a couple of times. Over its purring rumble, he called out, "Hang on." Whatever was going on with her, she wasn't hanging on, so he snagged her flailing hand with one of his and secured it to his waist as he leaned for the turn onto the highway. He'd take her to his place.

"Mates, maid! How mean you that? No mates for you
Unless you were of gentler, milder mould."
~Hortensio, in The Taming of the Shrew, Act I, Scene 1, William
Shakespeare

Something scratched Pete's foot. He woke in a panic. Someone was in his bed. Pete slid out the side of the bed and dropped to the cramped space between it and the wall, narrowing his eyes at the bump that remained under the covers.

What in the blue blazes? He groped for his jeans, pulling them on from a crouch. The wench must have snuck in here sometime during the night. He'd brought her to his fifth wheel in the wee hours of the morning. On the short drive over, she'd gone and fallen asleep, leaning dangerously to one side so that he'd had to prop her upright with one arm and drive with the other. Then he distinctly remembered laying her on the couch at the front end of his RV. Easier to clean vomit off the removable seat cover there than off his bed. Besides, he couldn't give her his bed because he would never be able to stretch out on that dinky seat. She, on the other hand, had fit perfectly.

He frowned at the mass of dark curls spilling across his bed sheet, the only part of her not covered by his black-and-red Harley Davidson blanket. Grabbing yesterday's T-shirt, he crawled out of the room and closed the folding door. He was pretty sure she hadn't tried anything on him during the night. But he didn't think much of a cheap move like that. Did she have no self-respect or decency? Peter Bartholomew Neufeld did not take advantage of vulnerable, inebriated women.

After a quick wash, he pulled breakfast fixings out of his fridge and found his frypan. The chick would be in no condition to eat anything yet, so he started coffee and dropped only enough eggs and venison sausage for himself into the pan.

Only a couple of minutes later, the folding door slid open. "Do you have to bang around like that?"

Pete looked up from the sizzling meat to find O'Dell standing in the bedroom doorway, barefoot, holding her hands on either side of her head of crazy hair. She spoke in a harsh whisper, her eyes screwed shut against the morning light streaming into the main window. Evidently, she operated on the principle that what was his was hers, too. She'd commandeered one of his denim shirts.

"Need the biffy." She disappeared into the tiny bathroom, closing the door.

"You better not be puking in there!" he called out. He shuddered at the cleanup it would take in that small space, where the mess would get on everything.

In a few minutes, she emerged. "Quit your yelling. And don't worry. No vomit on your precious shirt."

Her bare legs and the two buttons undone at the neck that let the shirt slide off one tawny shoulder did a number on Pete's nerve endings. Maybe he was finally ready to look for a wife, but this time it was going to be someone stable and nurturing, someone he could trust implicitly with a child. He certainly wasn't about to hook up with some bird that flew in from who-knew-where. He turned his back on her. "Go put your own clothes on. Then you can have a Gatorade. It'll help with the hangover."

"*Jawohl*, commandant!" She slammed the folding door across the opening as much as possible, given the limp state of the closing mechanism.

Bet her sore old noggin was hurting bad. He opened the fridge again for a sports drink, loosened the lid, grabbed a glass from the cupboard, and set both on the table across from the small stovetop.

When she came through the door, he thrust a thumb behind him. "Drink up. Got you my favourite flavour, blue cherry."

"Cherries aren't blue." She poured a glass and took a sip. "Gross! Tastes like cough syrup."

He watched from the corner of eye as she read the nutrition notes on the bottle. "This stuff has thirty-six grams of sugar. I don't do sugar."

He laughed. "You think all that pink gin you were guzzling last night was sugar free? Drink it. Trust me, it'll help. And by the way, name's Pete Neufeld."

She hmphed but polished off the glass, then sat down at the table. O'Dell grimaced as she turned her head, slowly surveying the RV. "The nineties called. They want their décor back."

"You no like?" He scoffed. "Nothin' the matter with the place that a good woman couldn't fix." He smirked.

She snorted, then winced at her own sudden move. "You'd need a lot more than a decrepit old fifth wheel to lure a good woman into your evil clutches."

Pete turned the sausages, then cracked three eggs into the pan beside them. "Which means the woman that's currently in my evil clutches is . . . not good?" He tossed a sly look her way. "By the way, shall I cook you a couple of eggs?"

"The thought of anything that heavy makes me feel sick." Frowning, she poured the rest of the drink into her tumbler.

"Protein would be good for you. So maybe later, then." He chose a plate from the cupboard and a fork from the drawer, served himself his breakfast, salted and peppered it liberally, and sat across from her. When he looked up, she was watching him, a faint sneer on her face. "If it makes you sick, you don't have to watch."

O'Dell shifted her gaze out the window, sipping her Gatorade and squinting against the light. She reached for the window blind wand and lowered the blind. Abruptly, she narrowed her eyes at him. "You dumped me on a vinyl couch last night. Are you trying to kill me? That stuff gives off toxic fumes."

"Yeah, well, you were giving off some pretty toxic fumes last night yourself. Toxic puke breath, not to mention plenty of fuming back there in the pub." He chuckled, pleased with his wordplay.

She raked him with a look of scorn. "Aren't you clever. I was talking about vinyl chloride and volatile organic compounds."

He laughed. "I'd say *you* were the volatile organic compound last night. Fighting like a wildcat."

She averted her face but not before he caught the corner of her mouth quivering. She was hiding a smile, the first he'd squeezed out of her, such as it was. She was proud of that debacle?

After finishing the last of his meat and eggs, Pete leaned back on the seat and crossed his arms. "So, do you need anything else for the hangover?"

She lifted the empty Gatorade bottle. "Since you forced cough syrup on me for a headache, I'm not inclined to take any more of your medical advice." She downed the last of the drink.

Pushing his plate away, he rested his arms on the edge of the table. "Okay then, what's the plan for today?"

She shrugged, her full lips tightening at the corners.

"You must have come up here from Prince George for a reason. Most people come for the camping, but somehow I don't take you for the camping type." All he got from her was a grunt. "How 'bout, once we get some food into you, I drive you back to the bar for your car, and you can be on your way. Where are you from, anyway? And where were you headed?"

She still didn't answer.

"Look, I was just making conversation. You don't have to tell me. I'm not about to follow you and ambush you somewhere out there. All I wondered was what a woman might be doing on a road trip up here."

She muttered something about adventure, and the last bit sounded like "getting lost."

Pete frowned. It wasn't uncommon. People regularly came up from the south to "get lost in the bush"—fugitives from the law, crunchy-types with romantic notions about living off grid, loners escaping civilization. Some lasted, most didn't. Usually they weren't women alone, though. What was O'Dell's story? Didn't matter. None of his business.

"How 'bout I make you those eggs, eh?" He got up, taking his plate to the small sink before starting on her breakfast.

"But be thou armed for some unhappy words."
"Ay, to the proof; as mountains are for winds
That shake not, though they blow perpetually."
~Baptista and Petruchio, in The Taming of the Shrew, Act II, Scene
1, William Shakespeare

Things were different now. This time, O'Dell didn't need to snag a man with money. In the eight months since Chet's death, the estate had pretty much settled out. She had the ranch, and, with the cash payout from life insurance and survivor's benefits, she had a good reliable income. She eyed Pete up and down as he stooped over the miniscule kitchen sink washing his dishes. Not bad looking. Not bad at all, with his sandy hair and twinkling blue eyes. He had nice teeth, too. Beefy and tall. O'Dell didn't even come up to his shoulder. Tall was good. He must be at least six-five. He seemed like a decent guy in other ways, too. He hadn't even made any moves on her yet. And despite his shabby living arrangement, it was clean. Most importantly, all her insults and complaints hadn't made him mad no matter how obnoxious she'd been. She finished up the last of the eggs and toast he'd made for her, then rose and reached around him to slide her dishes into the sink. "You make a great scullery maid. I figured a bit more practice can't hurt."

He bent his head toward her with a wry look but kept washing. "Apparently, you're not aware of the old saying 'Those who will not work will not eat.'"

"Nope." She located her purse and escaped into the bathroom to do her makeup. Last night was the first time in forever that she hadn't followed her skin care regimen. She was just finishing up with setting spray when he called out.

"You ever coming outta there? It's shaping up to be a pretty day. What do you say to a scenic cruise around the area?"

O'Dell checked the mirror, satisfied with her face. *I am beautiful. I am enough. I am worthy of love and respect.* She stood on tiptoe to survey her somewhat rumpled outfit and frowned. She'd see about getting a change of clothes before going out anywhere. She opened the bathroom door and stepped out to find Pete already at the RV entrance. "Anything to see out there that I haven't already seen all across BC? Nothing but rocks, trees, and water."

He lifted an eyebrow, scanning her face. "True. Just like everyone has two eyes, a nose, and a mouth. But it's the arrangement of those that make it beautiful. Come on."

"Not so fast. I can't go anywhere looking like this."

He looked her up and down. "Yeah, you could start by washing off some of the paint. I'll wait."

Sniffing, she scorched him with a look. "I meant my clothes. I need my suitcase from my car. Can you get it?"

One of his nostrils lifted, and his mouth dropped open in disbelief. "You're kidding, right? One, you don't have the keys to get into your car. And, two, I can't carry a suitcase on my bike and drive at the same time." He shook his head. "'Fraid you'll have to come as you are."

"Can't you just drive me over so I can get my keys back from that witch at the bar and find what I need?"

"Bar doesn't open until four in the afternoon."

O'Dell stomped her foot.

Pete sneered. "Forget the clothes. You'll be fine. Come on, you wanted adventure? Let's go have one." Before O'Dell could protest, he strode out the door to a dog's enthusiastic barking and whimpering.

She stepped into the cute new boots she'd bought in Calgary her first night on the road, then followed him outdoors, where the smell of woodsmoke from other campsites drifted on the air.

Pete stood behind a late-model, silver pick-up parked in front of the RV and flanked by a shiny, high-end snowmobile on blocks. He'd been roughing up the sleek black coat of a Rottweiler. "Rocky, say howdy to Miss O'Dell No Last Name."

O'Dell approached without hesitation, scratching the large dog under the chin and crooning flattery. "It's Adrian. My last name." Rocky bunted her hand, apparently demanding a full-body massage.

"Nice to see a woman who's not afraid of a big dog."

"I've got a couple of them at home—not Rotties but a Boxer and a Lab. This one's just a big baby, aren't you, Rocky?" She pooched her lips and smooched the pup on the forehead.

"Okay, O'Dell Adrian, that's enough spoiling my mean guard dog. You'll ruin his reputation. Let's get on the road. Rocky's gonna stay here and watch my castle." He held out a helmet toward her.

Sighing, she put it on. So much for her work refluffing her flattened curls. Barely seated on the back of the bike, he shot out, circling the RV and aiming for the campground exit to the road. She clung to his waist, closing her eyes and leaning against his leather-clad back that blocked the wind. In a few minutes, he stopped at a small grocery store, dismounted, pulled off his helmet and gloves, and started for the door without a backward glance.

"Hey, wait a minute." She scrambled to catch up, fumbling with the strap on her helmet. "What are we doing here?"

"Picnic stuff." He grabbed cheese and buns, sliced ham, and a couple of tomatoes, adding a large bottle of ginger ale from the cooler near the checkout. Raising an eyebrow at her, he pointed at the rack of chocolate bars. "What's your pleasure?"

She stuck her fist on her hip. "I told you, I don't do sugar."

"Suit yourself." He piled a large chocolate nut bar onto the mound in front of the till. Once he'd paid, he strode out the door, ignoring her.

O'Dell scurried to keep up. He was packing the groceries into the two narrow saddle bags when she reached the motorcycle. "You mind letting me in on where we're going?"

"You'll see." The engine rumbled. "Hang on and watch for bears."

Bears? Yeah, right. O'Dell snuggled against him as they reached cruising speed, watching the scenery flit past. With the sun on her back and Pete's warmth in front, she relaxed like she hadn't since she'd started this road trip. Driving into the sunset until she reached the Pacific had been a cool idea when she'd come up with it on impulse three days ago. But the better highways didn't lead straight west; she'd had to accept that her car's compass had read northwest most of the distance. Besides, driving solo and navigating unfamiliar roads had tired her and stressed her more than she liked to admit. A lot different from her youthful hitchhiking days; now she was more cautious. She should probably be wary of the guy she was smushed up against, too. But a night and a morning together without any red flags swept that wariness away.

Leaving the main highway, the bike climbed and wound along a curving road crowded by towering trees. She caught occasional glimpses of the lake, turquoise blue, below them. At last they reached a lookout spot, where Pete parked in the dappled shade of some birches. He took off his helmet, hanging it from the handlebar, and did the same with hers when she passed it to him. Then he collected the food items from the bottom of the saddlebags into a denim sack and slung it on his back. "You carry the bottle." He thrust it at her.

"At least give me the grocery bag to put it in."

He handed it over, she stuck the pop into it to carry on her arm, and they sallied forth. Keeping up with his long strides wasn't easy. Dancing with him would be a workout. O'Dell swiped moisture from beneath her nose. Her boots were meant for cute, not comfort. "How much farther?" She was puffing now on the path through pine forest, the spongy bed of dead needles veined with tree roots.

"Just wait. Not far now."

He was right. Light suddenly burst through the cool shade of the trees onto a meadow dazzling with colour. Against the lightly swaying grass, blue Arctic lupines vied with scarlet Indian paintbrush and brilliant yellow mountain arnica like a Monet watercolour. The field of flowers sloped down to a shingle of pebbles that surrounded a glittering aquamarine lake. Beyond the water, a dark green forest stood guard against sentinel mauve and blue peaks topped with snow in the distance.

O'Dell gasped. Staring around in wonder, for a moment she abandoned her guard along with the bag containing the pop bottle. She ran a few steps into the blossoming glade, twirling with her arms outstretched, conscious of the picture she presented. She must look like Jennifer Lopez, romping around through the weeds.

"This is glorious!" She spun until she dropped, dizzy, into the grass, stretching out full length and letting the sun mingle the fragrances around her into a heady perfume. She peered back at Pete through the stems.

He stood at the edge of the meadow watching her, a mile-wide grin on his face as if he'd grown this garden of flowers just for her.

She sat up and arranged her face in a cute pout. "Well? Are you gonna stand there all day, letting those buns get moldy?"

"And where two raging fires meet together
They do consume the thing that feeds their fury."
~Petruchio, in The Taming of the Shrew, Act II, Scene 1, William
Shakespeare

This wasn't Pete's first lap around the track. He knew what O'Dell was doing, frolicking around in the flowers that way, showing her figure off. Thing was, it was working. She was a tantalizing piece of work, for all her frowny flirtatiousness. Just because he'd recently decided he could leave the past in the past and get serious about looking for a woman didn't mean he was above playing this game.

He sauntered out to where she sat, settling across from her in the grass and depositing the food bag between them.

O'Dell picked a pink blossom the size of a walnut from the turf beside her, sniffed it, and held it out for him to do the same. "I've never seen clover this big." Rising to a stand, she roamed the area, searching for more. After picking a handful of stems, she commenced weaving them together in a circle. When she placed it on her head, she posed with a coy look. "Aren't I fetching?"

"Very. About as fetching as my dog when he's chasing a stick." She snorted.

Flicking out his hunting knife, Pete opened the block of cheese and cut off a square. "How'd you like to make yourself useful and *fetch* the bag of buns."

She made a face. "Who was your slave last week?" She opened the bag and held out a bun to receive the cheese, as well as a slice of tomato he offered. Next she handed him the bottle of pop to open. "No cups?"

"Chug-a-lug," he ordered, sticking the bottle under her nose.

"Great planning."

"Hey. You saw the size of those saddle bags. You're lucky I remembered to buy a drink at all. 'Course, if it's too high in sugar content . . ." He withdrew the bottle.

She snatched it back. "It'll do." She took a swig, setting the bottle down and wrapping its base with the cloth bag to keep it upright. Suddenly, she jerked away from it with a yelp.

Pete dived for the bottle, saving it from toppling. "What's the matter with you?"

"A wasp!" She swatted the air frantically. "I hate wasps."

"You don't have anything to worry about. They're only attracted to sweets." The look on O'Dell's face made him laugh out loud. "Gotchya!" A thump on his arm opened his eyes wide.

He caught her wrist in the loose circle of his thumb and fingers, abruptly sober. "Hey. That's a game I don't play. It's a hard no to the fisticuffs . . ." He stared into the chocolate depths of her eyes, then down at her plump pink lips, for a moment ignoring the red flag of warning inside him. "But a definite yes to the backchat."

"Then let me go." She tugged unconvincingly at his grasp, her gaze still fixed on him.

Releasing her hand, he angled away from her. "Hmph. We're like an old married couple, sniping away at each other."

"So, *husband*, are you going to share that chocolate bar or not?" She took a bite of her sandwich.

"When I'm good and ready. I reckon I'll have another of these buns." He took his time fixing the sandwich, laying the ham on thick and placing the tomatoes just so, simply to bug her. Her impatient sighing slowed him even further.

"Would you like another drink?" she asked.

Pete raised his eyebrows at her new, kind tone. "Sure, that'd be nice."

"Get it yourself!" O'Dell cackled, setting the bottle well out of his reach.

"Some *wife* you are." He rose to his knees and swiped the pop from her hand.

Like a balloon deflating, the pep seeped out of her, leaving her small and uncertain. She sat cross-legged, propping her elbows on her knees and gazing across the lake. Something in the set of her mouth softened. "Just so you know, I'm not in the habit of drinking as much as I did last night."

He wasn't about to be fooled a second time by her abrupt change in attitude. "That's good."

"It's just . . . I've been on an adventure for the past few days. Thought I'd drive west until I hit the ocean. I've never seen it." Pensive, the longing in her voice seemed genuine. "When I was seven, my dad told me we were going out west to play in the waves. I was so excited." She sighed. "But he left my mom and me the very next week."

Pete stretched out, leaning on one elbow and munching his sandwich. Confiding an old hurt like that was more than he expected, considering how their morning had gone. "Well, as long as we're confessing, I'm not in the habit of bringing women home with me from bars, either."

She snuck a furtive look at him over her bun before taking a bite. Swallowing, she added, "Just so you know, I'm also not in the habit of crawling into bed with strange men."

"Glad to hear it. That could be a dangerous practice."

She looked away. "But I don't think I was a very good one." Her dejected expression remained, and it wasn't contrived.

"What? What are you talking about?"

"You called me wife. I don't think I was a very good wife."

Pete sat up, alarmed. "You're married?" He hadn't noticed a ring.

"I was. For thirteen years. Until eight months ago. My husband was killed in a car crash with his dad and brother."

"Whoa. That's bad news. I'm really sorry." The hand that held his bun went slack.

"You're not the only one. Let's just say I have some regrets about how I treated Chet. I wasn't always the nicest."

He couldn't help a chuckle. "Why doesn't that surprise me?"

O'Dell turned on him, eyes blazing. "Hey, no fair!"

He held up his palms. "You're right. That was a low blow."

"Just when we were having a moment."

"Yeah. Me and my mouth." He chewed in silence for a few moments. "Any kids?"

O'Dell stiffened. "I'd rather not talk about it."

"Sure, of course. I can understand that." His own children were a topic he kept deeply buried himself. Insect buzz and the breeze whispering in the trees filled the silence that followed. Eventually, he unwrapped the candy bar and broke it in half, handing one piece to O'Dell.

"Thanks." She took it with both hands, breathing in the aroma before closing her eyes on the first bite. "Mm."

He ventured a sneak attack. "I thought you didn't do sugar."

"I reserve the right to make exceptions," she replied tartly.

"Seeing too much sadness hath congeal'd your blood
And melancholy is the nurse of frenzy."
~The Taming of the Shrew, Induction, Scene 2, William
Shakespeare

After their lunch, they wandered down to the lake. O'Dell could feel the cool air emanating off its surface from several feet away.

"Take off your shoes and socks, and roll up your jeans." Pete shed his leather vest, unlaced his own boots, and hobbled barefoot onto the sharp-pebbled beach.

O'Dell unzipped her boots, laughing at the sight of his snow-white feet and awkward gait. "Tenderfoot!"

"You dare to laugh, wench?" He scooped water and flung it at her, the pure, icy droplets sprinkling around her like diamonds in the sunlight. She flinched and splashed back. Soon they were both spattered with damp.

"That's some cold," Pete said at last. He pranced gingerly over the rocky shore till he reached the grass, where he sat down to let the sun dry him off.

O'Dell followed and sat close beside him. "Look at our feet. It's like we're wearing socks. Mine are red, but yours are purple." She shivered despite the mild day.

He circled her with one arm, conveying his warmth, then squinted into the sun. "We're a ways from town out here, and you still want to get your car keys. What say we head back and see if Marian's opened the bar yet?"

The spot was so beautiful and his nearness so cozy that O'Dell resisted breaking the spell. But the ground was hard. She sighed. "I guess so."

Together they donned their socks and shoes and returned to the flattened foliage where they'd picnicked. Packing the leftovers into the bag, Pete reached out to pass O'Dell her purse. He let go before she'd fully grasped hold, and it tumbled into the grass, scattering its contents.

She scrambled to gather her things, her cosmetics, sunglasses, lotions, and other private items. She pawed through the bag, then stood frowning at the ground.

"What?"

"My wallet. I don't see it." She eyed him suspiciously.

Pete raised his palms. "Hey, I didn't notice it either. Let me have a closer look." He crawled around on his hands and knees and finally caught sight of the leather case, half hidden by a tussock of daisy-like arnica. It had fallen open to the photo of her kids—two dark-haired, big-eyed girls and a sandy-haired boy missing his front teeth.

"Give me that." O'Dell snatched the billfold, stuffing it into her purse.

"You've got kids?" he burst out, open mouthed. He rose to tower over her. "Where are they?" he barked. "Have you lost your mind? Or just your moral compass? What kind of mother hops in a car and goes joyriding all over creation when she's got young kids? A woman's place is with her children."

Startled, O'Dell went into defense mode. "Oh! Big He-Man knows what everyone else should be doing. Where do you get off telling a woman what her place should be? Moral compass, my eye! You have a kid. I saw the picture in your bedroom. So, why aren't you with her?"

He grunted like he'd been punched in the gut. "Never mind."

"Never mind? I will so mind! You can't just insult me that way when you know nothing about me. I'm a good mom! I'm super attentive and loving and—" O'Dell glared at him, but he wasn't listening. "I just . . . I had to get away. I had some things I needed to work out for myself. Don't worry, I made sure my kids are in good hands." She closed her bag with an emphatic zip, her lips clamped tight.

Pete was a pillar, ossified in the centre of the clearing like a statue. The flowers bent in reverence.

O'Dell shifted foot to foot. "So, are we leaving or what?"

"Sit down."

"What do you mean, sit down? I've gotta get back to town for my keys. You're the one that—"

"Shut up and sit down, woman." He pointed to the ground, his fierce brow lowered.

O'Dell promptly sat, watchful and waiting.

Pete crouched in front of her, leveling a stern look at her. "You were never supposed to be in my bedroom."

She cringed under his glare and the male authority radiating off him.

"That picture you saw? That was twelve years ago. The third birthday of my daughter, Melly. She was born with a heart defect—bicuspid aortic valve. Causes problems with opening and closing. We had to monitor her closely—lots of doctor visits." He slumped to a crouch, looking away as his voice lost strength. "We thought she was doing well but, a few days after that party, she got infective endocarditis . . . And just like that, she was gone. Three years old forever."

O'Dell hadn't counted on this revelation of deep pain. She could almost see the wound in his heart throbbing through his vest. Also, he'd said "we." If he was married, where was the wife? "I don't know what to say."

Wearily, he got to his feet. "Come on. Let's see about those keys." He turned and plodded back the way they'd come. O'Dell followed meekly.

Her boots pinched, but she didn't complain. A wasp buzzed past, and she waved it away without a word. Instead, she absorbed the disapproval, or exasperation, or disappointment—whatever it was that rippled off his back at her. It accused even as she excused.

She hadn't run away from her kids. Just this once, she had needed time to herself. Men had no idea of the stress level created by the endless demands of children and their constant crises. Everyone needed a break at times, didn't they? But the tearful face of her own three-year-old, Summer, left at her grandma's place, came before O'Dell. What would it be like to lose a child like that? Then Willow's serious, knowing face appeared, too, and Arrow's, both of them charging her with neglect by their looks. Yet she missed them. She couldn't live without them.

Pete and O'Dell left the sunny field, walking through tree shade until they arrived at the widened shoulder of the road where they'd parked the bike.

He picked up his helmet, then paused. "In all that ruckus last night and the bickering this morning, I never asked you where you're from."

"Central Alberta. I own a ranch out east of Red Deer."

He stroked his beard, calculating. "Look, I'm off work at the mill until next week, and I've got another few sick days coming to me. Time enough for a trip to the Prairies. I'm going to take you back to your kids."

O'Dell clasped her hands in front of her, objecting. "You don't have to do that. I can manage on my own. Besides, I still haven't seen the ocean, and that was the whole point of this trip."

"The ocean be hanged!" Pete huffed, rolling his eyes, then fixing her with an exasperated glare. "I am driving you back home to your children where you belong, and that's that. They need you." He handed her the helmet, clapped on his own, and straddled the motorcycle. "Hop on and let's go."

Obediently, she climbed aboard. Everything had changed, shifted before her eyes. She had lost the upper hand. Pete was not a lapdog to attend to her every whim. He was a Rottweiler with his own strong sense of moral rectitude. Shaken, she hardly knew how to act around him now. Yet his assertiveness made her feel safe. It had been a long time since her will had bent to anyone, if it ever had.

In a last, faint show of independence, she tried merely hanging onto the bike seat strap between the two of them, but it wasn't a secure hold. She soon gave up, unable to wrap her head around what had just happened even as she wrapped her arms around Pete.

"Why are our bodies soft and weak and smooth,
Unapt to toil and trouble in this world,
But that our soft conditions and our hearts,
Should well agree with our external parts?"
~ Katherine, in The Taming of the Shrew, Act V, Scene 2,
William Shakespeare

This is how, on a Tuesday evening in late June, Pete and O'Dell happened to drive into her mother-in-law's farmyard. Out front, the sunshine gleamed on the shiny hair of three-year-old Summer and five-year-old Arrow, who stood up from their sandbox play, watching the car's approach. When their mother leaped out of the car and ran to greet them, they flung themselves at her, clasping her legs. She crouched to enfold them in her arms.

With a swelling heart, Pete watched the reunion, a tender joining he had never had the chance to see with his own wife and children. O'Dell knew that now. He'd told her the rest of the story as they shared the driving on the road southeast, the long-lingering daylight shining bright through the rear window of her car.

"But you said your wife was pregnant when Melly passed?" O'Dell tilted her head for his answer. Her manner was deferential, cautious, when she asked.

Pete kept his eyes on the highway ahead, hating to relive this worst chapter of his life by telling. But O'Dell needed to know. Needed to know the pain of rejection, loss, and helplessness of the one who gets left behind. If he could prevent those three children of hers from experiencing a similar pain, he would tell it. "Yup. A week after Melly's funeral, I found out we had another child on the way. But first I found out our marriage was over."

There was a soft intake of breath from the passenger seat. Grateful that O'Dell had the grace to recognize the devastation he'd just revealed, Pete nodded and went on. "Nothing I said, or apologized for, or promised would change her mind. All she said was she was done. When I asked about the baby, she said her appointment was already made. Bicuspid aortic valve is an inheritable condition." He turned to her, his eyes narrowed, testing her.

"Appointment?" She wasn't picking up what he was putting down.

Pete gripped the steering wheel hard, recalling the helpless rage that had overtaken him at the news. "To terminate. She didn't want to take the risk of another child with a heart defect."

"Oh . . ." O'Dell breathed the word out long, resting her hand on his arm. "I think I get now why you were so bent on taking me back home." She pushed her hair back from her face. "You couldn't convince her to cancel?"

"Tried. She went through with it anyway. On February 14 of all days, a day that's supposed to be all about love. The baby would have been born sometime in September."

O'Dell stroked his arm, following the direction the hair grew. Something about that simple motion soothed him, dissipating the old grief. "I'm so sorry for your loss."

Pete shrugged. "You get used to things."

She pressed his arm urgently. "Not something like that you shouldn't. You never get used to betrayal or the death of a loved one."

He looked at her for as long as he could before he had to concentrate again on the road. "I think you're right. Thanks for saying so." After that, he held her hand.

Now he sat watching O'Dell squeeze her children to her. The older girl, Willow, came cautiously out the door. When O'Dell saw her, she beckoned her over to join the group hug.

A deep satisfaction filled him. He had done a good thing. And by the joy on her face, he knew that O'Dell thought he had done good, too. It had been a bit touch and go there, the moment he started ordering her around the way he had. Despite his intimidating biker looks, tyranny wasn't his way. But it had worked. O'Dell had tamed right down and followed his lead. She must have known she was way out where she didn't belong.

As the miles and the mountains had flown by and they'd talked about their lives, their past, their hopes, Pete saw a different side of her. What a surprise it was to find that Drunk Chick, also known as the "bird that flew in from who-knew-where," alias O'Dell Marie Adrian, was the face that came into focus out of the shadows. The indistinct wife he had so lately realized his need of had a name.

Soon O'Dell stood to wave him over. The children's grandmother had stepped outside, all smiles. Should he intrude on this family moment? Was it fair to these kids to introduce another man into their lives when they had so recently lost their father? Yet he wanted nothing more than to step into those shoes to take care of their mother and of them. It was all happening fast, he knew that. But he was certain O'Dell felt the same way. And the thought of having a family to work for and love salved the wound in his heart.

He would let the children lead, playing games with them only if they wanted, being cautious with his joking to prevent hurt feelings, treading softly with the older girl, who looked like a sensitive sort. And maybe one day, he would take the four of them to play in those ocean waves that O'Dell had missed out on.

He reached for the door handle, leaving the stuffy car where he sat alone to enter the enveloping warmth of a ready-made family and home.

A Note from the Author

Dear Reader:

A woman's place . . . it's a contentious issue these days, isn't it? Biblical instructions on women's roles are mocked and ignored if they're mentioned at all. Evidently, resistance to these commands is nothing new. The quiet and gentle spirit that God cherishes in a woman has never come naturally. But let's not make the mistake of thinking that a woman "tamed" is a woman without wit, or intellect, or agency. God uses our personality, talents, and natural bent for His good purposes. I've had the privilege of knowing gentle, godly women who are accomplished, strong, and influential precisely because of their quieted spirit.

Shakespeare's brazen, insolent Katherine in *The Taming of the Shrew* was the perfect literary allusion for my character, O'Dell, who first appeared in my novel *Unbound*. I had left her there, a troubled, angry young widow, stressed out by the demands of her children yet looking for a man. She made another brief appearance in the epilogue of *Tethered*, married to a faithful man who loved her despite the Bell's palsy that marred her pretty face. This story fills in the gap from "there to here."

I hope you enjoyed the banter, brooding, and blessing of watching O'Dell be gentled. May the Lord increase His fruit in our lives, including gentleness, to make us more like Himself.

Your friend,

Eleanor

ACKNOWLEDGEMENTS

My mother's gentle spirit has been my lifelong inspiration. Though she has been gone now for three years, her teachings ring in my mind and heart, for which I thank the Lord. I'm grateful for the many ways He has "gentled" me over the years and how He continues to do so.

I owe much to my English and creative writing teachers and professors over the years. Their correction and encouragement gave me confidence to try.

Thank you to my Mosaic sisters, who spur me on to grow in the craft and business of writing; to Brenda Bryant Anderson, who freely shares her vast knowledge; and to Deb Elkink, who has taught me so much through her precise and careful editing.

ABOUT THE AUTHOR

From her home in central Alberta, Canada, Eleanor Bertin has a passion for studying and memorizing Scripture. Inspired by the depths of God's love and mercy to humanity, she writes fiction that ponders the place where life's perplexities meet faith's certainties.

Before raising and home educating a family of seven children for thirty years, Eleanor received a college diploma in Communications and worked in agriculture journalism. She returned to writing in 2016 and has since published five novels, as well as the memoir, *Pall of Silence*, about her late son, Paul. She and her husband of forty-four years are the grandparents of ten amazing grandchildren. Along with their youngest son, Timothy, who has Down syndrome, they live in the Before of a century home.

TITLES BY
ELEANOR BERTIN

THE MOSAIC COLLECTION: NOVELS

The Ties That Bind Series
Lifelines

Unbound

Tethered

Burning Bright Series
Flame of Mercy

Flicker of Trust

Flare of Doubt

THE MOSAIC COLLECTION: ANTHOLOGY STORIES

"Like Wool" in *Hope is Born*

"Love & Unexpected Stress Responses" in *A Star Will Rise*

"How Life Begins" in *All Things New*

"Christmas at the Crossroads" in *A Whisper of Peace*

"Grounded" in *Before Summer's End*

"A Portion of Grace" in *Song of Grace*
"Who Sends the Rain?" in *Dancing in the Rain*
"No Night There" in *The Heart of Christmas*
"Meg and the E-Monster" in *A Thrill in the Air*
"Not by Chance" in *Sounds Like a Plan*
"Unremarkable Sue" in *A Weary World Rejoices*
"Call Me Birdie" in *BirdSong*
"L'il Trip to Paradise" in *Skipping Winter*

Standalone (Non-Fiction)
Pall of Silence: My Journey from Tragedy to Trust

You Always Were My Favourite
AN IN THE SHADOWS NOVELLA
SARA DAVISON

YOU ALWAYS WERE MY FAVOURITE

Sara Davison

Carly Travers is counting the days until she can marry the love of her life, Alain Temauri. Only one thing mars her happiness—the distance that has always existed between her and her sisters. When their father sends them on a quest well off the beaten path, the three of them must lean on each other if they hope to complete the challenge and discover the treasure awaiting them at the end. A gift far greater than any they could have imagined.

And now these three remain: faith, hope and love.

But the greatest of these is love.

~ I Corinthians 13:13 (NIV)

To Luke, Julia, and Seth
You are all my favourite.

ONE

Present day

Invitations sent. Venue booked. Dress purchased. Check. Check. Check.

Carly Travers ran her finger down the screen, ensuring that each task had been taken care of. Flowers. Band. Caterer. All done.

She reached the last item she had typed into the Excel spreadsheet weeks earlier. The tip of her finger stilled next to the word: Bridesmaids.

Her stomach tightened. Alain, her fiancé of four months, wanted his three brothers—two biological and one, Xaviar, whom they had all essentially adopted into the family a year and a half ago—to stand up with him. That meant she needed three bridesmaids. Not a problem. Although she was the only child of a single mom, she had plenty of friends to choose from. Carly had already asked her best friend, Tory Ellison, to be her maid of honour. That left two spots to fill.

The problem was that she'd delayed making this decision so long time was running out. The wedding was June 6th, less than two months away. Carly yanked open the top drawer of her desk, tugged out a large, pink spiral notebook, and flipped it open to the page where she'd scrawled a list of possibilities. As she'd done with the spreadsheet on the computer, she ran her finger down the names, considering each one. All good friends, any of whom would be happy to join the wedding party, she was sure.

So why couldn't she pick one?

With a sigh of exasperation, she grabbed her phone, called up her list of contacts, and tapped on Stephanie, the first name she'd written in her notebook. The tip of her finger hovered above the receiver icon for a full ten seconds before she hit the back button to get out of the contacts section. "Argh." Carly tossed her cell onto the desk, shoved enough of the paper clutter Alain teased her endlessly about out of the way that she could prop her elbow on the wood, and lowered her forehead to her palm.

"Not getting cold feet, are you?"

Alain's teasing voice released the tension tightening up every muscle, and she lifted her head and spun the black leather desk chair around to face him. "Absolutely not. I'm counting the days until we get married. Forty-eight, to be exact."

He grinned. "Good. Me too." Gripping both armrests, her fiancé leaned in to kiss her. His lips were soft and warm and, by the time he straightened, her heart was pounding and her cheeks were flushed. Definitely counting the moments.

He hadn't cut his hair since they'd returned from getting engaged in Tahiti four months earlier. She liked the longer curls and the wire-framed glasses. Very English professor like.

Alain glanced at the open notebook. "Any luck finding your bridesmaids?"

She grimaced. "Not yet."

He crouched in front of her and rested his hands on her knees, his dark eyes searching hers. "Why don't you call them?"

Her throat tightened. "Who?"

Alain tilted his head, one dark curl nearly touching the collar of his plaid flannel shirt. "Your sisters."

All right, the whole only-child-to-a-single-mother thing wasn't entirely accurate. At best, it was a half truth. She had been the only child of her single mother, who had passed when Carly was seven, but she had two half sisters—one born to her father's first wife and the other to his current one. Carly was his eldest child, although he and her mother had never married.

Despite dear old Dad's best efforts, she and Phoebe and Scarlett weren't very connected. The fact of the matter was that she hadn't seen either of her sisters for months. Hadn't heard from them, either, beyond the odd cursory text. "They're not on the list."

Alain tucked a strand of blonde hair behind her ear. "I see that. Did you even invite them to the wedding?"

She sighed and tugged open the small drawer of her desk. Lifting out two ivory envelopes rimmed in gold, she held them up to show him. "I will. I just haven't gotten around to it."

"Could that be because you know you'd feel better if you called and invited them in person? Maybe even asked them to stand up with you?"

One of the things she loved the most about Alain was how well he knew her. It was also one of the things she loved the least. "Maybe."

"They're family, love."

Carly sighed. "Just because we're family doesn't automatically mean we're close."

"I know that." Sadness drifted into his voice, and she mentally kicked herself. Of course he knew that. Better than most. He and

Tane and Rav's dad was an abusive alcoholic who'd been in prison for years after killing a kid while driving drunk.

She set the invitations back in the drawer and took his face in her hands. "I'm sorry. My situation is nothing like yours, I know. Scarlett and Phoebe aren't bad people. We just . . . don't have anything in common."

"You have your dad."

When she didn't answer, he reached up and clasped her fingers. "You did invite him and Nell, didn't you?"

"I sent them an invitation last week but haven't heard back yet."

"I'm sure you will soon." He squeezed her fingers before straightening. "I should get home. But you'll think about talking to your sisters, right?"

As she had thought about little else for weeks, she had no problem making the promise. "I will."

"Good." Alain pressed a kiss to the top of her head. "I'll pick you up at ten tomorrow for the cake tasting."

"Sounds good." If anything could perk up her spirits, it was cake. "I'll—" The vibrating of her cell phone cut her off, and she shot a look at the screen. Her brow furrowed. "It's a text from Phoebe."

He grinned. "Must be a sign."

Carly wasn't so sure. It was unlikely her sister was reaching out simply to catch up. But what could she want? She pursed her lips. Only one way to find out. She grabbed her phone. The message was short, but she had to read the words over three times before they would sink in.

Alain touched her shoulder. "What is it?"

She swallowed. "It's my dad. He's in the hospital."

TWO

September 1993

Arlo Stone ran his fingers across his forehead. The lights were hot and, given the size of the intimate venue he and his band were performing in, the temperature in the packed room was rising rapidly. Not that he was complaining about the number of people who'd shown up to see him and the other members of his folk band, Lone Trail. Numbers had risen dramatically since they'd released "Way Off Track" six months earlier, the only song of theirs that had made it to number one. The only one that had cracked the top twenty, in fact.

That was fine. They'd only been performing a couple of years, and so far just in Canada. They were paying their dues like everyone had to in their business. If they stayed focused and committed, launched an American tour before too long, they'd get there one day.

Assuming he could get through tonight's show.

His throat tightened, and he turned his head to cough, pressing a fist to his mouth so the mic wouldn't catch the sound.

As he straightened around on the high wooden stool, his eyes locked with those of a young woman in the front row. She tilted her head slightly, studying him. Could she tell?

His dad's raspy words still rang in his head. Felix Stone was every bit the singer Arlo was, although he'd never been one to perform for others. He'd called Arlo an hour ago, his voice thick with sorrow. *I'm sorry, kid. It's your mother. She's gone.*

Blinking rapidly, Arlo glanced down at the fingers plucking out a melody on his guitar. When he looked up, the woman's gaze remained fastened on him, her long, blonde hair cascading over one shoulder.

Focused. Right.

This was a critical time for Lone Trail. They'd made a pact to avoid the whole women-alcohol-drugs trap so many performers fell into. No hotel room overdoses or Beatles-style breakups for them. Although plenty of female fans waited outside whatever venue they were performing at, he and Jim and Davey would only smile and wave and get into their van to drive to the hotel.

Tonight would be no different. Except that, tonight, everything was different. His mother was no longer in the world, which meant that the world—his world, anyway—had gone suddenly dark.

He rubbed his palm over the deep ache in his chest before returning his fingers to the strings. Summoning every bit of resilience he had, he began softly crooning the words to "Hard Times Come Again No More," one of his dad's top ten songs. A small smile crossed his lips. Man, his dad loved Arlo Guthrie. Presented the idea to Arlo's mother that they name their long-awaited son after the man. Thankfully, Arlo's mother had been amenable to the idea. Of course she had been. His dad would never have insisted on the name if she hadn't been—he'd lived to make her happy.

An only child, Arlo had spent much of his growing-up years sprawled on the carpet in the living room, his mom and dad doing dishes or working on a puzzle or sitting close on the couch, hands clasped. The three of them had listened to Guthrie's *Alice's Restaurant* so often they'd pretty much worn down the grooves on the old album.

They listened to other artists too—the Beatles, Beach Boys, Donovan, Jefferson Airplane, Herbie Hancock. Ella Fitzgerald, too, and, over and over, Merle Haggard's *Mama Tried*. His parents didn't worry much about genre, but they were sticklers for real, raw, authentic voices and lyrics.

They had a lot of gospel albums in the bins lining the shelves the way books did in most people's homes. Albums like Johnny Cash's *The Holy Land* or *Gospel Time* by Ruth Brown. Something about the soulful sound and the lyrics on those albums reached further down inside Arlo than any of the other songs they listened to. Even so, the grip they'd had on him loosened as the years passed. By the time he himself was writing and performing, the echoes of those worshipful words had pretty much faded completely.

Tonight, though, Elvis Presley's "How Great Thou Art"—his mother's favourite—played quietly in the back of his mind even as he sang the words of another. "Tis the song, the sigh of the weary. Hard times, hard times, come again no more."

But hard times *had* come. And he *was* weary. His gaze drifted to the woman again. The small smile she offered gave him the courage to push back his shoulders and finish the song and then the show before stumbling from the stage.

He and Davey and Jim loaded their equipment into the van. At one in the morning, the air was cool, and a September breeze swept across the deserted parking lot, clearing the cobwebs from his mind. He hadn't told his bandmates about his mother yet. Still needed to work out the news in his own head before he could talk about it or figure out what it might mean for the rest of the tour. He slid the side door closed and lifted a hand. "I think I'll walk to the hotel. See you in the morning."

It wasn't an unusual move for him, and the guys nodded and climbed into the front seats. In seconds, he was alone in the parking lot.

The stars above Hope, British Columbia, an hour and a half from his hometown of Maple Ridge, tried valiantly to break through the clouds to offer tiny pinpricks of twinkling light. Shoving his hands into the front pockets of his jeans, Arlo gazed up at them. *I see the stars, I hear the rolling thunder, Thy power throughout the universe displayed.*

Funny, he hadn't thought about God in a long time. Not since leaving home a decade earlier. Maybe even before that. Why tonight, when God had just ripped from him one of the people Arlo cared about the most? *Awesome wonder* was definitely not what he was feeling in this moment.

"You're sad, aren't you?"

Arlo whirled around. The woman from the front row stood a few feet from him. She wore a pink denim jacket over a black Lone Trail T-shirt and had wrapped a pink-and-black scarf around her neck. He glanced behind her. Was she out here all alone?

Without looking back, she flicked her fingers over one shoulder. "I told my friends I needed to check on someone and would take a cab home."

When no response came to his mind, she tipped her head in his direction. "You. I'm checking on you. In case that wasn't clear."

"Oh." His forehead wrinkled. "Do we know each other?"

She tipped her head from side to side. "Not in the traditional sense, no, in that we've never actually met. I'm sad too, though, so you could say that part of me recognized that part of you."

Arlo almost laughed. Interesting logic. "Well, I appreciate you checking on me, but I'm fine."

She didn't answer, only raised her eyebrows. His shoulders slumped. "All right. I'm not fine. But I'll get over it."

"What I saw and heard from you tonight didn't look like something you'd just *get over*."

She wasn't wrong. Still, he doubted that spilling out his heart to a perfect stranger—even one who shared his sorrow—would help. And there was that pact he'd made with his bandmates . . .

The woman stepped closer. "Look. I know this is weird. Full disclosure, I'm a big fan of Lone Trail, so I do know a lot more about you than you know about me. Sometimes that helps, though, don't you think? There's freedom in talking to someone you don't know, someone you'll likely never see again. Probably why so many people are willing to share their woes with a bartender or pay a stranger two hundred dollars an hour to listen to their troubles."

Hmm. "Maybe."

That one word, noncommittal as it was, appeared to be all the encouragement the woman needed. She held out her hand. "My name's Solace."

It was his turn to raise his eyebrows. "Really?"

She laughed, a sweet sound that eased the ache in his chest even as it set all kinds of alarm bells ringing in his head. "True story. My parents were a couple of hippies."

Against his better judgment, Arlo wrapped his fingers around hers. "Mine too." His voice had gone raspy again, and she tightened her grip, her eyes welded on his the way they had been when he was performing.

Then she nodded slightly, as though she'd figured out the source of his grief without him having to reveal it, a thought that disconcerted him as much as it offered comfort. She let go of him and slid her hand through the crook of his elbow. "Come on. I know a place with great coffee. You can share your woes with me. No charge."

Arlo managed a weak grin. Despite the cool evening, her fingers were warm through the sleeve of his denim shirt.

They sat in the coffee shop for hours. True to her name, the woman did offer him a solace he desperately needed that night. So much so that, when they left the café, he abandoned every bit of good sense, the truths on those gospel albums he'd grown up with, and the pact he had made with Davey and Jim, and invited her back to his hotel room for the night.

When he woke up the next morning, Solace was gone.

THREE

Present day

Carly rapped softly on the partially open hospital room door. Alain's hand, warm between her shoulder blades, gave her courage as she pushed it far enough to step inside. Her stepmother, Nell, sat in a chair on the far side of the bed, holding her dad's hand. They both looked over when Carly and Alain walked into the room.

Worry lines were etched across Nell's forehead, but she smiled at them. "Carly. Alain. Hi. Come on in."

Carly made her way to the near side of the bed and gripped top rail. Her dad was hooked up to a heart monitor and an IV, but he managed his usual wry grin as he touched her hand with his before lowering it to the light blue blanket. "Hi, sweetheart."

"Hi, Dad. How are you doing?"

"I'm okay. Really. The doctor said that, with the right medication and a few lifestyle changes, you'll be stuck with me for quite a while yet."

The thought of a world without her dad rocked her, and she wrapped her fingers around the railing to hold herself steady. "I certainly hope so. I need you to be at my wedding."

He waved his hand feebly through the air. "Don't you worry about that. Nothing could keep me away. Now tell us how the plans are going."

Since he clearly didn't want to talk about his health—she'd have to get more details from Nell later—Carly shared what they had been up to.

He kept his blue eyes fixed on hers as she talked about flowers and cake and the dinner menu. Although she suspected what he really wanted to know was if Phoebe and Scarlett were involved in the ceremony, she held out hope that, in his current state, he would let her off the hook and not ask.

By the time Alain finished describing the resort where they planned to honeymoon, her dad's eyes looked heavy. They should go and let him rest. Carly was about to tell him that when he covered her hand with his. "Will your sisters stand up with you?"

So much for being let off the hook. It bothered him that the three of them were distant, she knew. "I'm not sure yet. I haven't completely decided."

He patted her fingers. By the time he'd returned his hand to the blanket, his eyes were fully closed.

Nell had clung to his other hand the entire time they'd been talking, but she let him go now and stood. "I'll walk you out."

Carly nodded. "We'll come back soon, Dad."

He opened his eyes. "Don't come here. It's no place for a visit. I'll be home in a few days, and we can see each other there." The grin he offered Alain was a shadow of the one he'd given her when she first came in. "Bring that crazy Xaviar with you. He's good medicine."

Alain chuckled. "That's true. And I will."

If she hadn't been so worried about her father, Carly might have smiled. Instead, she kissed her dad on the forehead and followed Nell from the room.

Alain's unofficially adopted younger brother *was* good medicine. He'd been through a lot, including his older brother letting him take the blame for his drug-dealing and then not stepping in when Xaviar was sent to prison for his brother's crimes. Then his dad had cut him off, leaving Xaviar completely alone in the world.

If Rav hadn't met him during a trip to Tahiti and brought him home, who knew what might have happened to Xaviar? And the rest of them would have missed out on the privilege of knowing him and the joy he'd brought their family.

Family. Her chest squeezed. What had happened with her father had shown her how quickly life could change. Was she missing out on the privilege of time with Phoebe and Scarlett? Her dad's health was all she could think about in this moment but, with her and Alain's wedding approaching quickly, she couldn't put off reaching out to her sisters much longer.

FOUR

Arlo's walk of shame lasted two years. When he couldn't carry the burden any longer, he broke down and went to church—a place whose doors he hadn't darkened since he was a teenager. There he encountered the God of his youth and found redemption and, for the first time in as long as he could remember, at least a tentative peace.

He also found Viviana Mylonas.

The two of them married eight months later. Lone Trail disbanded on amicable terms, since Davey was also married with a baby and Jim was engaged.

Arlo continued to write and sing but only for himself, in the small studio at the back of his music store. He'd bought the store from a friend of his dad's who'd run the place for forty years without ever updating anything but his record collection. The pipes groaned and water stains marred the walls, partially hidden behind old concert and movie posters. Arlo loved the place—his second home growing up—and refused to change a thing.

A year after they got married, Viviana gave birth to their first child. When a nurse set a tiny, red-faced Phoebe Ruth in his hands, Arlo's heart was lost. *After all my failings, Lord, thank you for the gift of this precious child.* It felt to him as though God had restored, as he had promised, the years the locusts had stolen, and Arlo could not have been more grateful.

Then one afternoon the store bells jangled. He glanced over from the miniscule table in the children's corner where he was having high tea with four-year-old Phoebe. A man he didn't recognize stood on the mat inside the door. While he had numerous regulars, a new customer was a bit of an oddity.

Arlo set his tiny teacup on its tiny floral saucer and flicked one of his daughter's dark braids over her shoulder. "I'll be right back, princess. Keep an eye on our guests, would you?" He nodded at Holly the rag doll and Jiminy the teddy bear propped on the other two chairs at the low table.

Phoebe nodded solemnly, and he smiled at her before pushing to his feet and heading for the middle-aged man who was strolling toward them. He wore a navy suit and red-and-white-striped tie in jarring contrast to the standard, heavy-metal T-shirt and ripped jeans most of Arlo's customers favoured.

Arlo stepped behind the counter. "Can I help you?"

"Mr. Arlo Stone?"

"That's right."

"My name is Gordon Smith from the law firm Smith, Jacobs, and Callahan."

"Okay." Arlo drew out the word. The man's voice was grave, and his chest tightened. What could this possibly be about? Was someone suing him? If so, they were likely to be disappointed—the whole *you can't get blood from a rock* thing. Of course, he did have his share of the Lone Trail money tied up in investments in case of emergency, but the store barely brought in enough for them to live on.

Mr. Smith set his briefcase on the counter and hit the buttons with both thumbs to pop open the clasps. Arlo glanced over his shoulder. Phoebe was pouring a cup of "coffee" for Jiminy and speaking quite seriously to her guests. Otherwise, the store was empty. While Arlo wasn't typically thankful for that state of affairs, in the moment he was glad no one was there to witness . . . whatever this was.

The lawyer withdrew a brown legal folder, nudged the briefcase to one side, and set the folder on the counter. After flipping it open, he tugged out a sheet of paper. "Regretfully, I am here to inform you of the recent death of Solace Travers who, I believe, was an acquaintance of yours?"

Shock jolted through Arlo so strongly that his palms lifted and then smacked back down on the countertop.

"You okay, Daddy?"

Arlo shifted sideways, propping a hip against the counter to steady himself. "I'm fine, sweetheart. If you want, you can get the cookies from the kitchen. I'll be there in a minute."

"Okay." Phoebe stood and skipped toward the area in the back with a sink, microwave, and bar fridge.

He watched her a moment, hoping the delay would allow his heart time to slow its painful thudding. It didn't. Arlo straightened around to face his visitor. "Sorry about that." With his fingers, he swiped at the small beads of sweat that had formed on his forehead. "As for Solace, I don't know if I'd call her an acquaintance. We met only once, eight years ago."

"Once was enough, apparently."

The man's tone was dry, and Arlo lowered his hand to the countertop. "Excuse me?"

The lawyer held up the piece of paper. "Are you aware that Ms. Travers gave birth to a girl in June of 1994?"

Arlo did the math quickly in his head before briefly pressing his eyes shut. "I was not aware of that, no."

"At the time, the name of the father was left off the birth certificate, but Ms. Travers did leave a will in which you are named as biological father and sole custodian of the child, Carly Autumn Travers. I'm here to see if you are willing to accept that guardianship. Otherwise, you can sign this waiver relinquishing any rights to your daughter."

The ground beneath his feet trembled as though the ongoing threat of seismic activity along the Queen Charlotte Fault was coming to fruition. He gripped the edge of the counter with both hands to keep from swaying. "What will happen to her if I sign?"

"She'll remain with Child Services, who will do their best to find a good home for her."

Arlo's head spun. No way could he let his child remain in the foster system, especially one who was likely already too old for anyone to want her. *I want her.* The thought caught him off guard, but he couldn't dispute it. This was his child, his daughter, every bit as much as Phoebe was, despite the circumstances of her conception. He had to be the one to take care of her, to raise her.

Viviana. Their marriage had been rocky from the start. For months before the wedding, he had wrestled with himself over confessing his one-night stand to her. Two weeks before the big day, he'd finally mustered up the courage. It hadn't gone well. Viviana was furious that the encounter with Solace had happened at all and even more furious that he hadn't told her about it sooner.

During the forty-eight hours of stony silence that followed, he'd been sure the wedding was off.

Eventually, she informed him she'd decided to forgive him and go through with it but, whenever she was upset with him, she would throw the transgression in his face. Arlo had hoped that when their child was born their relationship would settle, but it had been four years and they had yet to find their footing.

For whatever reason—whether she still couldn't let go of the past or simply hadn't wanted to be a mother—she'd never shared his joy over their sweet girl. She fed and clothed Phoebe and spoke to her when necessary, although even that was usually a reprimand. The rest of the time she was content to leave their daughter to his care while she returned to her work as manager of a large bank.

How would she react to the news that he had another child? Not well, he suspected, although hopefully she would come around. They could raise Carly and Phoebe together, sisters who would no doubt grow up to be each other's best friends. More redemption from a gracious and forgiving God. The thudding in his chest eased. "I'll need to speak with my wife, but I'm almost positive we will want to take Carly."

The lawyer paused as though that was not the response he'd expected. Slowly, he returned the paper to the file, closed it, and set the folder in the briefcase. "Very well." He dug around in the inside pocket of his jacket before tugging out a business card and setting it on the counter. "You have my number. Call me when you've made up your mind."

Arlo nodded and followed him to the entrance on shaky legs. "Can I ask what happened to Solace?"

"She passed two weeks ago. Breast cancer."

The man's words were curt, matter of fact, but they hurt something deep in Arlo's chest. Despite the shame and guilt associated with the night they'd spent together, Solace had been lovely. He'd only ever blamed himself for what had happened between them. Although . . . why had she never contacted him to let him know she was expecting his child? Heat coursed through his chest.

Mr. Smith nodded curtly before hauling open the door, setting the bells jangling again. Mrs. Coleman, who owned the convenience store across the street, was at her usual post, one finger holding the blind away from the frame as she peered outside. Arlo raised a hand in her direction. As always, her only response was to let the blind go, leaving it to bang against her large front window as he closed the door.

He turned and leaned against the back of it. What had just happened? In the course of a five-minute meeting, his life had completely changed. Confusion and grief mingled in his chest, cooling the heat. Likely he would never know why Solace had kept this secret from him. No sense driving himself crazy over the reasons for her choices.

What had she gone through the last few years, fighting that terrible disease? What had Carly gone through? She'd be seven, old enough to know what was going on. He and Viviana would have to be extra patient and loving with the young girl who would be coming to them traumatized and grief stricken.

Arlo pushed away from the door, the growing excitement he felt over having another child tempered by apprehension about the coming confrontation with his wife. Viviana would have to understand. He could endure even more days of silence and nights on the couch if it meant that, in the end, his wife would eventually come around and embrace Carly as her own.

He tried and failed to ignore the question insinuating itself into his brain as he headed for the back corner and the tea and cookies waiting for him at the doll-sized table.

What if she never did?

FIVE

Present Day

Carly and her stepmother reached the front exit, Alain trailing behind them. "I'll bring the car around," he offered, then hugged Nell before disappearing out the revolving door.

"Sit with me a minute?" Nell nodded to a bench, one of many in the expansive lobby.

"Sure." Carly followed her over to the metal bench.

Nell slid her bag off her shoulder, setting it between them. "I have something for you. From your dad." She rifled through the bag and then pulled out a small, brown leather box.

Carly held out her hand, and Nell set the box on her palm. For a few seconds, Carly only studied it, then she undid the bronze clasp and lifted the lid. Catching her bottom lip in her teeth, she touched the item inside. The bronze compass her father had given her shortly before her eighth birthday. She lifted it out and set the box on the bench. When she pressed her thumb to the knob extending from the front of the compact, the lid sprang open.

The sight of the light green arrow shifting slightly from right to left before settling in place unleashed a flood of memories, carried along on a rush of emotions like twigs caught up in a raging river.

Not wanting to confront either the memories or the emotions here, in a public place, she started to close the lid. Then something on the inside of it caught her eye and she stilled. Words had been engraved there since the last time she'd held the compass. How old would she have been, seventeen or eighteen? Her dad had taught her how to use it in the wild, creating maps and directing her and her sisters to head a particular number of steps in a certain direction.

He'd guide them from one landmark to another until they reached the end of their quest and found whatever treasure he'd hidden for them. The three of them had loved those adventures as much as he had. What had happened to drive them all apart? She couldn't even remember now.

Shoving the thought aside, Carly tipped the compass back so she could read the words, written in elegant cursive. *You always were my favourite. Dad*

Carly blinked. She was? That was news. She snapped the lid closed. What was she supposed to do with this?

When she looked up, Nell held out a cream-coloured envelope. "This should explain everything. Take it with you and read it when you're ready."

Carly took it from her. *My darling Carly* was scrawled across the front of it in her father's handwriting. Her throat tightened. Was this about what was happening with her dad? Was he in worse shape than he was letting on?

Nell rested a hand on her forearm. "He'll be okay, Carly. I'll take good care of him, I promise."

Carly swiped a rogue tear from her cheek. Her stepmother had always been able to tell what she was thinking and feeling, even when she tried to hide it from her. She covered the soft, warm fingers with hers. "I'm really happy he found you, Nell."

Nell smiled. "I am too."

"You'll let me know if Dad gets worse?"

"You know I will."

Clutching the envelope, Carly stood. "I'd better go. Alain will be waiting."

Nell hugged her. When she stepped back, she held Carly's forearms. "I'm glad you found Alain as well. He's a good man, Carly."

The warmth that spread through her chest lifted some of the heaviness. "I know."

Nell squeezed her arms before letting her go. "I'll see you soon." She shot a pointed look at the envelope. "Once you've done everything you need to do."

Carly nodded and stuck the letter into her bag before heading for the revolving door. As soon as she stepped outside, she caught a glimpse of Alain standing next to his car. A light spring rain was falling, the drops cool against her flushed cheeks. When their eyes met, he shook the water from his hair and lifted both hands to the sides, a rueful grin on his face. Carly laughed, a memory washing over her like more soothing rain.

The evening they met, Alain had rushed into her bookstore soaking wet from a sudden west coast downpour. He'd stood on the mat just inside the door, arms lifted away from his body, rivulets of water sliding down the lenses of his glasses, drops falling from the ends of his glistening hair.

His dark eyes met hers, and they both laughed. Carly had been about to close the shop and head home, since all the other customers had gone. Instead, she directed him to the couch in front of her gas fireplace, fetched him a cup of tea, and the two of them sat and talked about literature and life for hours.

Questions buzzed through her head as Alain held the car door and she slid onto the front seat. What had her father written to her? And what did the compass have to do with it?

Had Nell given Phoebe and Scarlett something from Dad as well? Maybe she should call them, ask if they were okay and talk to them about the wedding. Or maybe she should read the letter first to find out what she was dealing with.

As though he could sense she was on the verge of spiralling again, Alain reached for her hand. His touch calmed her, and she drew in the first deep breath she'd taken since Nell had texted her. One step at a time. As soon as they got home, she would read the letter, and then she could figure out where to go from there.

SIX

October 2001

Arlo sat in the rocking chair in the corner of Phoebe's bedroom, his hands gripping the wooden arms until his knuckles gleamed white in the soft glow of the small lamp next to her bed.

He should go downstairs, talk to Viviana, but he couldn't tear his gaze from his daughter. Her cheeks were flushed and her long, dark hair spread across the pillow as she clutched a stuffed pink dinosaur in one arm.

Most nights he'd read two or three books to her. Tonight, he had started and finished six of them, until his little girl's eyelids were heavy and she'd rested her head against his chest. Then he had lifted her into his arms and carried her to bed.

Now he sat in the chair gazing around the room, picturing the space with another bed, another child sleeping in it. Their house was small and had only two bedrooms, so the girls would have to share. Maybe they could get bunkbeds to allow enough floor space for them to play.

Christmas was coming in a couple of months. Did he have time to make that doll house he'd been considering? Would Carly still play with doll houses, or was she too old? His chest squeezed. He had missed out on so much of her life. All those moments he'd had with Phoebe—bringing her home from the hospital, getting up with her in the night, her first steps, her first words. Every milestone big and small had passed by in Carly's life without her father there to witness them. Did she believe that was Arlo's choice?

What had Solace told their daughter about him? That he had willingly walked away from them both? If so, they might be getting a girl angrier and far more traumatized than Arlo had considered.

Even so, the thought of his elder daughter here, in this room, under the same roof as him filled him with a deep joy that outweighed any trepidation about how he could possibly make it up to her for missing so much of her life.

Speaking of trepidation . . . With a deep sigh, Arlo pushed to his feet, kissed Phoebe on the forehead, and crossed the room. Time to get this conversation with his wife over with. The sooner they talked, the sooner the countdown to her eventual acceptance of the situation would begin. Not to mention that the longer he delayed, the longer Carly would be left in the foster system. That thought propelled him out the door and down the stairs.

When he'd nearly reached the bottom, he caught a glimpse of his wife on the couch in the living room. She was wrapped in a blanket, her feet propped on the cushion in front of her, deeply engrossed in whatever show she was watching. He took a few seconds to study her. Phoebe had gotten her beautiful dark hair and eyes and her olive skin tone from her Greek mother. His daughter's personality was much sunnier, however.

Not long into their marriage, Arlo began to realize what kind of a person his wife was, how self-absorbed. Somehow she had kept that part of herself largely hidden until she unexpectedly became pregnant with Phoebe. For months, he blamed the hormones, the disruption to her life and work that she hadn't asked for, and the physical discomfort she was experiencing to explain why she had morphed into a different woman than the one he had dated and married.

By the time Phoebe was two, with his wife only becoming more narcissistic as the months passed, not less, Arlo was forced to admit that this was the true Viviana. The thought of clearing space in her life and schedule for yet another surprise child likely wouldn't sit well, but she'd have to understand.

When he walked into the room, she didn't take her eyes from the screen. "Is she asleep?"

"Yes." Arlo settled at the far end of the couch. "Could we talk?"

She blew out an irritated breath. "It's been a long day. I just wanted to relax for a bit."

"I know. I'm sorry to interrupt, but this is important."

Something in his voice must have snagged her attention, because she pointed the remote at the television and pressed pause before shifting around to look at him. "What is it?"

His mouth had gone dry, but Arlo didn't want to go to the kitchen for water in case she turned the show on and refused to pause it again. "Remember when I told you about that woman I spent the night with before I returned to church and met you?"

Her features darkened. One of her demands when she agreed to go through with the wedding was that he never mention that night again, even though she brought it up herself on a regular basis. "It's doubtful I would forget my husband cheating on me."

His jaw tightened. He had never cheated on Viviana and never would. Still, although he hadn't been a Christian at the time and had repented and been forgiven for his past, she had always insisted on framing that night in those terms. She spoke again before he could respond to the charge, which was likely for the best. "Why are you bringing it up now?"

He drew in a steadying breath. "Because a lawyer came to see me today to let me know that Solace has died."

Although he didn't expect Viviana to feel badly about that, he also didn't expect the interest that sparked in her eyes. She clicked off the TV, tossed the remote onto the coffee table, and bent her knee on the couch so she could fully face him. "Why would a lawyer come see you? Did she leave you something?"

"In a manner of speaking. Nothing of any monetary value, though."

Her shoulders slumped. "What, then?"

The moment of truth. Arlo unclenched his fists and rubbed damp palms over the front of his jeans. "She left me a daughter."

His wife stared at him, her mouth slightly open, for several agonizing seconds, as though she couldn't comprehend what he had said. Then her eyes narrowed to glittering slits. "You have another daughter?"

"Apparently, yes."

"Did you know?"

"Of course not. I never even suspected such a thing, or I would have told you. Today was the first time I heard about her."

Her cheeks flushed an angry red. "You said this woman left her to you. Does that mean you're expected to take care of this . . . stranger?"

"She's not a stranger, Viviana. She's my child."

"Whom you have never met. Which makes her a complete stranger. And she's certainly not *my* child. If you think for one second that I am going to take on someone else's brat, then you—"

"Stop." As tumultuous as their marriage had been, Arlo had rarely been furious with his wife. Frustrated, yes. Sad and lonely and disappointed that the two of them never could seem to bridge the chasm between them, definitely. He wasn't a man given to anger, however, so for the most part he had accepted the state of things and tried to be as evenly keeled as possible when dealing with her. Tonight, though, an intense rage gripped him at the idea that she could call an innocent child, a young girl who had grown up without a father and who had just lost her mother, such a thing. "You will not speak about her that way."

Her cheeks mottled and her eyes blazing, his wife shoved to her feet. "Get out of this house."

Arlo's chest clenched as he stood. "You don't mean that."

"I most certainly do. It's bad enough that I've had to live with your infidelity all these years and that you saddled me with one child I didn't want. I refuse to take on another one."

He shot a look toward the stairs. Was Phoebe still asleep? "Lower your voice, please."

"I'll speak as loudly as I want. And if you aren't out of this house in thirty seconds, I will scream loudly enough for Phoebe and the rest of the neighbourhood to hear."

There would be no reasoning with her tonight. Maybe, once she calmed down, they could discuss the situation like rational adults. "Fine. I'll go. But let me take Phoebe with me." The last thing he wanted was to leave his little girl with Viviana when his wife was out of her head with anger and resentment.

"Absolutely not. You gave up any right to her when you chose to have a child with another woman." She pointed at the door. "Go. Now."

Gave up any right? Was she suggesting that she might keep Phoebe from him? Deep cold gripped him, turning his blood to ice. "Viviana."

"Go." As promised, her voice rose.

He needed to leave now before she terrified their child. Or someone called the police. Being arrested might mean Children's Aid wouldn't let him take Carly. He could lose both his children.

"All right, all right. But we'll talk tomorrow." Arlo headed for the entrance. Thankfully, his wallet and keys were on the table in the front foyer. He kept a toothbrush in the small apartment above the store, along with a few items of clothing that he stored there in case of tea party spillage. He could make do with what he had for a few days if necessary.

His wife pushed past him to stalk to the door and fling it open. "We'll talk if and when I am ready to talk. Or maybe you'll simply hear from *my* lawyer."

Arlo grabbed his jacket from the closet, leaving the hanger swinging wildly as he stepped outside. He scrambled to come up with something, anything, to say that might calm her down but, before he could form the words, she slammed the door in his face.

For a few seconds, he stood, his jacket clutched in one hand, staring at the red door he'd painted only weeks ago. As much as he had known his wife would not accept the news well, he could not have foreseen that their conversation would go as badly as it had or that he would end up here, outside the small home the two of them had scrimped and saved to purchase a year ago.

Arlo shook off the thought as he turned and descended the porch stairs. All that mattered tonight was that Phoebe was okay. His heart ached at the thought of her waking up and calling for him if he wasn't there to answer, but what could he do? He had to respect Viviana's wishes. For now.

Even so, if she tried to keep his younger daughter from him, Arlo would fight for his little girl with everything he had.

SEVEN

Carly sat at the desk in her room, running a finger over the scrawling words on the front of the envelope Nell had given her. *My dearest Carly.*

For some reason, she was reluctant to open the letter. What if, despite Dad's declaration that he was perfectly fine and she wouldn't lose him for a long time, he was writing to tell her that what he had was serious and that he might not have a lot of time left. She couldn't bear it. She and her father had missed the first few years of her life. Even after they were united, their life paths had only run parallel to each other. Gradually they veered closer and closer until they at last intersected. Eventually, their two paths became inextricably entwined. What would she do if she lost him?

Read it.

Good advice. Likely what he had written had nothing to do with his health but something else entirely. She'd never know if she didn't open the letter.

With a heavy exhalation of breath, she reached for the opener on her desk and slid it along the top of the envelope until she could see the folded piece of cream paper inside.

Maybe she should have taken Alain up on his offer to stay while she read it. It was late, though, and he had a long drive home, so she'd sent him on his way. Carly tugged the paper free and dropped the envelope onto her desk. Settling against the back of her chair, she unfolded the paper and began to read.

Dearest Carly,
It's time for another Stone Family Challenge—#50, to be exact. We've had fun with these, haven't we?

She lowered the paper to her knee, her mind flitting to the first ever challenge, a treasure-hunt-type quest her father had created for her. The two of them carrying out that challenge together had changed everything between them. Would this one do the same?

She set the paper on the desk and leaned forward to read.

Here are the conditions of the challenge:
1. *Go on your own to the head of the Woebegone Trail at 10 a.m. on Saturday, June 14th.*

2. *Bring only the following items: hiking boots, sunscreen, insect repellent, bear spray, water, snacks, your compass, and an open mind and heart.*

3. *Beginning at the sign with a map of the trail, use your compass to follow the steps below. When you reach the initial destination marked with an X, you will find your first treasure.*

Near the bottom of the page, he had included a long list of steps leading from one landmark to the next. Four bigger destinations had been marked with X's. At the end of the list, he had added, *You can do this!*

Carly sincerely hoped that was true. She and her sisters had never failed to complete a Stone Family Challenge, but their dad had always been there with them, encouraging them, allowing them to go slightly off track and try to find their way back but stepping in if they veered too far off course.

She had never attempted to complete a challenge on her own. *Could* she do it?

This was Thursday, so in two days she would find out the answer to that question.

All she knew for sure was that, if this was something her father wanted her to do, she would do everything in her power to complete the quest and discover whatever it was that was waiting for her at the end.

EIGHT

October 2001

Arlo tossed the sponge into the ceramic dish next to the sink. He'd spent all day scrubbing and mopping and vacuuming the apartment above the store until every surface gleamed.

At the harsh buzzing of the doorbell from down at street level, he swiped his hands on the new dish towel hanging over the handle of the stove and then strode for the door. Was he ready? He almost laughed. How was he supposed to prepare himself to meet his seven-year-old daughter for the first time? It didn't even matter how he was doing, only how Carly was. What had the social worker told her about what was happening?

Lord, help. I have no idea how to deal with a girl who is hurting so badly. Give me wisdom. Still sending desperate pleas heavenward, Arlo reached the bottom of the stairs and pulled open the door.

Carly looked like her mother, as blonde and blue eyed as Phoebe was dark. They both had his cheekbones, though. Phoebe also had Arlo's smile. As Carly was staring at the bottom step where a chunk of concrete had broken off years ago, he had no idea if she did as well. Lord willing, he would find out before too long.

In the two days since Viviana had kicked him out of the house, Arlo had called the lawyer to let him know he would not be signing away the rights to his daughter. Then he had spent a few hours setting up a cot, dresser, and bookshelf for her. There only was one bedroom, but that was fine. He could sleep on the couch for the short amount of time they would be here. He still believed that he and Viviana could work things out and she would allow him to bring Carly home. In the meantime, he needed to make this space as comfortable and welcoming as possible.

With no idea what Carly, or any seven-year-old girl, would like, he'd stood in front of a wall of bedding at the local box store for fifteen minutes, debating with himself. In the end, he'd chosen pale green sheets over pink and then added a soft pillow and a comforter covered in flowers to the cart. Maybe she was too old for it, but he couldn't resist the soft stuffed monkey he found in the toy department.

He hadn't trusted himself to choose what books she might like and relied on a saleslady who apparently had six- and nine-year-old granddaughters and who assured him that his daughter would love The Unicorn Academy and Junie B. Jones. Arlo bought both series and tossed in a sketchbook and box of pencil crayons for good measure.

Their town of Maple Ridge was situated on the Fraser River and surrounded by the Golden Ears mountains. The sun sparkling on the water and gleaming off the majestic peaks of British Columbia assuaged Arlo's inner turmoil. *Lord, any chance you could make this go well?* Clutching the steering wheel tightly in both hands, he breathed the prayer as he left the outskirts and maneuvered his ancient Chevy along Highway One, headed east toward Hope, the town less than two hours away where, unbeknownst to him, his daughter had spent her first seven years.

Help Carly as she makes this transition. Please help the two of us to get along and for her to feel comfortable with me. And please soften Viviana's heart toward her. And toward me. Help the four of us to become a family.

It felt impossible, but nothing was impossible with God, right?

The tightness in his chest eased as he pulled up in front of the CAS office in Hope. An hour later, he'd signed a bunch of paperwork and gotten a whole lot of advice and encouragement from the social worker, Ellen, a woman about his age who, somewhat startlingly, wore a pink T-shirt beneath overalls covered in flowers. Not the most professional look but likely much more appealing to the children she worked with than a blazer and dress pants would be.

She was extremely kind and spoke highly of Carly, which made Arlo unreasonably proud, as though he'd somehow had anything to do with his daughter turning out the way she had. She had then promised to pick his daughter up from school and bring her to his place, which likely was better than his plan—to go to the school and pull Carly out of class because he couldn't wait another minute to meet her.

Now here his daughter was, in front of him. Arlo realized suddenly that he was gazing at her, mesmerized, and had yet to say a word. He cleared his throat and stepped back. "Hi. Welcome. Come on in."

The social worker smiled at him before resting a hand on Carly's back. "Let's go upstairs, sweetie. Your dad can show you your room."

Still not looking at him, Carly allowed the woman to guide her up the steps. She remained silent as Arlo showed them around.

When they finished the very brief tour, he crouched in front of her. "I'm glad you're here, Carly. If you need anything, just ask me, okay?"

She hesitated before nodding slightly, her gaze still averted.

"Are you hungry?"

She shook her head.

Ellen slid an arm around her shoulders. "Why don't you go and get settled in your room, Carly. I need to talk to your dad for a minute. I'll say goodbye before I leave, okay?"

His daughter nodded again before trudging to her room and closing the door.

Arlo offered the social worker a helpless look.

She smiled again. "It will take time for her to adjust, but she will. All you have to do is be there for her and be as patient and kind as you possibly can."

"I will." He glanced around. "I know the place isn't much, but I'm hoping it will be temporary."

Ellen held up a hand. "You aren't adopting or fostering Carly; she's your daughter. As long as she is safe and healthy, you don't have to explain yourself to me. In fact, your association with Children's Aid has officially ended, barring any reports of issues, of course, which I don't foresee." She hesitated before unzipping her leather across-the-chest bag and pulling out a business card. "Having said that, I've spent quite a bit of time with Carly over the last couple of weeks. There's something about her." She looked up at him, a sheepish grin on her face. "I have a lot of experience with helping parents and children through the transition period as they get used to each other and the huge changes in their lives. If you have any questions or need advice about anything, please don't hesitate to call." She held out the card.

Arlo took it and set it on the corner of the small Formica table in the kitchen. "Thank you. I appreciate it. I feel like I'm in over my head here."

"Of course you do. So does Carly. If you give her—and yourself—a lot of grace, I'm confident you will find your way to each other."

Find their way to each other. Arlo liked the sound of that. His father had given him a compass when he turned twelve and told him that with it he could find his way anywhere. Arlo had spent a lot of time in the woods after that, learning how to use it and how to navigate unfamiliar landscapes, keeping his eyes on that arrow guiding him to where he needed to go.

The reason he'd returned to church after what happened with Solace was that he realized he had lost his true north—the one who not only knew the way Arlo needed to go but was Himself the way, the path he needed to follow.

Following Jesus hadn't failed him yet, so he would trust Him now to guide him and Carly through whatever rough terrain lay ahead.

NINE

Present day

Carly arrived at the sign at the top of Woebegone Trail—an advanced hiking trail that was rarely used, as it was way off the beaten path. The paint was peeling from the large wooden sign at the entrance, and it was covered in vines and spider webs. Was it even safe to strike off here alone?

Open mind and heart, Carly.

Right. Neither was her strong suit, but she would attempt to follow her father's directions. He wouldn't put her in danger.

She set her backpack on an old, rotting bench next to the sign and dug through it, checking to make sure she had everything on the list. All the items were tucked safely inside with the exception of the bear spray, which she had clipped to her belt in case she needed it. Which she sincerely hoped she wouldn't.

Since there was no phone on the list, Carly had, somewhat reluctantly, left hers in the glove box of her car, determined to do this right. Alain knew she didn't plan to take it with her, so he wouldn't expect to hear from her until she had completed her list of instructions. Which included waiting until ten a.m. to start along the trail, following her compass and measuring her steps until she reached the first X on the map. According to the rough sketch her father had made, that X indicated a large rock next to the stream that wound along beside the trail.

A car door slammed in the distance, and she frowned. No other vehicles had been parked in the small lot fifty metres behind her, and Carly had really hoped she wouldn't encounter any people today. At least, if they were hostile, she could use the bear spray on them.

As footsteps approached, she slid her arm through one of the backpack straps and slung it over her shoulder. She'd let whoever it was go on ahead, wait a few minutes, and then follow after them.

A woman came into view, her long, dark hair tamed into two braids hanging beneath a beige ball cap. Carly squinted. "Phoebe?"

Her middle sister tilted her head to the side. "Carly?" She sounded as surprised as Carly. What, exactly, was their dad up to?

Phoebe closed the gap between them and stopped in front of her. "What are you doing here?"

"Same as you, I'm guessing. Did Dad send you?"

"He did. Nell gave me a letter when I went to see him in the hospital."

"Me too. What did yours say?" A cool breeze ruffled the leaves overhead, and Carly did up the zipper on her light blue hoodie.

"Not much. Just that I was supposed to come here at ten o'clock this morning and that I'd find out what I was supposed to do when I arrived. Oh, and he gave me a list of things to bring."

"Anything unusual?"

Phoebe slid a pack off her shoulders and set it on the bench. She unzipped the small pocket on the front, tugged out the same piece of cream-coloured paper as Carly's, and opened it. "Nothing out of the ordinary, other than an open mind and heart."

Carly laughed. "Those were on my list as well. Along with my compass."

"Hmm. Do you suppose he also told—" Another car door slammed, and Phoebe grinned. "Never mind. I believe that answers my question."

"What do you think Dad's up to?"

Her sister shrugged. "No idea. But I'm guessing we're about to find out."

The two of them waited as the sound of hiking boots tromping over grass and loose gravel grew louder. Carly caught a flash of red as her baby sister came into view.

Scarlett shook her head as she approached, her long, red ponytail swishing against the back of her pale green jacket. "I should have known I'd find you two waiting here."

Always more effusive than Carly or Phoebe, Scarlett swept in to complete their Stone sister triangle, pulling the other two into a hug. Even if they had never been BFFs, Carly returned the hug, the warmth easing the last of the morning chill from her bones.

Scarlett stepped back. "All right. What's this all about?"

Carly pulled the folded letter from her back pocket. "Apparently we're about to set out on The Stone Family Challenge #50."

Phoebe let out a low whistle. "Wow. Fifty. Really?"

"That's what Dad said in his note."

"We've never done a challenge without him. Do you think we can?" Scarlett propped one hiking boot on the bench and bent forward to retie the lace.

"We don't have a choice." Carly held the letter out to Phoebe. "Here. You read the instructions, okay? I'll work the compass, and

Scarlett can count the steps and make sure I don't walk into a tree or a rock or anything else."

"All right. Let's do this." Scarlett stuck a hand into the middle of the circle. After a brief hesitation, Carly covered it, and Phoebe laid hers on top. "*Go Stones* on three," Scarlett instructed.

Grateful no one was around to witness their little cheering session, Carly counted to three. Open mind and heart, right? With her dad's words echoing through her mind, she shouted "Go Stones" along with her sisters. Their battle cry must have disturbed a flock of turkey vultures, as they rose from the evergreens around them, flapping huge wings as they circled overhead before flying off. Carly watched them a moment, in awe of their massive wingspans. Hopefully the presence of vultures at the start of their quest wasn't an ominous sign.

She shook off the slight sense of foreboding. "Okay, Phoebe. Where are we going first?"

Her sister gave her the direction and degrees and the number of steps, and Scarlett counted out loud as Carly started forward. Two minutes later, they reached the first small destination, a metal pole marking the edge of the trail. From there they picked their way carefully over roots and thick vines to the next stop, a Charlie-Brown-Christmas-tree evergreen with drooping branches. Clearly Dad was taking them one small step at a time to ensure they didn't veer off course, which was fine with Carly.

After forty-five minutes of making their way through thick underbrush, she caught a glimmer of white on the west side of the path. Adrenaline shot through her. "There's the rock." She pointed to the big stone ten metres ahead of them. "Dad wrote that he left something there for us."

Scarlett pumped a fist in the air. "Treasure number one. Way to go, Carly."

Her sister's words warmed her, and she picked up her pace, eager to discover what awaited them at their first stop. When they reached it, the three of them dumped their backpacks on the rock. Carly closed the compass before setting it next to the packs so her sisters wouldn't see the inscription and feel hurt. She was still working it out herself, since it didn't seem like something her father would do, singling any one of them out like that and expressing favouritism.

The three of them searched around the base of the rock and a few feet out until Phoebe cried, "Found it!" She held up a plastic box before jogging back to them. "It was hidden in the long grass."

"Here." Carly took the box and set it on the rock next to their packs. "Let's make sure you didn't pick up any ticks." She reached for Phoebe's hands and lifted them so she could check her sister's arms and front. Scarlett went around behind and brushed off Phoebe's shoulders and jacket and legs before stepping back. "I don't see anything."

"Me neither." Carly let go of Phoebe's hands.

"Thanks." Phoebe lowered her arms and then reached for the box. "Should I open it?"

"Sure." Carly waved a hand toward it. "You found it."

Her sister popped the plastic tabs and lifted the lid, and all three of them leaned closer to peer inside.

TEN

October 2001

After Ellen the social worker had brought her to Arlo, Carly stayed in her room for two days, only coming out to use the washroom or grab the food he'd made for her and then retreating without a glance in his direction. For now, it was enough for Arlo that she was here.

The first night, once he was pretty sure she had fallen asleep, Arlo crept to the doorway of her room and stopped, propping one shoulder against the frame to gaze at her. Soft moonlight drifted through the white gauze curtains to fall across her face. The sight of her tear-stained cheeks tore at his heart, although he smiled when he realized she had wrapped an arm around the stuffed monkey and was holding it tightly against her chest. Hopefully it helped to have something to cling to when everything familiar had been ripped away.

Little by little, she came out of her shell. Since she had arrived on a Friday afternoon, her third morning with him was a school day. Arlo packed what he hoped was not only a healthy lunch but one she would like. Since he truly had no idea what her preferences were, he had to guess. It would take time, but he would learn her as he had Phoebe.

Once he'd filled the lunch bag covered in unicorns that he'd bought when he was shopping for bedding, he set it on the counter and glanced at the clock. They needed to leave in thirty minutes to get to the school in time to register her. As much as he hated to wake her, he'd need to soon or they would be late.

Before he could decide on his next move, Carly slipped from the bedroom and into the bathroom across the hall, her hands full of clothes. When she emerged a few minutes later, she was dressed in a light-green top—vindication for his choice of bedding colour—over white leggings. She'd pulled her long, blonde hair into a ponytail and looked ready to walk out the door. Whew.

Arlo did have practice doing hair, as he was the one who braided Phoebe's or put it into one or two ponytails or slid barrettes into the sides to keep it from her face, whatever the princess wished for. Somehow he doubted Carly was ready for that level of intimacy, however.

"Good morning, Carly." He smiled at her, trying not to make too much of the fact that she had willingly walked into a room he was in and not walked right back out.

"Good morning," she mumbled.

A bit early for her to call him *Dad*. Arlo got that. Baby steps. "Would you like cereal or toast for breakfast? Or I could make eggs."

He held his breath, waiting for her to tell him what she preferred to eat. He was like a man lost in the desert who'd come across an unexpected crack in a rock. He'd crawl to it on his hands and knees and gratefully drink any tiny drop of water he could extract from it.

"Toast." She hesitated before adding, "Please."

"All right." Arlo reached for the loaf of whole wheat bread on the counter. "Jam or peanut butter?"

"Jam."

"Got it." Arlo gestured to the table. "Go sit down and I'll bring it to you." He stuck two slices in the toaster and then grabbed the jar of raspberry jam from the fridge. Carly settled on the far side of the table, her back to the wall.

Arlo carried the toast and jam over and set it in front of her. "Would you like coffee with that, mademoiselle?"

His daughter giggled, a sound he hadn't expected to hear from her for a long time. "I don't drink coffee. I'm seven." Her eyes met his briefly before she looked down at her plate.

A victory. Two victories. Arlo would take them. "Orange juice, then?"

"Yes, please." She bit off the corner of a piece of toast and munched in silence. Arlo didn't push her to talk, just settled on the chair across from her and sipped his coffee while he waited for her to finish.

They arrived at school with barely enough time to get her registered before the bell rang. Mrs. Whitlow, the principal, asked a secretary to show Carly to her classroom. His daughter grabbed her backpack and followed the woman across the office.

Arlo watched her go, melancholy settling around his shoulders. How was it possible to miss someone he didn't know existed until a few days ago and with whom he had only exchanged a few words?

At the door, Carly stopped and turned. She didn't speak, only lifted a hand and then disappeared into the hallway.

Even so, the gesture, slight as it was, filled him with a warmth that carried him through the day until it was time to pick her up and take her home.

ELEVEN

Present day

The plastic box contained another envelope and a navy velvet bag.

Phoebe lifted out both. "This has your name on it." She handed the envelope to Carly.

Hmm. She took it and, in the absence of the letter opener she kept in her desk, carefully ripped the top open. Another cream-coloured piece of paper. She pulled it out, set the envelope on the rock, and opened the letter.

The message was short, and she read it silently in case it contained anything private.

> For Carly.
> *There's one who is the earth to me, cool grass beneath the trees,*
> *And roots so deep they hold against the gale.*
> *Although for time apart and moments missed my heart still grieves,*
> *The gift of her proves mercy does prevail.*
> All my love, Dad

Wow. Tears pricked her eyes. Had her dad written this? What was it, a poem? A song? It was personal, given the reference to the time they had spent apart before she came to live with him.

When she looked up, her sisters were watching her. Scarlett rested a hand on her forearm. "You don't have to share it with us if it's private."

"No, I want to." Carly read the lines, her voice catching on the words *moments missed*. How she wished she could talk to her mother one more time, ask her why she had chosen to keep her and her father from each other. Neither would ever know, as she had taken her reasons with her to the grave. How had Dad not been furious with her? If he had been, he'd never shown it. He'd only been patient and kind and loving, even in those early days when Carly couldn't make sense of everything that had happened, what she had lost and how much her life had changed. When she didn't yet know if she could love this man who was a stranger to her. She'd held out as long as she could but, in the end, couldn't stop herself from letting him into her life and her heart. And she had never regretted it.

An open mind and heart. She'd learned to develop that with her father but had never fully done so with her sisters. Why not?

She swallowed hard as she folded the paper and slid it into her back pocket.

Phoebe clasped her shoulder. "Are you okay?"

"Yeah. I think so. Just processing."

Her sister nodded and let her go. She had set the velvet bag on the rock, and Scarlett reached for it. "There's a piece of paper sticking out." She tugged on it, pulling it out far enough to reveal a name. "It's for you, Phoebe." She held the bag out to their middle sister, who pursed her lips as she accepted it.

Loosening the drawstring at the top, she reached in and pulled out the old Swiss metal military flashlight their dad had given her when she was a kid. Whenever one of their quests had kept them out after dark, Phoebe was called upon to use the flashlight that had belonged to Dad's grandpa, who'd gotten it while fighting in the Second World War.

Phoebe wrinkled her nose sheepishly. "I'd forgotten about this. I must have left it at home when I moved out." She turned it around in her hands, inspecting it from all angles. When she tipped it up to check out the bottom of the squat, square torch, she paused a moment before slowly lowering it. Using the clip on the back of the flashlight, she attached it to her waistband.

"I did the same with this." Carly held up the compass. "Nell gave it to me at the hospital."

"Yeah." Phoebe tugged on the flashlight to make sure it was secure. "I went to see him too. Do you think he's okay?"

Carly shrugged. "He says he is, but Nell promised to let me know if that changes." She nudged Scarlett in the ribs. "You see him the most. Have you noticed anything concerning recently?"

"I mean, maybe he's been more tired than usual. And he did start closing the store an hour earlier a few months ago, but nothing major."

"That's major enough for Dad." Carly spread the map out on top of the rock and set the compass on it. "Anyway, we better get going so we don't actually need to use that flashlight of Phoebe's."

They set off, the words Dad had written her playing on repeat in Carly's mind. She was like the earth to him? Like cool, shaded ground? How was it possible that he considered her a safe, welcoming refuge when she was the one who had upended his stable life by showing up on his doorstep? As hard as it was to comprehend, the idea dug as deeply into her as the roots he'd mentioned in his poem. Was she mistaken about his life being stable before she arrived? Maybe it had felt unsteady for him and she had somehow stabilized the ground beneath his feet.

Whatever he meant by it—and hopefully she'd have a chance to discuss it with him at some point—the imagery alleviated any guilt for upending his life that, until this moment, she hadn't realized she'd been carrying.

For the next couple of hours, Phoebe rhymed off directions as Scarlett counted and, once, grabbed Carly's backpack to halt her in her tracks and keep her from stepping into a hole, likely the opening to some kind of animal den. Yikes. She could easily have turned her ankle. If Dad had instructed her sisters to leave their phones behind as well, they needed to be extra careful not to get hurt or the other two would have to carry the injured party out of the woods or leave her behind as they hustled back to their vehicles. Neither was an appealing option, and Carly took to glancing from the compass to the ground as she walked.

Thoughts of her phone got her thinking of Alain and how much she'd love to hear his voice right now. Was he worrying? He'd suggested, more than once, that he could come with her today, especially after learning that she would be out in the wild with no way to reach him. A big part of her had wanted to accept his offer, but she needed to do this alone. Or, as it had turned out, with her sisters. Since his first question would be whether Carly had spoken to them about the wedding, she really needed to do that if the right moment presented—

Scarlett grabbed her arm. "Freeze," she hissed.

Phoebe stopped next to Carly, whose nerves were jangling. "What is it?"

Slowly, Scarlett raised her arm to point up into a tree. "Cougar."

TWELVE

November 2001

For two weeks, Viviana evaded Arlo's calls. He went to the house every single day when Carly was at school, but his wife either wasn't home or refused to answer the door.

A deep ache settled in his chest, a longing to see Phoebe, feel her hand in his, make sure she was okay. *Lord, help me to be patient and wait for Viviana to be ready.* Although he prayed that prayer every day, he drew ever closer to calling the police or a lawyer and forcing his wife to let him see his child.

The pain was eased only by spending time with his other daughter. He and Carly still had a long way to go, but she was spending more time out of her room each day. Today, when he asked if she wanted to get pizza and watch a movie together since it was Friday evening, she had actually agreed.

The two of them sat at opposite ends of the worn couch in the makeshift bedroom/living room, her legs crossed beneath her and his heels propped on the coffee table. They were munching veggie pizza—her choice—and watching some animated feature Arlo couldn't concentrate on, as overwhelmed as he was by the two of them having this quality time together.

He allowed himself to be lulled into a dozy state of euphoria, enjoying the moment and, for once, not thinking about Phoebe or the state of his marriage. Suddenly Carly, her gaze firmly fixed on his boxy old TV with the rabbit ears, said in a voice he had to strain to hear, "Where were you?"

Arlo blinked and then slowly lowered his feet to the floor and swivelled around to face her. "Where was I when?" Unable to bring himself to put her on a bus with kids she didn't know when so much in her life was new and overwhelming, he'd driven Carly to school every day and picked her up after. Other than those few hours when she was in class, they had been under the same roof every moment.

"You know, when I was a baby and a kid. Where were you?"

Ah. He grabbed the remote from the coffee table and paused the movie, buying himself a few seconds. "What did your mom tell you?"

Still not looking at him, she shrugged. "She said you travelled for work and didn't have time to come home."

Ouch. Nothing about how he had no idea he had a child, then? *Lord, I need you now. Help me to know how to somehow heal her hurting heart.* "Carly." As loathe as he was to say anything against Solace, especially when she was no longer here to defend herself or answer for her actions, his daughter needed to know the truth if they were ever to, as the social worker had put it, *find their way to each other.*

For a few seconds, she didn't move. Then she slowly turned around, pulled her legs to her chest, and looked at him. "What?"

"What your mom told you wasn't quite right."

Her eyes narrowed slightly like she was preparing to leap to her mother's defense. "You weren't travelling for work?"

"I mean, I was in a band for a while, so yes, I did travel. But that wasn't why I didn't come see you."

"Then why?" She wrapped her arms tighter around her legs, as though bracing herself for even worse news. That he didn't want to be bothered with a kid and had no interest in keeping her, maybe. Another reason Arlo needed to come clean with her.

"I'm not sure why, but your mom never told me about you. I didn't know I had a daughter until a couple of days before Ellen brought you here to live with me. If I had known, if I had the slightest idea that you existed, I would have come to see you every day. You would never have been able to get rid of me."

Remarkably, her lips twitched, although she didn't quite smile. "Really?"

"Yes. Absolutely."

"Do you have to go away again?"

The slight tremor in her voice wrecked him. Had she been worried about him leaving her? Arlo shook his head firmly. "No. Never. I have a music store downstairs, and I work there now so I don't travel anymore." *Give me the words. Help me to get through to her.* He closed the lid of the pizza box, the feel of the smooth cardboard beneath his fingers grounding him. "Look, Carly. It breaks my heart that I missed the first seven years of your life. I don't plan to miss another minute. I'm not going anywhere. Except maybe home to live with my wife and your younger sister, Phoebe. But whether I'm here or there, you'll be with me. Pinkie swear." He held up his little finger. Was Carly too old for pinkie swearing? He and Phoebe did it all the time, but their situation was vastly different. He and his older daughter had never touched, even briefly. Was it too soon for her to—

Carly let go of her legs and leaned forward to hook her finger around his. Arlo held his breath, scared to move in case he broke the sacredness of this moment, of her warm hand pressed to his.

After a few seconds, she pulled back.

It took everything Arlo had to inject nonchalance into his voice as he nodded at the pizza box. "Want the last piece?"

"Sure."

He lifted the lid and she grabbed the slice and then settled back against the arm of the couch. "How old is your other daughter?"

"She's four."

"Why don't you live at home with her and your wife?"

Arlo had kind of been hoping they were done with painful conversations for the evening. "My wife, Viviana, and I had a fight a while ago, and she asked me to leave."

"Are you getting a divorce?" Carly picked a green pepper off the slice and tipped her head back to drop it into her mouth.

He rubbed a hand over his chest and then glanced down at the bit of tomato sauce he'd smeared across his grey T-shirt. "I'm not sure. I hope not."

"Do you still love her?"

He started to say that yes, of course he loved his wife, then stopped. Did he? He'd known for a long time that their marriage was a mistake. He genuinely doubted that she loved him now, if she ever had. Still, he was committed to her and to the vows he had made and would never willingly walk away. Was that the same thing?

"I—"

The shrill buzzing of the doorbell cut him off. Just as well, since he really wasn't sure how he'd planned to end that sentence.

Carly set the pizza slice on top of the box. "Who's that?"

"I have no idea." Arlo stood and brushed crumbs off his T-shirt and the front of his jeans. "I'll go check." He scooped up the remote from the coffee table and hit the play button. "You watch the movie, and I'll join you as soon as I talk to whoever it is, okay?"

"Okay." Carly propped her slippered feet on the coffee table the way Arlo had earlier. She looked considerably more comfortable than she had since arriving. Had she only been waiting for him to reassure her that he wouldn't leave her again?

Whatever it was, they did seem to have crossed some kind of bridge. Arlo prayed they could keep making their way along the path, however overgrown with weeds and brambles it might be.

He shot her one last glance before starting down the stairs. At the bottom, he pulled open the door. Viviana and Phoebe stood on the sidewalk. Arlo's gaze snagged on the big, red suitcase his wife clutched in one hand, but before he could speak, his young daughter launched herself at him. "Daddy!"

Arlo scooped her up and hugged her to his chest. He had never been apart from Phoebe for longer than a few hours, and he'd missed her desperately. "Hi, princess." He met Viviana's dark eyes above Phoebe's curls. "Hey, Viv."

The old nickname he hadn't used in a long time did nothing to soften the hardness in her eyes. "Is *she* here?" She jerked her chin toward the top floor of the building.

Arlo lowered Phoebe to the ground. "Why don't you go upstairs, sweetheart? There's a girl up there whose name is Carly. You can watch a movie with her until I come up."

Phoebe nodded and slipped past him to scramble up the steps. Not exactly the way he would have chosen for his daughters to meet, but he needed to speak with Viviana, and he didn't trust her not to say something that might permanently damage their daughter. When she'd gone, he turned back to his wife. "Can we talk?"

She held out the suitcase. "There's nothing to talk about. I hope the three of you will be very happy together."

If she tried, she couldn't make the sentiment ring any less true. Prickles of shock tingled across his skin as Arlo reached out numbly to take the suitcase from her. "Are you saying we can't come home?"

"That's right." Viviana took a step back and held up both hands as though washing them of her family. "You made your choice, Arlo. You chose another woman's daughter. So I'm choosing too. I'm choosing to begin a brand-new life. One that doesn't include you and it doesn't include Phoebe."

THIRTEEN

Present day

Carly stared at the wild cat, stretched out on a limb, its tail and one leg hanging off the side of the branch. That meant it was relaxed, not preparing to pounce, right?

She had no idea. Dad had taught them what to do if they ever encountered a bear, which they had done one time on a family quest. It was a black bear, not a grizzly, so they'd all made themselves as big as they could and created as much noise as possible, and the bear had turned and ambled away into the trees.

They never had seen a cougar, though, and she couldn't remember if he told them how to handle it if they did. Was there such a thing as cougar spray? Would bear spray work or only make it madder?

"What do we do?" Phoebe sounded fairly calm, thankfully, and neither she nor Scarlett were moving. Since the cougar wasn't either, not even flicking its tail, freezing in place might at least buy them time to form a plan. They couldn't stand here forever, though. It would be dark in a few hours, which would give the nocturnal cat a serious advantage over them if the teeth and claws weren't already enough to tip the scales.

"I'm not sure," Carly whispered. "Scarlett?"

Her baby sister shook her head slightly. "No clue."

Carly's breaths were coming in short, shallow gasps, and she forced herself to take a deeper one so she could think more clearly. *Jesus, could you help us get out of this?*

Her relationship with God was strong now, although it hadn't always been. She'd never known her mom to go to church, but thankfully she hadn't objected when Carly's friend invited her to go. Carly had given her life to Jesus when she was six. Then, shortly after, her mom got sick and within a few months was gone.

When she went to stay with her dad, she closed her eyes as he said grace, and she still prayed before bed, but for a long time those prayers ran along the lines of "Thanks for everything, God, except why did you take my mom away from me?" She kept God at a distance the way she did her dad. But the gentle, unwavering love of both drew her back. Would He help them now?

"He doesn't seem that interested in us." A bit of a stretch, since the big cat hadn't taken its eyes from them since Scarlett first pointed him out. Still, he didn't appear inclined to do anything about it. "I suggest we slowly take a wide circle around him, moving as quietly as we can."

"Got it." Phoebe carefully unclipped the bear spray from her waist.

Scarlett nodded and grabbed her can as well.

Better than nothing, Carly guessed, so she stuck the compass and map into her jacket pocket and tugged her spray free. Then she nodded to their right. Phoebe took a cautious step in that direction. Carly watched the cat, but he didn't react to the movement. Painstakingly slowly, the three of them made their way through the thick underbrush, freezing once when Scarlett stepped on a twig, the snap echoing like gunfire through the quiet woods.

The cat never moved, and eventually they were far enough past him that Carly let out the breath she'd been holding. "I think we're good."

"Well," Scarlett kept her voice low as she returned the bear spray to her belt, "that was interesting."

"A little too interesting." Phoebe pressed one hand over her heart but kept the other tightly wrapped around the can.

That suited Carly. She needed to free her hands up to use the map and compass, but it wouldn't hurt for at least one of them to have a deterrent at the ready in case the cougar was playing some kind of cat and mouse game and suddenly sprang at them from behind.

Twenty minutes later, they arrived at their next big destination—another worn bench, this one covered in tree-hugger graffiti messages like *take only memories, leave only footprints* and *there is no planet B*. Delinquents.

Both her sisters slid off and dumped their packs on the bench before flopping down next to them. Carly settled on a stump across from them and set her pack on the ground, balancing the map and compass on top of it. Then she tugged the water bottle from a side pocket and took a long drink. Her sisters did the same.

Balancing the bottle between her knees, she reached into the other side pocket and pulled out three protein bars. She tossed two of them to her sisters before opening the third one. "Are you guys doing okay? No blisters or anything?"

"I'm fine so far." Phoebe took another swig of water before lowering the bottle to the bench between her and Scarlett and ripping off the top of the protein bar package.

Scarlett stretched her booted feet out in front of her. "Me too."

"Good." Carly scrambled to think of another topic of conversation. The sun hanging just above the tops of the trees concerned her, since they did have quite a hike back to their cars, and she had no desire to be stuck in the woods after dark. They did need to take a break so they'd have enough energy to get to wherever this crazy quest was taking them, though. "How's school going, Scarlett?"

Their youngest sister was finishing up her Master of Music at the University of British Columbia. While they all had decent voices, Scarlett was the only one who had inherited their father's ability to pick up and play any instrument.

"Fine."

"You're almost done, right? Any idea what you'll do next?" Carly took another bite of her protein bar.

Scarlett levelled a heated look at her. "Do you really care?"

FOURTEEN

January 2002

The three of them settled into something of a routine. Arlo had hoped his two daughters would bond from the start, but that might have been overly optimistic, given the trauma they had both been through. Although Phoebe had always been closer to Arlo, having a mother—albeit a cold, distant one—ripped away without warning had to leave a gaping wound. Even the loss of their mothers had not so far proven to be enough common ground for the girls to connect.

Viviana appeared to be in earnest in her desire to distance herself not only from him but from their child. Papers had arrived by courier a few days after she dropped Phoebe off—a petition for divorce along with a signed legal document waiving any right to their daughter. Arlo had full custody and no visitation was requested. As much as it hurt his heart that Phoebe would know her mother wanted nothing to do with her, it did make things cleaner.

Not that anything about his failed marriage felt clean, only messy and heartbreaking and sad. Could he have done more to make Viviana happy? To make their marriage work? Looking back, he realized a big part of the reason he had married her was that he believed her when she told him she loved him and he hoped maybe that love was proof that God had forgiven him and was redeeming his past. Had he been wrong?

Every night after the girls fell sleep, Arlo spent a long time on his knees, face pressed to the couch cushions, hands clasped above his head as he asked God those very questions. In the stillness of their darkness-draped apartment, no answers came.

One realization did take shape in his consciousness. Viviana wasn't the precious gift he'd been given after the mistakes he'd made in his past. Carly was. His surprise daughter was irrefutable proof that God forgave, redeemed, and turned mourning into dancing. That truth—and the unexpected presence of Carly in his life—brought him back to solid ground after years of trudging through shifting sands. With every moment they spent together, more deep roots formed beneath his feet, anchoring him to his little place in the world. Taking care of these girls, loving them, protecting them—that was his calling in life, his mission. One he accepted gladly and with deep gratitude to God.

To give Carly space to adjust, he set up a small bed in the corner of the living room and surrounded it with screen dividers as a temporary space for Phoebe. Hopefully one day they would be comfortable enough with each other that he could finally set up those bunk beds for them. Or maybe he should cash out some of that Lone Trail money and find a bigger place for the three of them to live.

Three months after Carly entered his life, the doorbell buzzed late one night. Arlo had been lying on the couch staring at the ceiling, one arm flung across his forehead, but he bolted upright at the sound and glanced at his alarm clock. Just after midnight. Who would be at his door at this time of night?

He clambered to his feet and stood a moment, listening for any hint the sound had woken Carly or Phoebe. When he was satisfied it hadn't, he crossed the room, tugged on his running shoes, and started down the stairs in his black T-shirt and grey track pants.

When he pulled open the door, two police officers stood on the sidewalk. It had been snowing all day, and a gust of wind whipped up a mini tornado of flakes that swirled around the man and woman in uniform.

Arlo wrapped his arms around his torso, trying to brace himself against more than the bitter cold. "Can I help you?"

The woman dipped her head. "Arlo Stone?"

"Yes."

"We're here because you were listed as next of kin for Viviana Mylonas."

Her maiden name. His wife had gone back to her maiden name. Arlo's brain hyper-focused on that one detail so he wouldn't have to deal with the other words the cop had said. *Next of kin*. Next of kin were never notified for a good reason, only a bad one, and he wasn't ready to hear it yet.

"We're very sorry to tell you that Ms. Mylonas was killed in an automobile accident earlier this evening."

Maiden name. Maiden name. Maiden name. The words wove around him like chainmail. She'd dropped his surname as quickly and easily as she had dropped him. Why? She'd always said she loved the sound of Viviana Stone. So why—

"Mr. Stone?"

Arlo blinked. "Yes?"

She took a step closer. "Did you hear what I said?"

"You said Mylonas." His voice sounded faint and faraway in his ears.

The woman shot a look at her colleague. He cleared his throat. "Did you hear my partner say that Viviana Mylonas was—"

Arlo flung up a hand. He couldn't bear for them to say the words again. "I heard."

The female officer glanced at a notebook she held in gloved fingers. "We understand that Ms. Mylonas had a child."

"That's correct." The world was spinning around him, and Arlo pressed a hand to the door frame.

"Is the minor being taken care of?"

The words were beginning to sound unintelligible, as though the officers were speaking in another language that he needed to translate for it to hold any meaning. After a few more seconds, during which the male cop shifted from one foot to the other a few times, Arlo managed to get out, "Yes. I have full custody of our daughter. She's here with me."

"All right then." The woman pulled a business card from the pocket of her heavy navy coat and held it out to him. "When you're ready, call the station and the administrator can give you more information."

His fingers felt frostbitten, and Arlo clenched and unclenched them two or three times before he could reach out and grasp the card. "All right."

The officer touched his elbow. "I'm sorry, Mr. Stone."

His throat tightened. "Thank you." He stepped back and closed the door, unable to summon the energy to care if he had cut them off before they were finished with him.

His knees buckled twice on the way up, and he leaned heavily on the railing so he could make it to his apartment and over to the couch. Arlo had no idea how long he sat, staring out the window at the snow swirling through the dim light cast by the streetlamp in front of the store.

Viviana was gone. If he'd been harboring any thoughts that she might have a change of heart, that she would decide she wanted to be part of Phoebe's life if not his, that faint hope was gone. He was a widower. A single dad. And his daughters would both grow up without a mother to guide them.

Would any of them be able to find their way home again?

FIFTEEN

Present day

Carly slowly lowered the protein bar to her leg. "Of course I care. Why would you ask that?"

"Because not one of us has ever expressed a genuine interest in the others' lives. We only talk on a surface level. I have deeper conversations with my barista, for Pete's sake."

Ouch. Scarlett's words—and her uncharacteristically cold tone—hurt, although Carly couldn't dispute them. The few bites of protein bar she'd taken weren't sitting very well.

"Scarlett." Phoebe, the peacemaker, rested a hand on the backpack between them as though beseeching her sister not to stir up trouble.

"No, she's right, Phoebe." Carly tucked the wrapper around the remainder of her bar and dropped it into her pack. "We don't talk to each other. Really talk. We never have. I'm not sure why."

"Me neither." Scarlett stared at the bar in her hand as though the answer might be written across the packaging. "I've always wondered why neither of you particularly liked me."

Carly glanced at Phoebe, who looked as shocked as she felt. Carly shifted to face Scarlett. "What are you talking about? We love you. You're our sister."

Scarlett waved a hand through the air. "I know you love me. You have to. We're family. But liking family is entirely different. That's something you choose to do. Or choose not to do, in our case. I've never really understood it, since Mom and Dad have always tried so hard to create opportunities for us to be close, like our family challenges."

In the quiet that followed, Carly wrapped her fingers around the water bottle. A mosquito buzzed near her ear, and she swiped it away absentmindedly. Her head was spinning. Was Scarlett right that the three of them didn't like each other? Why not? Something her sister said tweaked a revelation. Carly's instinct was to rebel against it, since it revealed a decidedly ungodly side of herself, a pettiness she was not proud of. "Maybe that has something to do with it."

"What?" Scarlett tipped her head, her ponytail draped over one shoulder.

"What you just said about Nell being our mom. I've never consciously thought about this but, if I'm being completely honest, maybe a small, deep-down part of myself is a bit jealous of the fact that you have a mother and I don't."

"But she's always treated you and Phoebe like her own daughters."

"She has, absolutely. She couldn't have been a better stepmom. Still, I'm beginning to wonder if I ever actually dealt with losing my own mother. Which is on me, not on you or Nell."

"At least your mother didn't dump you on a doorstep and walk away."

Carly whirled toward her other sister. She couldn't remember ever hearing that level of bitterness in Phoebe's voice. "What do you mean? Your mother died in a car crash, didn't she?"

"Yeah, a few months later. But I overheard Dad and Nell talking on the phone one evening, and he told her that my mom kicked him out of the house and then brought me to the apartment one night, handed me over, and told him she was done with both of us."

Scarlett's cheeks paled. "Why would she do such a horrible thing?"

Phoebe didn't answer, only gazed down at the fingers she had clasped tightly in her lap.

Carly felt the silence like a slap to her face. "It was because of me, wasn't it?"

SIXTEEN

April 2002

Arlo took care of the final arrangements laid out in Viviana's will. Even when he found out she hadn't died alone, that the driver of the car had been a male co-worker of hers whom Arlo had always been leery of, he pressed on, ensuring every detail she had requested was carried out.

They laid her to rest at a small graveside ceremony attended only by a few friends and colleagues and her father and sister, who barely said a word to Arlo. What had Viviana told them about him or the state of their marriage? They didn't ask about Phoebe, so he didn't offer any information or issue an invitation for them to see her. As soon as the minister finished, they turned and walked away.

Time for him to end that chapter of his life and focus on a new one.

With every passing week, Carly spent more time out of her room, even joining him and Phoebe for a movie on Friday nights, although she rarely shifted from her position pressed to the arm at the far end of the couch, a pillow clutched in front of her like a barrier.

Those couple of feet might as well have been two kilometres.

Other than those few precious seconds when she had wrapped her little finger around his, she and Arlo had never touched.

Occasionally he had reached out to help her put on her coat or free her ponytail from her collar, but she had stepped beyond his reach and done it herself. He understood—or was trying desperately to understand, at least—but the distance between them broke his heart, and he had no idea how to breach it.

Earlier this evening, they'd watched an old classic—*Mary Poppins*. When Phoebe got up and danced along with Dick Van Dyke and the chimney sweeps—they might have watched the movie a few too many times—Arlo observed Carly from the corner of his eye. She continued to face the TV, although her gaze did slide from the screen to Phoebe a few times. She edged slightly closer to the front of her seat, too, as though tempted to get up and join her sister. Nothing would have made Arlo happier, but then the song ended and Phoebe collapsed to the carpet in a fit of giggles, her chest heaving. Carly settled back into the corner of the couch and wrapped her arms more tightly around the fluffy blue pillow.

How could he reach her?

The two girls had gone to bed half an hour ago. With a heavy sigh, Arlo finished drying the popcorn bowl, set it in the cupboard, and then wandered along the hallway to Carly's room. He paused outside it, his ear close to the wood, but heard nothing. Despite how helpless he felt to get through to her, it still brought him joy knowing she was there, that she existed and was part of his life. When he checked on Phoebe, she was breathing deeply, her dark hair spread across the pillow and both arms flung above her head.

A fierce protectiveness for both his daughters gripped him. All he wanted was to take care of them, to find a way to make them happy, to teach them about God and the world around them and the beauty of creation and how to be the best human beings they could possibly be.

If only he didn't have to do it alone.

Arlo grabbed a glass from the cupboard, filled it with water, then turned to lean back against the counter. A small, white card stuck to the side of the fridge with a pizza place magnet caught his eye, and he set the glass down and meandered over to it. With the tip of his finger, he traced the name on the card. Ellen McMaster, RSW.

Hmm. The social worker had told him to call her if he had any questions. Was she thinking more along the lines of what time he should send Carly to bed or how many servings of vegetables she should have in a day, or would it be okay to call and ask her how to bridge the seemingly insurmountable emotional and physical canyons between them?

Arlo glanced at his watch. 9:45. Too late to call, obviously. He'd muddled along thus far without seeking help, so he could muddle along a while longer, couldn't he? Holding the magnet in place with his left hand, he snatched the card out from under it with his right. No. He couldn't wait another day, another hour, without at least attempting to get advice. If this Ellen person was off duty or didn't want to be bothered, she could simply refuse to answer the phone. He'd call back on Monday during regular business hours like an emotionally regulated person who wasn't on the brink of tearing his hair out by the roots.

Arlo paused on the landing outside his apartment, listening for any movement. When he heard nothing, he pulled the door closed behind him and made his way down the stairs. After settling on the third one from the bottom and resting his socked feet on the cold cement floor, he pulled the flip phone from the pocket of his black sweatpants and held the card up as he typed the number in with his thumb.

It rang four times, his heart sinking lower with each ring. All right, fair enough. The woman had boundaries. He'd respect that. Arlo started to hit the button to disconnect the call when a female voice rose from the device. "Hello?"

He pressed the phone to his ear. "Hi. Is this Ellen McMaster?"

"That depends. May I ask who's calling?"

Her voice held more amusement than annoyance, thankfully. Arlo propped his elbows on his knees and rested his forehead on his palm. "Sorry. It's Arlo Stone. I'm not sure if you remember me, but—"

"Arlo. Of course I remember you. And sweet Carly. How's she doing?"

"I'm not sure, which is what I'm calling you about. I realize it's late, so if you want me to call back next week, I can."

"No, it's fine." Something creaked, as though she was settling onto a chair or couch. "I'm just sitting here with a cup of tea, unwinding. I've got time. Tell me what's happening."

Arlo wasn't about to refuse an invitation like that. He told Ellen how things had been going and about how distant Carly still was. Her responses were so warm and inviting that he found himself sharing about Solace and about Viviana's death and how hard it had been to explain to Phoebe that she would never see her mother again. How desperately he wanted his girls to get along but had no idea how to draw them closer. By the time he finished pouring out his heart, an hour had passed, and he pressed a shoulder to the wall and rested the side of his head against the cool brick. "I'm open to any and all suggestions you might have."

"Okay, wow. Let me start by saying that you've taken on a lot, Arlo. And you've lost a lot. So my first piece of advice is that you take a big breath and then slowly let it out."

Arlo pushed away from the wall and did as she suggested. It did help, relieving some of the tenseness from his muscles. "Okay, that was good. What else have you got?"

She laughed, the sound doing more to relax him than the deep breathing had. "The way I see it, Carly's probably struggling to feel like part of the family. Even though she knows in her head that you're her dad, she doesn't know you. And she doesn't know her sister. What she does know is that you and Phoebe are close, one unit. I'm sure she feels every bit as helpless to break into that unit as you do to pull her inside."

Huh. That made sense. "What should I do?"

"You're already doing a lot of it. Being there, reassuring her that she is safe and wanted and that you'll never leave or send her away, is huge. That gives the three of you a foundation to build on. Now you need to start constructing the walls around you brick by brick until you've created a home where all three of you feel as though you belong."

"All right." Arlo drew out the words, no real idea what those bricks would look like or where he could get his hands on one. "Any idea where I should start?"

"Well, *belonging* is an ambiguous feeling, difficult to define or picture. I find it's always helpful for a child to have something physical, something tangible, to hold onto and look at. A daily, visual reminder that they are where they should be and with the people they're meant to be with."

"That makes sense." Arlo wracked his brain. What could he give Carly that would remind her every time she looked at it that she was part of this family, that she could trust that her dad and sister wanted her with them and would always be there for her? "Out of curiosity, what kinds of items make good bricks?"

She laughed again and, for the first time since the cops had shown up at his door, Arlo laughed too. The heaviness that had pressed down on him since that night lifted, and he caught faint glimmers of light, like sunshine breaking through the heavy leaves and branches hanging over that wild, overgrown path he and his daughters were on.

"Do you have something that's been in your family for a while, maybe something passed down from one of your parents or grandparents? Something that means a lot to you?"

"I have a few outdoor survival tools my dad's father left to him and that he passed along to me when I was twelve. Probably the only things I have that belonged to either of my parents." Other than their collection of albums, which wouldn't likely interest his daughter.

"Would you be willing to give one of them to Carly?"

"If you thought it might help her, then yes, in a heartbeat."

"I think it could. Make sure she knows where it came from and that it means a lot to you, but you want her to have it. That could go a long way toward making her feel wanted and special."

"She is."

"Then give her the gift along with plenty of time and attention and safe boundaries and love. I truly believe that, if you do that, she will eventually come around."

"I can do that."

"I know you can. Call me whenever you doubt it, and I'll remind you. And Arlo? We're not really supposed to say this, but I'll be praying for all of you."

More of the heaviness lifted. He wasn't completely alone. He'd always known that God was with him. There was no way he'd have made it this far without Him. Still, the support of another human being, even over the phone, was an unspeakable comfort. "I appreciate your prayers. And your advice. Thanks, Ellen."

"Actually, my friends call me Nell."

"Nell, then. And my friends call me, well, Arlo. Not much you can do with that name."

She laughed again, a sound he would carry with him into whatever lay ahead.

Ever since the day the lawyer had come to his store to let him know he had a daughter, Arlo hadn't been sure he could truly do this, that he could be both father and mother to Carly and somehow give her the life and family and home she deserved.

Tonight, the soothing voice and laughter of the woman on the other end of the line offered something he'd been afraid to let himself feel until this moment.

Hope.

SEVENTEEN

Present day

"It wasn't your fault, Carly." Phoebe crumpled up her protein bar wrapper and carried it to a lidded trash can.

When she returned, she crouched in front of Carly. "I haven't let myself think about that conversation in years. Now that I'm looking back at our relationship, I can see I might have blamed you for my mom abandoning me, but that's not fair. You were a kid. You weren't responsible for what happened before you were even born."

"What did happen? I've never talked to Dad about it. The only thing I asked him was where he was when I was growing up. Mom told me he was busy and didn't have time for me. When I told him that, he assured me it wasn't true, that he didn't know I existed or he would have come to find me right away."

Phoebe sighed. "Do you really want to know?"

"No." She pressed her hands to the cool rock on either side of her. "But I'm thirty-two years old. Maybe it's time I hear the truth."

"All right then. Your mom came to a concert of Dad's one night. Right before he went on stage, his father called to let him know his mother had died that day. He was incredibly sad, of course, and I guess your mom could see that. When he came out to the parking lot after, she was waiting for him. Sounds like she'd lost people close to her and understood his pain. The two of them went for coffee and got talking and eventually ended up back at his hotel room."

Carly's throat tightened. "That doesn't sound like either of them."

"Well, I never knew your mom, but it wasn't like Dad, for sure. He had drifted away from his faith at that point, though, and he made a bad decision. I heard him tell Nell that it was the only time he'd ever done anything like that and he'd regretted it right away. He didn't say anything against your mom. It seems they were both simply seeking comfort and found it in each other that night."

"Wow. You must have been listening to them for a long time. Little sneak."

Phoebe offered her a weak smile. "I didn't mean to listen in. I got up to get a glass of water, and Dad hadn't closed the apartment door tightly. I heard his voice and went looking for him. When I realized he was on the phone, I started to turn away, but then I caught my name and stayed."

"Did he catch you?"

"No. I heard him say goodbye and hurried back to my room before he came upstairs."

"So he has no idea you heard what you did."

"That's right."

"Wow, Phoebes." Carly had never called her sister that, but it felt right. "That was a lot for you to carry around."

"I guess. I never intended to tell you but, when you admitted you might be jealous of Scarlett, I realized that I likely am too. Nell is such a loving mother, and obviously mine wasn't. At all. And

Dad and I were so close before you came into our lives that maybe I've always subconsciously carried a bit of resentment around because of that as well."

She leaned back on her haunches, spinning around so she could draw Scarlett into the conversation. "I need to ask both of you for forgiveness."

Scarlett shook her head. "No, you don't. I get it. As you were talking, Phoebes, I realized that I'm also to blame. I've always considered it your fault, yours and Carly's, that there is so much distance between us. It's time for me to stop playing the victim and accept my part in it. I think I envied both of you the time you had with just Dad before I was born. I know you missed out on a lot of that, Carly. Still, the three of you were so tight before Dad married Mom and I came along. I've always struggled to figure out where I belong. I can see now that I took my frustration out on you guys. I accused you of not liking me, but the truth is I never acted as though I liked either of you either. Part of that was probably because I was hurt, but I could have made more of an effort. So, I'm sorry."

Carly rubbed her cold fingers over her forehead. "I'm starting to see that I should probably talk to someone who can help me deal with losing my mom and believing for so long that Dad wanted nothing to do with me."

Phoebe nodded. "I think I need to do the same. Maybe we can pray for each other, that we'll all be able to let go of the past and look forward to a future together."

"I like that."

"So do I." Scarlett stood and slid her arms through the straps of her backpack.

Given the warmth of the moment, it might have been a good time to bring up the wedding. The sun was starting to sink dangerously low, though. They needed to get moving if they didn't want to spend the night out here.

Even with that ominous thought, Carly felt lighter than she had, well, ever. Maybe one conversation wouldn't miraculously heal her relationship with her sisters. Still, it felt as though the three of them had reached their first big X and found a gift waiting for them—the gift of each other.

EIGHTEEN

May 2002

The following Saturday, Arlo's old bandmate Davey came to the door with his wife, Hannah, and their two boys to pick up Phoebe for the day.

She'd been to their place a hundred times, so she went with them happily. Arlo stood in the doorway at street level watching them go, Phoebe clutching Davey's and his wife's hands and skipping, her ponytail bouncing against her pink jacket.

Smiling, he went back inside. Today was the day. Carly would turn eight in a few weeks, but Arlo couldn't wait that long to start building the wall around the three of them that might one day, Lord willing, feel like a real home. A real family.

He'd just flipped the pancakes in the frying pan when Carly wandered into the room, rubbing one eye with her fist. She looked so adorable that Arlo had to grip the handle of the pan tightly to keep himself from going over and scooping her into a hug. How would she react to that? Would that be laying a brick on that foundation of theirs or heaving the thing at her? He'd ask Ellen—Nell—her thoughts on that the next time they spoke. In the meantime, better err on the side of restraint.

"Good morning, Carly." He let go of the handle and turned off the burner.

"Morning," she mumbled. Unlike Phoebe, his elder daughter was not a morning person. Took after him in that regard. She nodded in the direction of Phoebe's chair. "Where is she?"

Arlo tried not to let it bother him that neither girl had used the other's name yet. "Phoebe?" He pulled open the fridge door and reached for the jug of maple syrup. "She's spending the day with friends." A thought occurred to him, and he closed the door, the jug dangling from one finger. "If you ever want to get together with friends, we can make that happen. You're welcome to have anyone come here that you'd like."

"My friends are at my old school." Carly trudged over to the table and flopped onto a seat.

"Well, that's only a couple of hours away. I could drive you there or we could pick them up."

"Maybe."

Arlo set a plate with a pancake and three strips of bacon in front of his daughter. "For today, I thought you and I could spend some time together." He watched her closely while trying hard not to look as though he was watching her for a reaction.

"Oh." Carly grabbed the syrup jug. "What are we going to do?" She sounded more interested than alarmed at the prospect of spending time alone with him. Progress.

He snagged the gift he'd set on top of the fridge and carried it over to her. "First, I want to give you this. Then I'll tell you what I have in mind."

She contemplated the box he'd wrapped in a bit of old brown paper from behind the counter in the store. "It's not my birthday yet."

"It will be soon. Consider this an early present."

She bit the inside of her lip for a few seconds and then set down the syrup and reached for it. It didn't take her long to rip off the paper to reveal a small leather box. She shot a look at Arlo and, when he nodded encouragement, she flipped the clasp and raised the lid. Her forehead wrinkled as she touched a finger to the item. "What is it?"

"It's a compass."

"Like for directions?"

"Exactly."

Carly ran the tip of her finger across the smooth metal top. "It looks old."

Arlo tried to gauge her tone. Not disdain, thankfully. Fascination, maybe? "It is old. It belonged to my grandfather. He gave it to my dad many years ago, who passed it along to me when I was a bit older than you." Arlo leaned forward and clasped his hands on the table between them. "This compass has been in the Stone family for a long time. It's been given as a gift to the oldest child in each generation. And that's you, Carly. You're the first one born in the next generation of our family. So this is rightfully yours."

She studied the compass a moment before nodding, once. "That's cool."

"Do you want to open it?"

"Sure." Carly lifted it out of the box and pressed the button on the front to release the lid. For a moment, she gazed at the needle, then she looked up at him. "How does it work?"

"Why don't you eat your breakfast and then I'll take you outside and show you."

Forty-five minutes later, they had walked to the park down the street, and Arlo was showing Carly how to spread out on a picnic table the hand-drawn map he'd made and then set the compass on it so it would be more accurate. He explained to her how compasses work and the difference between magnetic north and true north.

When she was ready, he gave her the instructions he'd written out the day before on a piece of lined paper he had torn from a notebook. Across the top of it he'd written *Stone Family Challenge #1.*

Carly caught on quickly and managed to get from one place on the map to another—the picnic table to a water fountain then over to a swing set, a basketball hoop, and the drain in the middle of a splash pad—with only minimal help from him when she occasionally ventured off course.

As Arlo followed her around, watching his daughter bite her tongue as she concentrated on lining up the needle on the compass just right and counting out the number of steps he'd instructed her to take in that direction and then lighting up like a firefly when she correctly identified the next spot on the map, he thanked Nell over and over in his mind.

For the first time, Carly had come out of herself. For the hour or so that it took her to complete his list of tasks, her eyes glowed and she laughed out loud several times. Earlier, he'd toyed with the idea of bringing his camera to capture the joy and wonder of each new discovery, but he had no desire to spook her into retreating again. So, they lived in the moment, the two of them, Arlo praying fervently with each step toward a destination that they were also taking one step closer to each other. Time would tell.

In a small hole in a huge maple tree that she had to stand on her tiptoes to reach into, he had hidden another gift for her—a small cardboard box with a gold-plated bracelet in it. The treasure at the end of their "quest." The smile she offered him as he wrapped it around her wrist and fastened the clasp made every bit of effort to set up the challenge and every moment of angst since she had arrived far more than worth it.

As they settled onto seats in the old '50s-style ice cream shop in town, Arlo's heart was full. Carly giggled when a splotch of ice cream from her cone dripped onto the swirling, engraved CT on her bracelet, rewarding him with another smile when he wiped it off with a napkin from the silver dispenser in the middle of the table.

"Can we do that again sometime?" She licked a stray drop of bubble gum ice cream sliding down the side of her cone.

"Sure. That's why I called it the Stone Family Challenge #1. I'm hoping we can do a lot of these adventures together."

Her smile dimmed slightly. "My last name isn't Stone."

"I know. That's why I had the T engraved on your bracelet along with the C. You'll always be a Travers, like your mom." Arlo stuck the wooden spoon into the mound of moose tracks ice cream in his bowl and leaned forward. "Even so, you are my daughter, as much as Phoebe is. And you are her sister. Which means you are also a Stone. Both families make you who you are, and you will always be part of both, no matter what."

Ice cream dripped over her fingers, but Carly didn't seem to notice. "Will she come with us next time?"

All right, maybe this was the moment to push a little, get both his girls to stop hiding behind pronouns. "Who?"

She sent him an exasperated look that gave him insight into how it would be between them when she was a teenager—a prospect that both thrilled and terrified him—before exhaling. "Phoebe."

"Of course. I mean, sometimes it can just be you and me or her and me, but most of the time it will be the three of us. That's why it's called the Stone *Family* Challenge. It's meant to be something the family does together. Okay?"

Carly hesitated a few seconds before lifting her shoulders. "Fine."

Not his favourite word, but Arlo would take it. "Great. Thank you." He worked a handful of napkins free and swiped them over her sticky fingers. "Look, Carly. I know you grew up believing that I didn't have time for you and didn't care about being part of your life and that it might take time for you to let go of that. I understand, but I do hope you will try, because nothing could be further from the truth. I very much want you to be part of my life. A big part."

She pursed sticky lips, pink and blue from the ice cream. "Why?"

"Because I love you."

Her eyelids flickered as though she was trying to absorb that. "How could you? We just met."

"Because I'm your dad. It's part of the job description. So is wanting to take care of you and protect you from anything bad ever happening to you and doing whatever I can to make sure you are happy and healthy and growing up to be an amazing human being. Which I can already see you are. Your mom did a great job with you, but now it's my turn to do all that if you'll let me. Will you?"

Her blue eyes locked on his, and for the first time she didn't immediately look away. Already he had noticed that about her, that she took her time to consider her options carefully before making a decision. Not a bad trait at all. After a moment, she nodded again. "I'll try."

"That's all I ask. Thank you." Arlo grasped the spoon and shovelled a bite of ice cream into his mouth. "You know, I'm a bit envious of you."

"Why?"

"Because I never had a sister or brother, and I always wanted one. I know you had no idea you had a sister, but now you do, and that's a pretty big deal, right? Family is a gift from God, and it's a far better gift than anything we could give each other. If you choose to accept it, it can be like that compass—it can help guide and direct you through life. If you had refused to accept the gift of the compass, we wouldn't have been able to have fun on our quest today, and you wouldn't have discovered another beautiful gift." He lightly touched the tip of his finger to her bracelet before pulling back.

"Gifts from God are like that too. If we don't accept them, we miss out on all the beauty and joy He wants us to experience. And I know how much He wants that for you, because it's exactly what I wanted for you today. It made me incredibly happy when you accepted and used the gifts I gave you."

His daughter lifted her cone until it pretty much blocked her face before she mumbled, "She'll always be your favourite, though. Because she was first."

Arlo slumped back in his seat. How could he convince her otherwise? *Lord, help.* The two-word prayer had become his mantra from the moment he'd found out he had another daughter. "Carly, do you believe in God?"

She slowly lowered the cone. "Yes."

"Do you believe that He loves you and every single person in the world?"

"Yes. I learned that in Sunday school."

"Good. Because it's true. And He doesn't love any person more than any other person. It's kind of like everyone is His favourite, right?"

"I guess."

"If God gave you and Phoebe to me as gifts, don't you think He'll make sure that I have lots and lots of love for both of you, enough that you can both be my favourites? And if I ever have any other children, they can also be my favourites?"

Her blue eyes probed his intently. *Lord, help her too. Help her to understand.*

Finally, she broke away. "I suppose."

Not exactly convincing, but better than a no. "Just think about it. If you ever want to talk more about this or anything else, you can always come to me, okay?"

She nodded. "Okay."

Her ice cream was melting. Probably he'd given her more than enough to think about for this, their first time out together. Arlo grabbed more napkins and wiped off her fingers again. "I loved spending today with you, and I hope we can do it again soon."

"Me too." Carly licked a wayward clump of ice cream from her cone.

She did? That was promising, and even more than Arlo had dared hope for at the end of their day.

For now, he would take that gift from God and be grateful for every step forward the two of them were able to make.

NINETEEN

Present day

Carly pulled the map and compass out of her pack and gazed at it before looking up at Phoebe and Scarlett. "This bench marks the next big destination on the map, which means that Dad left something for us around here. Does anyone see what it could be?"

They searched for a couple of minutes before Scarlett, on her knees behind the bench, reached beneath it and pulled something away from the bottom of it, the sound of ripping tape disturbing the stillness that had fallen over the forest in the murky twilight.

"Here." She clambered to her feet and brushed off her knees. "Another letter." She held up an envelope. "This one's for Phoebe." In her other hand, she clutched an orange velvet bag. "This has my name on it, and I have a pretty good idea what it could be."

"Your lighter," Phoebe and Carly said at the same time.

When Scarlett turned twelve, Dad had given her a cool, antique lighter. He'd shown her how to start a fire out in the woods, and she was given that task from then on when they were on their quests. They'd all left their gifts from Dad at home, then, when they moved out. Had that hurt him? It must have.

Phoebe took Carly's spot on the stump as she carefully tore open the envelope and extracted the folded, cream-coloured paper inside. Carly walked off a few steps to give her a moment, her attention on Scarlett as her baby sister pulled the old lighter out of the bag. Scarlett's gaze narrowed slightly as she contemplated the object, but she didn't say anything, only stuck it and the bag into her backpack before slinging it over her shoulders again.

Carly shifted her attention to Phoebe. "You okay, Phoebes?"

When she looked up, her middle sister's eyes shimmered the way Carly's had after reading her own letter from Dad. "Yeah. I'm good. Listen to this." She cleared her throat.

For Phoebe.
The second is the ray of sun that pierces darkest sky,
To softly fall upon the narrow way.
Because of her I'll offer thanks until the day I die,
For grace that drew me in and bid me stay.
All my love, Dad

For a moment after she finished and returned the letter to the envelope, none of them spoke. Only the melancholy call of a mourning dove broke the silence.

Then Scarlett said, her voice slightly hoarse, "That's beautiful, Phoebes."

Carly nodded. "It really is." And apt, since Phoebe did radiate light wherever she went.

Phoebe stuck the envelope into her backpack and stood. "It's getting dark. We better keep moving."

Carly spread the map over the stone and set the compass on it. Long shadows fell over the paper, and she had to lean in to see the directions to their next stop. It was about to get a lot more dangerous to make their way along the uneven ground. "Did either of you bring your phone?"

Phoebe shook her head. "I left it in the car, since it wasn't on Dad's list."

"Me too." Scarlett lifted an empty hand. "I doubt we'd get a signal out here anyway."

"All right then. Careful where you're walking." Carly studied the compass, getting her bearings. Her fingers shook slightly. The falling darkness had brought plummeting temperatures with it, and none of them were dressed warmly enough. All the more reason to get moving. She started along the rough path.

They moved from landmark to landmark, the woods growing increasingly dark. Finally, Phoebe tugged on Carly's backpack to slow her. "Let me walk next to you, Carly. I've got the flashlight."

With that soft glow falling across the pathway ahead of them, they made their way toward the next destination. Suddenly, Phoebe let out a sharp cry and skidded to a halt. Carly jerked her head up from the compass but couldn't see anything amiss.

"What is it?" Scarlett came up to stand on the other side of Phoebe.

"Snake." Phoebe pressed a hand to her chest. Of the three of them, she always had been the most squeamish when it came to creepy crawly things.

Carly's muscles tightened. "Rattler?"

"I don't know." Phoebe waved a hand toward the woods on their left. "It slithered across the path and disappeared into the trees so quickly I couldn't see."

Scarlett cocked her head in the direction Phoebe had indicated. "Listen."

The three of them stood in silence a moment, until Scarlett straightened. "No rattle. I think we're good."

"Maybe that guy'll get him." Carly pointed to a dark shape gliding overhead. A soft hooting sound drifted down to them. An owl.

"I hope so." A shudder moved through Phoebe that likely had little to do with the frigid temperatures.

Scarlett adjusted the strap that had slid down Phoebe's shoulder when she jerked to a stop. "Remember what Dad always said about snakes and spiders."

"They're way more afraid of us than we are of them." The three of them spoke in unison, which did manage to bring a smile to Phoebe's face.

"We better keep going." Carly held the compass and map in the light from the flashlight and studied them a moment. "Next stop is only a couple of hundred metres away."

Phoebe started forward, her head lowered, her gaze fixed on the trail. No doubt she was watching the ground closely in case another snake decided to slither past. Several more minutes passed before gravel crunched beneath their hiking boots, and Carly looked up from the compass.

A road. Excellent. They had reached civilization.

TWENTY

August 2002

Nell had called Arlo late one night a few days after he'd given Carly the compass. His heart leapt at the sight of her name on the screen. Because she was his lifeline out here in the rough waters of this situation he and the girls found themselves in, he told himself.

In any case, after making sure his daughters were both asleep, he stepped out of the apartment and hit the connect button.

"Hey, Nell."

"Hi, Lo." She laughed. "Nope. Thought I'd try it out, but you're right. There's no good way to shorten your name. What were your parents thinking?"

"They were thinking that they loved Arlo Guthrie."

"Ah. That's it. I'll call you Guthrie."

Arlo grinned wryly as he lowered himself to a step. "That's not shorter."

"I know, but the length isn't the point. It just has to be an *orra* name."

"*Orra?*"

"Yeah. My dad's Scottish, and he taught me that word. It means something that is only used occasionally. In this case, it's a name only one other person would call you."

They were *orra* name friends now? He had absolutely no problem with that. "Well, all right then. Guthrie it is. But only for you."

In the slight pause that followed, warmth crept up his neck. Too much? Before he could apologize or backtrack, she said, "I like that," and his shoulders relaxed.

"Me too."

"Did you have a chance to give Carly her gift?"

"I did, last Saturday. I gave her a compass."

"That's very cool."

"Exactly what she said."

"That sounds promising. It went well?"

"Really well, I think. I showed her how to use it, and she successfully completed the first-ever Stone Family Challenge."

Her quiet laugh drifted over the line. "Okay, I'll bite. What is a Stone Family Challenge?"

"It's a quest for treasure, of course. I made her a map, and she followed it from point to point in the park using the compass. The final destination was a maple tree, where I'd hidden a surprise in a hole in the trunk."

"What surprise?"

"A gold bracelet. I had CT engraved on it so she'd know that, while I hoped she would start to feel part of the Stone family, I wasn't trying to erase her Travers side. She's both."

"Okay, overachiever. I see you really took my suggestion and ran with it."

"I tried." Since she had mentioned that she would be praying for them, he added, "I prayed about it a lot, and that was the idea that came to me."

"It was a good one. I'm really happy it went so well."

"Me too. Thank you for talking me through that, Nell."

"Anytime, Guthrie."

Their conversation still filled him with warmth weeks later, whenever he thought about it. Which he did far more often than he should, probably. The truth was, he missed her. Missed her laugh and the sound of her voice late at night, when the silence in the apartment was deafening. Which was crazy, right? How could you miss someone you barely knew?

Of course, she was the one who had decreed them *orro* friends, so she must feel the connection between them as well, even though they'd only had a few conversations.

Arlo set a stack of '70s albums on top of a box and began filing them alphabetically in the bins that lined the shelves in his store. *Déjà Vu* by Crosby, Stills, Nash, and Young. Should he call her? *The Long Run* by The Eagles. Definitely not. *Say You Will* by Fleetwood Mac. He had no pressing reason to bother her at the moment. *Private Eyes* by Hall and Oates. He'd already taken up enough of her time. *Dazed and Confused* by the Yardbirds. Wait. He checked the album cover again. He must have been dazed and confused when he'd put these in order. The Yardbirds definitely needed to be closer to the bottom of the pile.

Ah well. He carried the record to the end of the row and slid it into place before returning to grab The Kinks' *Low Budget* album.

Ha. Exactly why he was misfiling albums—he couldn't afford to hire more staff for the store.

Which he should consider doing so he could stay open in the evenings, something he'd stopped doing since his daughters came to live with him. Not that he would trade a minute with them for the few measly extra bucks he might earn in a week by extending his hours.

He hefted the pile of albums and shuffled a few feet to the right to begin filing the next lot. For several minutes, he was able to push thoughts of Nell out of his head as he lost himself in the covers and the memories they invoked of concerts and evenings spent listening to music with his parents.

The bells above the door jangled and, yanked back to the present, he glanced over. Nell. His heart leapt the way it had when she called. What was she doing here?

Arlo dropped Pink Floyd's *Obscured by Clouds* in between *The Dark Side of the Moon* and *Wish You Were Here*—the irony not lost on him—before turning in her direction. "Hey, Nell."

"Guthrie." Her smile was warm as she approached. "So this is your store."

"Yep."

She cast a look around. "Nice."

That one word filled him with inordinate pleasure. The first couple of times they'd met in person, Arlo had been so distracted by finding out he had another daughter that he hadn't really been able to take note of Nell. Now, he drank in every detail. The strawberry-blonde hair that bounced lightly against her shoulders, the smattering of freckles across her nose, the big hazel eyes. He did remember the flower-strewn overalls she'd been wearing when he went to the CAS office. Her outfit today was no less subdued. Lime-green capris with a bright yellow T-shirt covered in birds. If a warm summer day were a person, it would look exactly like Nell.

He watched as she wandered over to the bins of albums and began flipping idly through them.

"Looking for a particular record?"

"I am, actually." She moved a couple of bins to the right and started going through that one.

"Anything I can help you with?"

Her back to him, she waved a hand over her shoulder. "I'm good."

Even given their limited association, he believed that to be true. "All right then." Leaning back against the counter, he crossed his arms over his chest, content to observe her as she made her way down the row of bins. By the time she was halfway down the aisle, he had a pretty good idea of the object of her search.

His suspicions were confirmed when she let out a triumphant "Aha!" and whirled around, brandishing in both hands a copy of *Way Off Track*, Lone Trail's top selling album—top selling, of course, being a relative term.

Arlo grinned. "You've been researching me."

She lowered the record to peer over the top of it at him, mock affront on her face. "I've been doing my due diligence, making sure my charge is in safe hands."

"I thought you said you didn't have to do that with Carly, since she's actually my daughter and not from the system."

A fascinating flush turned her cheeks pink. "This is more of a personal due diligence than an official one. There's something about Carly. Although we didn't spend a lot of time together, I felt a strong connection to her. I needed to make sure I'd handed her over to a decent man."

Arlo's lips twitched. "And?"

She walked a half circle around him before stopping in front of him and meeting his gaze. "You check out. So far."

"I'm glad to hear it."

"How's sweet Carly doing, anyway?"

"I mean, it's slow going. But we're making progress." His daughters had started referring to each other by name, at least, which was something. Carly hadn't yet called him Dad, but he was working at appreciating every small win.

"Good. It's a journey. But you appear to be heading in the right direction."

"I hope so. Don't stop praying."

"I won't." Her smile filled him with an intense warmth he wasn't sure he had ever experienced. Not even with either of the women he shared a child with. Which was interesting. And sad. But mostly interesting.

Nell set the album on the counter next to him. "How is Phoebe coping with all this?"

It touched Arlo deeply that she would ask about his other daughter, the one she had never met. "Pretty good, I think. It was a tough conversation, letting her know that her mother was gone and she wouldn't see her again, but I think she kind of gets it."

"That's a lot of change for a young girl."

"I know. She's been clingier than usual, which is understandable." Arlo exhaled as he drove his fingers through his hair. "I'm just trying to be there for them both, let them know how much I love them."

"That's the best thing you can do for them. Once they feel completely secure in your love, it will be easier for them to love each other."

Arlo nodded. As much as her presence sent his heart racing in the best possible way, having her here filled him with peace, and he was suddenly desperate to keep her from leaving too soon. "Can I make you a cup of tea?"

"Sure." Nell followed him to the back of the store.

He made them peppermint tea and, once she'd laughingly declined his offer to sit at the tiny pink table where he and Phoebe had their tea parties, they settled on bean bag chairs and talked and laughed all afternoon, until he realized it was nearly three o'clock and he needed to pick up the girls. Clambering to his feet, he held out a hand to pull her up. "I think I need an *orro* name for you."

She tilted her head as she looked up at him, her fingers still warm in his. "I told you that you could call me Nell."

"Yeah, but you said all your friends call you that, and only one person gets to call you by an *orro* name. Like you with Guthrie," he added pointedly.

Nell laughed. "You're right. It's only fair. What's it to be then?"

"Has anyone ever shortened Ellen to Len?"

"Actually no, that's a new one."

"That's it, then." He brushed a soft, red curl back from her cheek. "Len."

"All right. But only for you."

He got why she hadn't responded when he'd said that to her. There was something so powerful in those four words that no answer felt adequate. For a minute, neither of them moved. Then she cleared her throat and reached for the album. "I'm taking this. Although"—she gazed down at it—"I don't have a record player."

Arlo shook his head. "You have no idea what you've been missing." Grinning, he rounded the counter. "Here. I have a small one you can take." He pulled out the white portable one he'd let people listen to records on before he set up a better system with headphones along the far wall. This one hadn't been used in a couple of years, and he grabbed a cloth and swiped the dust off the top of the case. "A warning, though. It will spoil you for any other way of listening to music."

"Noted. What do I owe you?" Nell unzipped her bag.

Arlo rested a hand on top of the player. "You don't owe me anything. I owe you. You have no idea what it means to me to have someone I can call when life gets overwhelming, how much it has helped to feel like I'm not completely alone in this."

She touched the side of her hand to his. "You're not."

When he nodded, tingles of electricity travelling across his hand and up his arm, she zipped her bag and adjusted the strap higher on her shoulder. "Well, thank you. This buys you a few more sessions, at least, so call anytime, okay?"

"I will. And thanks for coming by. It was really good to see you. Len."

She offered him one last smile as she gripped the handle of the record player and heaved it off the counter. "You too, Guthrie."

A couple of evenings later, Arlo called her, and they chatted about their days and their growing-up years and very little about everything he was going through, which was a nice break. After that, sitting on the stairs in the still of the late evenings and talking to her on the phone became a near-nightly event.

As he and Carly and Phoebe settled into a rhythm and both girls appeared to be adjusting, even if they weren't exactly best friends yet, Arlo asked them if they would be okay if Nell joined them for the Stone Family Adventure #8. Carly was excited at the prospect, which confirmed for him Nell's words that she and Carly had connected during their brief time together, a thought that warmed his heart. Phoebe was more outgoing by nature, so she also readily agreed.

The next day, after the four of them had wandered deep into the woods, both girls suddenly got spooked at the sight of a massive furry spider that dropped down on a long strand of web directly in front of them. Phoebe grabbed his right hand and, for the first time ever, Carly grabbed his left. At the same time, both girls squealed, "Dad!"

A wave of emotion crashed over him. His older daughter was scared, and her instinct was to reach out for him and to call him Dad. That had to mean she was coming to understand he was her safe place, right? That he was there for her and always would be when she needed him? So much joy coursed through him that it took everything he had not to drop to a crouch and pull both girls into his arms.

Instead, he forced himself to speak calmly, assuring them that the spider was far more scared of them than they were of it. When the poor arachnid—equally spooked, no doubt—skittered into a hole in a tree, they struck out again. Neither girl let go of his hand.

Arlo glanced over his shoulder at Nell, his eyes wide with wonder. The hazel eyes that met his glowed. The fact that she clearly understood how momentous this moment was filled him with a deep, quiet excitement and affirmation of how special she was and how well she fit into the family.

Ten months later, after Arlo had asked for and received the blessing of both his daughters, he and Nell got engaged.

TWENTY-ONE

Present day

"Okay." Carly studied the map. "We're looking for a sign that says Rough Road. Should be right around here."

"I hope that's not a hint of things to come," Scarlett muttered as she peered into the darkness.

Carly might have laughed except that her sister sounded as though her teeth were chattering. They really needed to get somewhere warm. Somewhere with food, preferably. That half a protein bar wasn't cutting it anymore. As if on cue, her stomach rumbled.

"There!" Phoebe pointed across the road and maybe a dozen metres east.

The three of them crossed the dirt road and congregated at the base of the sign. Carly checked out the back of it to see if anything had been taped to it. Nothing. "All right. I assume we're looking for another envelope, at least. Possibly a velvet bag, although we all have the tools Dad gave us."

"This might be it." The beam from the flashlight caught a rock at the base of the sign. Something white gleamed at the edge of it. Phoebe nudged it aside with her hiking boot before crouching to pick up an envelope and a bag. A tiny piece of paper extended from the bag, and she slid it out. "Do not open until you reach the final destination." Whatever was in the velvet bag was small, and she tucked it into her jacket pocket and handed the envelope to Scarlett. "For you." She held the flashlight in Scarlett's direction.

Their little sister took the envelope and slid a nail beneath the flap to open it. After pulling the paper out, she scanned it and then drew in a deep breath and began to read.

> For Scarlett.
> *The last is fire that blazes hot, dispelling winter frost.*
> *Its golden flames invite this weary man*
> *To now and ever reach out for the hearth when tempest tossed*
> *And in its warmth find love and hope again.*
> All my love, Dad

Phoebe sighed. "It definitely sounds like a song, doesn't it?"

Scarlett clutched the paper to her chest. "It does. I didn't know Dad wrote songs anymore."

Carly rubbed her hands together, trying to warm them. "As far as I know, he hasn't written one in years, since before I came to live with him. Unless he's been composing in secret."

"Or maybe he's not doing as well as he says he is and wanted to write one more."

Scarlett's voice shook slightly, but Carly wasn't sure if that was pain at the thought or the deepening cold. Either way, they needed to keep moving. "We can talk to him about it when we see him. Let's try to finish this quest before we all freeze to death."

"Good plan." Phoebe swung the light around so Carly could read the map. "How much farther, can you tell?"

"It doesn't look like much, less than a kilometre. And mostly on the road, as far as I can—" Carly frowned and leaned closer to the flashlight. "Does that say *You always were my favourite?*"

"Oh. Yeah." In the soft glow of the flashlight, a sheepish look crossed Phoebe's face. "I didn't mention it because I thought it was a bit strange that Dad would say that."

"It would be, if he hadn't engraved the same thing inside the lid of my compass."

"And on my lighter." Scarlett snorted a laugh. "Tricky little trickster. What is his end game?"

"I'm not sure." A memory struck her, and Carly tightened her grip on the compass. "Him engraving that on each of the gifts he gave us just reminded me of a conversation I had with him the day of the first Stone Family Challenge."

Phoebe lowered the flashlight to her side. "What about?"

"Dad told me I was part of the family and he loved me, and I mentioned that you would always be his favourite because you were first. He asked if I believed that God loved everyone in the world the same, like they were all His favourites. When I agreed, he said, then don't you think God gives parents enough love for all their kids, so that each one can be their favourite?"

Although she couldn't see the words on the lid of the compass, she ran the pad of her thumb over them, feeling the engraving. "I didn't fully get that until this moment."

"He really means it, doesn't he?" Phoebe touched her finger to the flashlight as though, like Carly, she was trying to absorb that truth.

"I believe he does."

Scarlett sighed. "Makes our issues with each other feel pretty petty, doesn't it?"

Exactly what Carly had been thinking earlier. "It puts them in perspective, anyway." She was shivering, and her sisters weren't dressed any more warmly than she was. She nodded toward the east. "We better start walking."

It took about twenty minutes to reach the next landmark—a speed limit sign this time. After checking the map and compass, Carly directed them off the road and onto another patch of gravel punctuated with weeds. A wide trail, maybe? Or a rough driveway? A glimmer of light broke through the thick stand of trees in front of them, and she pointed to it. "That must be where we're going."

With the end in sight, they picked up the pace. Given the wider trail, they were able to walk next to each other. When they broke out of the woods, all three of them stopped abruptly.

Phoebe pressed her free hand to her cheek. "A cottage!"

"But whose cottage? Are we on private property?" Carly checked the map again. Had she miscalculated somewhere?

"Umm. I think it might be ours?" The small building was surrounded by a picket fence, and Scarlett strode forward to stop in front of the gate. "Shine the light here, Phoebe."

When the beam fell on the sign, Carly could make out the words written in elegant cursive on a metal plate attached to the gate. *Three Sisters Cottage.*

Phoebe drew in a sharp breath. "Three Sisters? Is that us? Did Dad actually get that cottage we were always pestering him about?"

"It looks like maybe he did." Carly closed the compass and tucked it and the map in the front pocket of her backpack. "Phoebes. Do you have the last bag?"

"Oh, right." Phoebe dug into her pocket and pulled out the bag. "You open it, Carly. You're the one who got us here."

"It was a group effort. I couldn't have done it without you guys. But okay." She took the bag and stuck her hand inside. A thin, rectangular box was nestled at the bottom of it, and she drew it out. Her fingers were so numb it took a couple of tries, but she was finally able to lift the lid. The glow of the flashlight reflected off a shiny silver key.

The gate creaked and she looked up. Scarlett pushed it open and then swept her hand in front of her, inviting Carly to go on ahead.

She dropped the empty box into the bag and shoved it in her pocket. "All right then. Let's check this place out."

TWENTY-TWO

September 2004

Arlo's third daughter arrived a week before his and Nell's second anniversary. Carly had just turned ten, and Phoebe was seven. The two of them stayed at Davey's for a couple of days so Arlo could be with Nell during the delivery and afterward, when all the bustling around and tests were done and they were finally alone with their new baby girl.

Arlo sat on the small bed next to his wife, one arm holding her close as she cradled their child in her arms. He tugged the blanket away from the baby's face so he could study her perfect features—tiny nose that would likely be freckled at some point, given her soft red curls—and big hazel eyes. Like Carly and Phoebe, this one had his cheekbones. Arlo hoped she would also be musical, although he had no problem with her otherwise being just like her mama. A wave of love for all four of his girls swept over him, and he tightened his hold on Nell, who rested her head on his shoulder.

"What will we call her, Len?" he murmured into her hair. They'd made a list of several possibilities but hadn't settled on one before their daughter decided to make an appearance two weeks early.

Nell looked up at him, her eyes sleepy but glowing with joy the way they so often were. "It's not on the list, and I know it's a bit on the nose, given her red hair, but every time I look at her, all I can think is that she's a Scarlett. Is that crazy?"

"Scarlett." Arlo tried the name on for size. Scarlett Stone did have a nice ring to it. And it truly suited their precious girl, now that she mentioned it. "I love it."

"You do?"

Whether he did or not, with his wife gazing up at him like that, there was nothing he wouldn't agree to. "I do."

"It's not the red hair as much as the set of her jaw. Your jaw. Like you, she looks ready to take on the world and anyone who might try to hurt someone she loves. She reminds me of Scarlett O'Hara. I can almost picture her standing in the middle of a field, raising her hand to the sky and vowing to never give up."

Huh. Now that she mentioned it, Arlo could see it. Although . . . was that how his wife saw him? Was that what he was like? "I've never really seen myself that way."

She shifted to look at him more fully. "Arlo. When I met you, I was introducing you to the seven-year-old daughter you didn't know you had. And your other daughter was about to come into your full-time care while her mother walked away from you both. I looked at you that day and, yes, you did appear a bit shell shocked, but you also had a set to your jaw, this steely determination. I knew you'd be just fine—as would Carly and Phoebe. And I was right."

He pressed a kiss to the top of her head. "Because of you."

"No. Because of you. And God." She offered him an impish grin. "And maybe a little bit me."

It was more than a little bit her, although it had also been a little bit him and, yes, a whole lot of God. Still, the woman had just given birth to his child. He wouldn't argue with her.

So, Scarlett Stone it was.

From the moment they brought Scarlett home to the small house they'd moved into when Arlo and Nell married, her sisters hardly seemed to know what to make of her. As they had always done with each other, they gave her a wide berth.

The years passed, and they all grew older and became their own people—Carly, the sweet, studious, reflective one, lover of literature and all things academic; Phoebe, the bright, bubbling, happy one surrounded by friends; and Scarlett, the ball of fire who lit up every room she entered. It was fascinating to Arlo, watching them become who they would be, the women God had created them to be.

He and Nell took the girls to church every week, and they were all slowly developing a faith. If they weren't as close as Arlo would have hoped, they got along tolerably well. He tried to be grateful for that, especially as they entered the teen years.

Even so, the desire of his heart was always that someday, as they continued to go on Stone Family Challenges and learn how to navigate rough terrain and thick underbrush, they would find their way to each other as well.

During Challenge #32, when the girls were fifteen, twelve, and five, the rough road they were hiking along took them past a small stone cottage surrounded by a white picket fence. Scarlett stopped and pressed her forehead to two posts, peering between them at the little house, smoke drifting from its chimney. "Daddy!"

Arlo stopped next to her and rested a hand on her red curls. "What is it, sweetheart?"

"We should get a cottage in the woods."

"That would be pretty cool." Carly had come up to stand on the other side of him without Arlo noticing.

"I agree," Phoebe chimed in from Scarlett's far side, gripping the tops of two of the picket fence posts as she gazed at the house.

Wow. His three daughters agreeing on anything was so rare that Arlo was tempted to give in on the spot. Buying a cottage was beyond his and Nell's means, however, although he couldn't bring himself to quash his daughters' dream outright.

He contemplated the cozy place. "You never know. Maybe it will be the treasure at the end of one of our quests someday."

It wasn't likely, although you never *did* know. If nothing else, the vague promise might keep the three of them interested in participating in their family challenges a few years longer. Or perhaps they'd simply forget they ever had this conversation, as kids were wont to do.

He shot a glance at his wife, who raised her eyebrows. When he lifted his shoulders, she gave him a smile as indulgent as any he ever bestowed on the girls. He did make an effort to avoid cute little houses in the woods when creating the next few family challenges. Occasionally, despite his efforts, they came across one here or there.

Each time, the girls renewed their request for a family cottage, and Arlo responded with a noncommittal "Maybe. Some day."

Nell was right, and he shouldn't even hint at the likelihood of such a thing. Even so, the beautiful idea of the cottage united his family, and he wasn't about to do anything to jeopardize that.

TWENTY-THREE

Present day

Carly stuck the key in the lock in the front door. Not until it turned beneath the pressure of her fingers did she begin to believe this might be real. She pushed open the door and stepped inside. Scarlett and Phoebe followed her.

The interior of the cottage was bathed in the soft glow of light from sconces mounted on every wall. There was a kitchen off to the left with stainless-steel appliances, and to the right soft leather furniture beckoned them to sit and relax after their long hike.

The couch and armchairs all faced a wall of stone with a big fireplace and gleaming wooden mantel as the centrepiece. A bin filled with pieces of wood sat next to the fireplace, and Scarlett started for it. "Let's get a fire going and maybe eat something and then we can take a look around."

It was cold enough in the cabin that neither Carly nor Phoebe protested. The two of them headed to the kitchen, where they found a fully stocked fridge. If they actually were trespassing on someone else's property—although, why would Dad have the key?—they were about to add robbery to their list of offences. Carly was hungry enough that she didn't care.

They put together a meal of salad, cheese, homemade chicken noodle soup they found in a bowl in the fridge and that reminded her suspiciously of the soup Nell often made, and thick slices from the loaf of fresh bread wrapped in paper on the counter. A container of brownies sat next to the bread, and they scarfed those down for dessert.

Finally, Scarlett leaned back in her chair, one hand pressed to her stomach. "That was the best meal I've ever eaten."

Carly laughed. "Me too." The dinners Dad or Nell made them after they'd spent the day hiking through the woods to complete a family challenge were always the best meals they'd ever eaten. The effects of fresh air, exercise, and triumph, she assumed. And she was feeling all three in this moment.

Phoebe pushed back her chair. "Let's explore."

It didn't take long. The cottage was snug and homey, with the open area taken up by the kitchen, a small washroom just inside the front door, and a large living area. Two doors on either side of the cabin led to bedrooms that each had their own small *en suite* bath. Perfect for their family.

When they had completed the tour, Scarlett went to check on the fire while Phoebe and Carly cleared the table.

As Phoebe filled the sink with water, Carly grabbed a dish towel and leaned against the counter to watch Scarlett work. She finished stirring up the flames and dropped the poker into a holder. Then she paused a moment, looking at something on the mantel, before reaching out and picking up an envelope.

Carly's pulse quickened. A message from Dad? Scarlett carried it to the kitchen and settled on a bar stool. "Look. Dad left us another note." She turned it around so Carly and Phoebe could read the front. *My Three Girls* was written across the front of it in his familiar handwriting.

"Open it, Scarlett." Phoebe dried her hands on the towel Carly still clutched in one hand before wandering over to stand across the counter from their sister. Carly set down the plate and towel and joined her.

Scarlett ripped the envelope carefully before extracting the piece of paper inside. She unfolded it and laid it flat on the counter between them. All three of them leaned in to read the words.

Earth and Sun and Fire,
these three remain alone.
And each one is my favourite,
For they are all my home.
Each of them will always be my home.

Carly's throat tightened. Why had Dad stopped writing songs? Were the ones he'd written when he was in his band as lovely? The second she got home, she was looking them up.

Phoebe touched her fingers to Carly's back. "It's gorgeous, isn't it?"

Carly nodded. "It really is. Clearly, Dad sees us as different, with unique characteristics and strengths, but he loves us all the same. Earth, sun, and fire. How could you choose which of those is better or more valuable? We need them all to survive, so I guess what he's saying is that he needs us too. We really are all his favourite."

Phoebe, the most tender-hearted of the three of them, swiped at a tear sliding down her cheek. "If he feels that strongly about us,

I can also see how it has hurt him over the years that we didn't feel the same about each other."

Scarlett reached over and covered each of their hands with hers. "I think we took the first few steps of that quest today, don't you?"

Carly nodded. "I do."

"Me too." Phoebe gave them a watery smile.

"Okay then." Carly pushed away from the counter. "Let's finish the dishes, and then we can relax in front of the fire. I recommend we don't start back through the woods tonight, not with snakes and cougars and who knows what else out there. Let's plan to sleep here and figure out how to get home tomorrow." Hopefully Alain wouldn't worry about her too much when she didn't check in tonight.

Scarlett started to round the counter, but Phoebe waved her away. "Go sit, Scarlett. There aren't many dishes. We'll join you in a minute."

She nodded and meandered over to the living area, stopping in front of a shelf of books built into the stone before making her way to a guitar on a stand in the corner. Picking it up, she carried it to the couch, where she settled it on her thigh and began softly strumming the strings.

Carly grabbed another plate from the rack and ran the towel over it. What was that melody? Not one she remembered hearing before. It was lovely, though, peaceful and rippling like water over stones. Phoebe had stopped washing a glass and was watching their sister as well.

Then Scarlett began to sing, low and soft. "There's one who is the earth to me . . ."

Carly's mouth dropped open slightly. It was their song. The one their dad had given them. Only the lyrics, though. How was Scarlett singing it? Occasionally she hummed a few bars, as though she'd forgotten the words, but she'd always had a killer memory, and she remembered a remarkable number of them.

Carly shot a look at Phoebe, whose dark eyes had widened. When she met Carly's gaze, she lifted her shoulders slightly.

Unwilling to interrupt the performance to ask how Scarlett was doing what she was doing, Carly only closed her eyes, taking in every word, every note that continued to flow like a slow-moving river sparkling with drops of sunlight.

By the time her baby sister finished, the words "Each of them will always be my home" still drifting on the air, all three had tears on their cheeks. For a moment, none of them moved, then Carly tossed the towel down and pressed her hands to the counter. "Scarlett. That was incredible. How did you do that?"

Scarlett lifted the guitar from her leg and leaned it against the arm of the couch. "I'm not sure. The melody just came to me as we were walking through the woods. I've been singing it in my head since we found the first verse, your verse, Carly."

"It's so beautiful."

"It's Dad's words."

Phoebe walked over to settle on the coffee table in front of her. "The words are powerful, but it wasn't only them. It was the combination of the words and the melody that gave them life. Like you created one and Dad the other, but they needed to find each other and be played on that exact instrument to become what they were meant to be."

Her words struck deep inside Carly like an arrow with a flaming tip, sparking a revelation. "Like us."

Scarlett tilted her head to the side, her red curls splashing over one shoulder. "What do you mean?"

"We have always existed around each other like powerful lyrics and a beautiful melody and an exquisite instrument. Only we've never made much of an effort to join all three together. Maybe, because of that, we've missed out on all the incredible music we could have been making together while we were growing up."

"Is it too late?" Phoebe's eyes still shimmered.

Scarlett shook her head vehemently. "Absolutely not. It's never too late. You and Carly, you're the treasure waiting at the end of my quest. Just because it's taken me a long time to find my way to you doesn't make the treasure any less valuable. In fact, like most treasures, maybe our friendship, our sisterhood, has only become more valuable with passing time."

"Yes." Carly walked over to sit on the table next to Phoebe. "Dad once told me that family was a gift from God that, like my compass, can help guide us through life." She reached for her sisters' hands. "I've never been grateful enough for that, but I'm starting to realize how incredible a gift it is. So I'd like to ask you both to stand up with me at my wedding."

Phoebe swiped a tear from her cheek with her shoulder. "I thought you'd never ask."

Scarlett let out a choked laugh. "Me neither. But I'd love to."

Carly squeezed her fingers. "I'm also going to need you to sing that song during the ceremony. And then you have to record it and share it with the world."

"I agree."

At the sound of a deep, male voice, Carly and Phoebe twisted around to peer back at the doorway. Dad stood in the opening, one shoulder propped against the frame, his hands in the front pockets of his jeans.

"Dad." Carly started to get up, but he waved a hand in her direction. "Sit. I'm coming over." He ambled across the room. When he reached them, he took their faces one by one in his hands and pressed a kiss to each of their heads before lowering himself onto the couch next to Scarlett.

She touched his forearm. "Are you okay?"

"I'm perfectly fine. Just needed the right medication. And I needed to see my girls together like this. That more than anything has healed this old heart of mine."

"I'm sorry it took us so long to find our way here." Carly swiped a thumb under her eye.

He shook his head. "You're here now. That's all that matters."

Phoebe swept an arm around the room, warm from the fire. "How did you do all this?"

He chuckled. "Lone Trail didn't exactly make heaps of money, but what I did bring in for royalties I handed over to Davey. He was the financial wizard among us, and Jim and I trusted him to invest our money wisely. Then, to be honest, I didn't give my holdings much more thought, since I doubted much would come of investing the bit of money we had. Imagine my surprise when Davey called a few months ago to let me know that in the '80s he'd invested heavily for all three of us in stocks for a new and little-known hardware company—Home Depot. Just had a feeling, he said. At the time, stocks cost about thirty-four cents apiece. Now, apparently, they're worth just shy of three hundred and eighty-five dollars, which is a pretty serious return on investment."

Phoebe let out a low whistle again, the way she had when Carly mentioned they were about to embark on their fiftieth family challenge.

"I know, right?" Dad grinned, the sight easing Carly's angst regarding his health. "Anyway, when I heard about this cottage a few weeks later, I called him to see if there was enough in my account to buy it. He let me know that Mom and I could purchase it outright and still have enough left for the future."

Carly bit her lip. "You shouldn't have spent that much of your savings on us."

"Why not? This place has been a dream of our family for years. One I wasn't sure I would ever be able to fulfil. Finding out that I could, that we could have this place where the five of us can spend time together and maybe fill with husbands and grandchildren one day, brought me far more joy than leaving that money sitting in the bank."

Scarlett hooked her arm through his. "I don't know how we can thank you except to promise you that we'll use it a lot. Together."

He rested his head against hers. "That's all the thanks I need."

Phoebe glanced over at the door. "Where's Nell?"

"She wanted to give the four of us some time together. She'll join us for breakfast in the morning." He turned to his youngest daughter. "Carly is right, Scarlett. You need to record that song. I've never heard anything more moving."

"Absolutely not."

He blinked. "You won't record it?"

"I will. But only if we make it a duet and you sing it with me. And my sisters have to do backup vocals on the chorus. This is the Stone Family Song #1 or it's not a song at all."

When their father spoke, his voice was husky. "All right then. A Stone Family song it is. And whether or not it ever makes it to the charts, I can tell you right now that it will always be my favourite."

You Always Were My Favourite
By Arlo Stone

There's one who is the earth to me, cool grass beneath the trees,
And roots so deep they hold against the gale.
Although for time apart and moments missed my heart still grieves,
The gift of her proves mercy does prevail.

The second is the ray of sun that pierces darkest sky,
To softly fall upon the narrow way.
Because of her I'll offer thanks until the day I die,
For grace that drew me in and bid me stay.

The last is fire that blazes hot, dispelling winter frost.
Its golden flames invite this weary man
To now and ever reach out for the hearth when tempest tossed
And in its warmth find love and hope again.

Earth and Sun and Fire,
these three remain alone.
And each one is my favourite,
For they are all my home.
Each of them will always be my home.

A Note From The Author

Dear Reader,

As always, thank you for taking the time to read "You Always Were My Favourite" and the other stories in this collection. We pray over all our anthologies, that God will use them to bring hope, peace, and encouragement to every person who reads them.

I hope that is what you have found in this story. That the idea of a God who loves us all more than we can ever begin to comprehend settles in your soul and gives you great joy today. May that love and joy and peace overflow to all those around you.

Our world is in great turmoil. Conflict and division are reflected in every conversation, certainly in every online interaction. As believers, we have a choice to make. We can contribute to the dark, swirling vortex. Or we can humbly offer, with God's help, light to push back the darkness, hope to overcome despair, joy to comfort those in sorrow, and a love that is so countercultural and revolutionary that it can change not only another person's day or heart but the world.

Arlo's deep, unwavering love for his girls, even as his heart hurt over the distance and division between them, is a pale reflection of the deep, unfathomable love of God for humanity. And if He loves us that much despite how often we hurt Him or choose the path that takes us away from Him, then may He give us the ability to do the same for others.

Blessings,

Sara

Acknowledgements

I struggled with this story. In all honesty, I have struggled with the last few stories I've written. The darkness in the world—the uncertainty, division, hatred, and suffering—can weigh on me heavily and make it extremely difficult for me to focus and to be creative.

And so my deepest thanks go to my Father God, who has invited me to cast all these things on Him because He cares for me. I learned that verse as a child and often take it for granted, but when I truly sit in the depth and beauty of those words, of that truth—that the Almighty God, creator and ruler of Heaven and Earth, cares for and about little old me—I can't begin to comprehend it. But I can be grateful for it. And I can take from it the strength and clarity and peace I need to live a life that reflects that care to others and to carry out the work He has called me to do. Which, in these times, is our greatest calling and response to the darkness.

Heartfelt thanks as well to my beloved Mosaic sisters, who without fail offer grace, support, encouragement, prayers, love, laughter, and—bless them!—extended deadlines. Being part of this community is one of the great gifts and joys of my life. Special thanks to my dear friend Deb Elkink, whose editing skills always make my writing better and give me the courage to send my work out into the world.

And thank you to Michael and my kids, whom God has graciously given to me as travelling companions along this always-an-adventure path of life. Thank you for having my back and for the many, many bricks you have all laid on the foundation to help create a home and family that is as safe, warm, comforting, and sheltering as the Three Sisters Cottage in the woods. I love you all.

About the Author

Sara Davison is the author of numerous romantic suspense series, as well as the standalone, *The Watcher*. A finalist for more than a dozen national writing awards, including the Christy Award, Davison is a HOLT Medallion, Cascade, and two-time Carol Award winner for romantic suspense. She lives in Ontario with her husband, Michael. Like every good Canadian, she loves coffee, hockey, poutine, and apologizing for no particular reason.

Get to know Sara better at https://ontheedgesuspense.com, or find her on Amazon, Instagram, BookBub, Goodreads, and Facebook.

TITLES BY
SARA DAVISON

THE MOSAIC COLLECTION: NOVELS

The Rose Tattoo Trilogy
Lost Down Deep

Written in Ink

Sharp Like Glass (forthcoming)

This Little Nowhere, Nothing Town (story collection)

two sparrows for a penny series
Every Star in the Sky

Every Flower of the Field

Every Bird That Falls

The Happiness of Bluebirds (story collection)

In the Shadows Series
The Color of Sky and Stone

THE MOSAIC COLLECTION: ANTHOLOGY STORIES

"Taste of Heaven" in *Hope is Born*

"Ten Bottles of Sand" in *Before Summer's End*

"Sixty Feet to Home" in *A Star Will Rise*

"I'd Like to Thank the Academy" in *Song of Grace*

"Star Light" in *The Heart of Christmas*

"Scarlet" in *All Things New*

"A Single Spark of Light" in *A Whisper of Peace*

"The Poppy" in *Dancing in the Rain*

"The Other Way" in *A Thrill in the Air*

"Five Things You Know About Me" in *Sounds Like a Plan*

"The Back Door Christmas Tour Company" in *A Weary World Rejoices*

"The Weekend" in *BirdSong*

"Only the Ocean Knows" in *Skipping Winter*

The Night Guardians Series

Vigilant

Guarded

Driven

Forged

The Day Draws Near Series

The End Begins

The Darkness Deepens

The Morning Star Rises

Standalone

The Watcher

Abroad

Deb Elkink

Abroad

Deb Elkink

Newlyweds Kallum and Trina visit Fez on a mercy mission, assigned to escort an orphan from Canada to the Moroccan grandmother the girl hasn't seen since toddlerhood. Foreigners in a land of ancient culture and conflicting creeds, the couple ends up delivering more than first expected.

A doctor's door should never be closed, a priest's door should
always be open.
(Victor Hugo, *Les Misérables*)

How beautiful are the feet of those who preach the gospel of peace,
Who bring glad tidings of good things!
~ Romans 10:15 (NKJV)

*For John and Cora, whose hospitality
introduced me to Morocco*

ABROAD

Kallum MacVicar stepped through the arched doorframe of the *riad* lodgings into the narrow, stone-walled passageway of Fez that echoed with the melodic chant of the call to prayer. He tipped his face up at the slice of midday sky and the tower of a minaret, the source of the alluring tones snaking through the age-worn streets.

"Weird." The petite eight-year-old girl beside him shuddered, then grabbed his hand as though she trusted him.

Kallum gave it a reassuring squeeze. "Can you make out any of the words?" Morocco was Bekka's homeland, after all, though she'd lived in Canada since she was not quite three.

She narrowed her eyes in concentration a moment. "I think so."

Kallum himself couldn't distinguish one Arabic syllable from the next, blurred together as they were in the eerie warbling. Not that he would understand anyway.

"Wait up." Trina pulled the heavy wooden door closed behind her as she joined them. "I had to dig in the suitcase for my sun hat." Fair of skin with a constellation of freckles sprinkled across her cute nose, his bride of six months took hold of the child's free hand as the three of them set off.

His bride. Kallum couldn't help grinning.

"What's with the goofy smirk?" Trina adjusted her shoulder bag ready to be filled, he was sure, with whatever deals she might score in the market. She'd craned her neck over flashes of the colorful bazaar as they'd made their way on foot through the *medina* an hour ago with directions from the cab driver, no taxis allowed in the medieval city center.

Kallum shrugged. "Just happy to finally be on our official honeymoon." Six months after the nuptials, sure, and burdened with their assignment—their *special delivery*—but all the sweeter for the wait.

"Hardly our honeymoon." Trina raised one skeptical brow towards Bekka. "Still, very exotic."

She winked at Kallum, and warmth flared up at his memory of the days of romance following their wedding, spent in the rustic MacVicar cabin in the foothills of Alberta. Which was all they could afford, what with Trina's med school loans, his own leftover debt from seminary studies in scriptural languages plus commercial pilot training, and the low income of their new career—not a recipe for monetary wealth.

During that bridal week, Kallum had brought Trina breakfast in bed every morning for seven June mornings. And every morning Shoeshine, his half-wild pet crow, had pecked at the window, begging in vain to come in. No elegant room service, no crisp sheets, but rather an outdoor biffy and a mountain stream bath. Yet Trina had complained not one bit, insisting she loved roughing it. Kallum turned his head to catch her profile—full lips gently curved, wisps of hair escaping her wide-brimmed hat. Trina's character was amazingly flexible, a necessary trait for the life they'd begun together.

"We haven't had time off since that week in spring," he said.

This brief stint in Fez—timeworn capital of Morocco in an area peopled for many long-ago centuries by North African wanderers of its deserts and valleys, plains and mountain peaks—was a break from the MacVicars' regular duties and just what they needed. Even if it did involve a project. Kallum slowed his natural pace to match Bekka's, a kid too small to carry her emotional load.

The trio trod along one shadowed avenue after another in the labyrinth of the *medina* until they reached an open square swarming with tourists in jeans and locals in loose tunics, sometimes with headscarf or turban. The *souk* merchants in their open-faced shops peddled piles of spices—saffron and paprika and cinnamon—or leather goods, dried figs, carpets, or jewelry. Chickens squawked from wire cages. Beneath a squat olive tree, a swarthy man hauled copper pots off a rickety, mule-drawn cart. Succulent aromas swirled.

"Hungry, pipsqueak?" His senses exploding, Kallum leaned in to be heard above the cacophony.

"Famished." The girl let go of his hand, stopping before a smoking grill. "Mommy used to make the best *kababs* ever . . ." Her sentence trailed off, and she peered up at Kallum with doleful brown eyes welling, suddenly somber. What could he say to make her feel better? His only experience with kids this young was as an uncle to his brother's progeny.

Trina dug into her purse and squatted down to Bekka's level, holding out coins. "You order."

"What if I forget the words?" Bekka shrank back, eyes darting. "I can't remember her voice."

"Hush. It's okay." Trina wrapped the sprite up in her capable arms and hugged her close. "You spoke Moroccan all the time with your mom. You'll soon remember." Then over the girl's head she mouthed "poor little waif" at Kallum

Trina would make a great mother one day. Not anytime too soon, though at twenty-nine she was of course making noises about eventually having a baby. Kallum wanted Trina all to himself—at least for a while longer. Hence his irritation about their sharing the hotel room with someone else's lost child.

But hadn't he himself once been a lost child of sorts? Lost at sea, lost in the woods, lost as he stumbled his way towards maturity?

The vendor in stained apron understood Bekka's timid order—three skewers of marinated beef—and Kallum and the girls rambled along the serpentine lanes nibbling on their makeshift supper. They stopped to haggle for earrings of Berber design and a handwoven scarf dyed red and orange with pomegranate and madder root. On their return to the hotel, Kallum bartered awkwardly for a chunk of pistachio nougat to share for dessert.

Reentering the *riad*, they were greeted by their gracious host, a young man who, dipping his head, identified himself as Youssef and gestured towards the inner courtyard. "Please sit for tea." They settled themselves on indigo-blue leather poufs before a low table, and Youssef tipped his pot of boiling water in a steaming stream high above etched glass tumblers stuffed with mint leaves. Winking, he pushed a bowl of sugar cubes in Bekka's direction. "We drink it very sweet."

Just then, the melancholic chanting of the *adhan* began again, descending upon them like a swirling fog. Youssef backed away from them and nipped into his office, emerging immediately with a small mat rolled beneath his elbow, its fringe tickling the air. He left through the main door—headed for the mosque, Kallum supposed.

Trina hung her straw sun hat on the hook inside their room door, then encouraged Bekka to brush her teeth and change into pajamas. The suite was spacious, the decor opulent—glass-blown lamp globes suspended on chains from the timbered ceiling, wall and window tapestries in rich hues, a parade of handmade suede camels plodding across the fireplace mantel. Heavy draperies drooped around the four-poster bed.

Trina hadn't grown up in luxury. Her family was so huge it filled most of a hamlet in southern Manitoba and spilled down into North Dakota. Dad and his Reimer brothers farmed; Mom and her Penner sisters nurtured. Babies proliferated. As the youngest daughter of eleven kids, Trina saw her sisters marry off one at a time to local guys who, like her blood brothers, worked the earth or toiled in the trades. Her announcement after graduating Rosenwalde High School that she'd been accepted into an undergrad premed program in the big city of Winnipeg had stunned them all into silence, but they'd outright objected—vociferously—three years later when she qualified for a partial scholarship that took her west to Alberta for the duration of her medical training. She would be too lonely out in the world, they said. She would fall away from church. Why would she want to be a doctor instead of a homemaker?

Trina flared her nostrils at the recalled absurdities. She settled down into a roomy wingback chair while Kallum, connecting his tablet to the *riad* WiFi, flopped onto the bed to scroll. What a surprise it had been to meet him when the whole family had given up on her marrying at all. Trina contemplated Kallum's muscular frame and irresistible ruggedness—his thick matt of rusty hair a bit too long, just how she liked it, and his chin nicely stubbled. His eyes, sadly not at the moment focused on her, left Trina short of breath more often than she admitted to him.

"I'm ready." Bekka, smelling of bubblegum toothpaste, slipped up next to the chair and threw her arms around Trina like her siblings' kids did whenever "Tante Katarina" came to Rosenwalde to visit.

Trina embraced her in return. "Should I tell you a story?" What would the girl's bedtime routine be, having had a mother so sick for so long?

"Yes, please." Bekka wormed her way into the space left on the armchair, and Trina began.

"I once heard about a crow named Shoeshine who could talk . . ."

As she recounted the tale to the motherless, fatherless girl, Trina couldn't stem the tide of random pictures streaming through her mind of her own teeming childhood—playing hide-and-seek on the farm on soft summer evenings with dozens of cousins, helping to fry enough *portzelkje* fritters to fill all the yawning mouths on New Year's Eve, taking up the first four-going-on-five full-length pews on Sunday mornings. And now telling stories to a little girl as she, when a little girl, had been told stories by older sisters, aunts, mother—all who were still cozy at home with each other this winter on their southern Manitoba farms.

Had Trina escaped family only to be missing family?

Kallum squinted through the bedroom's dimness towards Trina and Bekka, the two snoozing peacefully under the blankets of the king-sized bed. He sighed and shifted position again on the antique sofa, head bolstered by velvet cushions and legs propped up against the armrest at the other end. The couch, not intended for anyone his height, had been made up for Bekka with bedding by the *riad* staff. But, as night approached, the child's sorrows had overwhelmed her again—How could they not?—and Trina had snuggled her into sleep under luxuriously embroidered covers that should have ensconced him.

Ah, well, all for a righteous cause. Bekka would be reunited with her grandmother soon, freeing up Kallum and Trina to carry on with their five-day stay in Fez, offered gratis by their organization, Northern Canadian Mercy Mission. None of their coworkers back home at NCMM had been available, or even suitable, for the babysitting task.

Kallum bundled the pillow under his neck and settled back to ponder exactly what that task demanded.

Bekka, properly spelled "B-e-k-h-t-a" in her own language with a throaty pronunciation unattainable by Kallum, had been born in Fez. Her father had soon died in a military border skirmish, and her mother—already quietly festering with hidden cancer—had obeyed the wishes of the family matron to flee to Canada for their safety, prosperity, and individual freedoms. The small-town church sponsoring the destitute mother-daughter pair was situated in northern Alberta far from any Middle Eastern populace, let alone a Moroccan fellowship. Five years in Canada had been long enough for the girl to become facile in English with no trace of an accent, and yet, as Kallum had read in her file, she also spoke the two dialects of her mother—both Arabic and the Tamazight of her nomadic Berber forebears.

The international flight from Edmonton had taken more than twenty hours including connection stops, with Bekka holding up well given her situation, her losses. She'd napped, head on Trina's shoulder. When awake, she'd chatted about this and that, mentioning her grandma now and then, apparently retaining snippets from toddlerhood or maybe simply repeating her mother's accounts.

Along the way, Bekka had sung a simple Moroccan lullaby, unrecognizable to him except for a couple of words that sounded strangely familiar. He asked her to translate. Her Tamazight *yemma* echoed the Hebrew *em* for "mommy"; her *tinok* could be found in Talmudic literature meaning "child." He'd noticed that Bekka, for further comfort, fondled a photo of her mom kept tucked into the illustrated children's Bible she'd won for verse memory at NCMM camp last summer, according to Trina, who'd given up a week to act as the camp's attending medic.

A precious week of their early wedded bliss. A self-pitying sigh puffed past his lips. For seven long nights in August, a mere two months after the church ceremony, Trina had left Kallum home to suffer alone after he'd waited so many years in relative chastity. Yet all the while, from their first meeting, Trina had been true to the Greek root of her name—*katharos* or "pure"—and the passion she freely gave to him within the bounds of matrimony proved further that her integrity was above reproach.

Kallum blinked through the room's gloom as his wife mumbled indistinctly in her sleep, probably longing for him. He chuckled at his own ego, his own impatience. It turned out he wasn't irresistible; after all, Trina had chosen an eight-year-old girl over him as a bedmate.

He turned his wandering, nighttime thoughts back to the problem of Bekka. NCMM had done all the necessary footwork after her mother's funeral. They'd looked into the governmental requirements to learn that the girl's visa to Canada was expiring, and they'd followed up on the maternal letter of authorization naming Bekka's grandmother, Dihya, as official guardian. No one opposed the behest; no other family members, if they existed, intervened. And the Moroccan pastor, according to NCMM, would be available to help them hand the girl over to her granny tomorrow. Or, rather—Kallum checked his watch—later today. Then, obligations fulfilled, he and Trina would be free to enjoy the vacation this assignment offered them.

Vacation, *vacāre*, Latin for "to be free."

Kallum shook his head to expel its ever-present pedantry and punched his pillow back into position. No one here would need tutelage in his ancient languages. He could take a break from his unconscious translation for a few days and just enjoy his wife, couldn't he?

Trina, lying so comfortably across the room from him, was unlike anyone Kallum had ever met. At thirty-one, he'd been pretty much a confirmed bachelor. He hadn't actively dated over the preceding decade, occupied as he'd been with studies and with flying supplies, medicine, and the gospel into remote communities.

A confirmed bachelor until, that was, the single locum physician, having just completed her rural residency and serving the northern populace, needed a lift up to Yellowknife, birthing love at first sight.

Besides Trina's stunning outer beauty—with long, buttery-blonde hair and fabulous curves that clothing couldn't hide—she'd impressed him with her ease in communicating with the First Nations population, picking up phrases in Chipewyan and Nakoda to help her treat a gushing wound or drain an abscess. She became his regular passenger and joined the ministry herself upon their marriage, the bush-pilot scholar and the compassionate physician making a valuable team.

What an adventure marriage was proving to be!

Kallum finally dozed off, sheer weariness overcoming the jet lag, only to be awakened at daybreak by the dismal tones moaned out in a minor key by the *muezzin* of the nearby mosque, the *adhan* once again summoning the city's faithful to bow before their god.

After a restful sleep and an invigorating shower, Trina brushed out Bekka's shiny, dark tresses as they sat alone in the room, on the bed beneath its tasseled canopy, warmed by the morning sunlight streaking through the *riad* window. Pity that many Moroccan women hid such locks beneath a *hijab,* though Trina had noted that not all the ladies in the *medina* yesterday wore the scarf. But it was mostly tourists who went bare headed.

Trina silently counted out the strokes: *twenty-seven, twenty-eight, twenty-nine . . .*

What was the significance of covering hair with a *hijab* or lower face with a *niqab* or—as Trina had caught sight of once—completely obscuring the body in a *burqa?* Were these meant to cloak a female from her holy god in an attempt to appease him, submit to him? Or maybe it was more about modesty, hiding femininity from lustful male scrutiny. This was likely, considering the way a man and his buddy had leered at Trina in her normal street clothes yesterday.

Forty-six, forty-seven, forty-eight . . .

However, come to think of it, several conservative women in Trina's own childhood home town—pious, even sanctimonious—also wore "prayer veils," those black cotton kerchiefs fastened with clips or more frivolous lace doilies pinned at the back. Not Trina's mom or aunts, who stood against the remains of legalistic standards brought over to Canada from Europe and Russia long ago. They'd found release from rigid ritual through a relationship with Christ. Nevertheless, legalism had held Trina captive for a while in her early teens, in the Rosenwalde Church Youth, when she'd bought into her friends' misbegotten beliefs of group identity or, better, slavish conformity.

She tightened her lips in thought as she continued brushing Bekka's glossy locks long past the fifty requested by the girl.

The symbolism of head coverings wasn't unscriptural in itself—Trina indeed humbled herself to this day, in spirit, under the authority of God—but how quickly a religious symbol could entrap one in a cultural quagmire. Spiritual belief was always the basis of thoughts, feelings, actions.

As for Trina, her proverbial *veil* had been rent in two long ago. Nowadays she came into the presence of her God boldly, head and heart uncovered, to repent and request and raise her praise.

Sudden tears stung. She squinched her eyes shut to dissipate them and put down her brush, gathering Bekka's hair into a thick rope.

"Are you excited about seeing your grandmother again?"

"I sure am!" Bekka's body quivered. She turned her head to look straight at Trina. "Are we going to her house this morning?"

"You recall her house here in Fez?" Trina doubted that, given Bekka's age at the time of her departure. Then again, she herself cherished lucid thoughts of the frilly pink bedroom curtains she'd glimpsed through crib bars as a toddler.

"It was more of an apartment, really." Bekka caught the edge of her lip in her teeth. "Kind of crumbly and old, not at all like where Mommy and I live—um, *lived*—in Alberta."

"Well, we're getting together with your grandma's pastor today so that he can connect us with Dihya. We don't actually have her street address—only the pastor's private home where the church has been meeting." Trina fastened Bekka's hair with an elastic. "Hope we don't get into any trouble."

Trina clamped her mouth shut. She hadn't meant to say that last sentence aloud. No need to worry the girl further.

Bekka squished her plush kitten stuffy to her chest. "Mom told me we'd have friends here."

Trina certainly hoped so. Pastor Amastan Ohana's English was only rudimentary, she'd been told. Other than the documentation necessary to bring Bekka into the country, neither she nor Kallum had been copied on any communication between Fez and the NCMM.

Bekka bounced out of bed to dress, and Trina realized she'd been holding her breath, anticipating tears from the girl. Perhaps her own emotions were spiraling again. Trina hadn't had a good cry since the stress of her final qualifying exams while simultaneously planning a wedding. She forced herself to relax into a slouch, then sucked in a fresh lungful of air, held her breath to the count of four, and blew it out fully. She wasn't used to feeling so jittery. She made her silent request to God, and immediate peace flooded her soul.

Kallum opened the door, returning from his reconnaissance of the hotel.

"What an architecturally beautiful place, centuries old yet in pristine condition." He held out the crook of his elbow to her. "Let me take you to the breakfast room." He led her and Bekka on a twisting tour past other guestroom doors, through narrow hallways and sitting areas, across intricate mosaic floors, down a stairwell decorated with a silk wall hanging, under a domed ceiling, and in front of a private fountain enclosed in an alcove.

"What artistry." Trina took in the palette of brilliant colors, the workmanship of ages. "But so much repetition of geometric shapes make me dizzy."

"Apparently, in Islam, portraying human and animal figures is strictly forbidden. Lots of swirls and arabesques in the designs, though. And calligraphy. What was it G.K. Chesterton's Moorish character said?"

Trina hid her grin. Kallum was fond of spouting words from some writer or other.

"Ah, yes," he continued, picking up an accent, "'No trace of ze Man form. No trace of ze Animal form. All decoration as goo-ood as the goo-oodest of carpets; it harms not.'" He pushed his nose close to a great lacquered door, maybe examining its carving for signs of life—a lamb or a dove or a man upon a cross.

Her husband was as fascinating to her as he seemed fascinated with her. Trina took in his tall, athletic form bent forward, his eyes a rich shade of amber sharpened now in concentration. Her belly did a flip, and she drew nearer to him, letting her arm brush his side for the tingle it gave her, close enough to catch his scent.

Kallum's ability to recollect the written word was the second thing that had attracted Trina, and it continued to amaze her. He was a walking library, fond of declaring that hermeneutics tied the ages together, steeped as he was in such theoretical aspects as syntax and semantics and synchronicity. And not just with regards to his formal education in the archaic languages he couldn't properly speak—Greek, Hebrew, Latin—but even when it came to novels he'd read. Especially those with theological themes.

Trina, on the other hand, was no lectern linguist. She loved living languages and absorbed them during her everyday doings.

She could converse in creditable French—a secondary language appearing on many signs here in Fez—in addition to Spanish, German, and blossoming Japanese. At home, she'd been trying to teach Kallum a few words in Cree, or at least some Scots, but he'd largely lost the dialects of his parents' forebears. Though he boasted that he spoke a smattering of various tongues, the truth was that he had no ear for current oral languages; his brain was locked on visual definitions from analytical lexicons and exhaustive concordances—very helpful for manuscript exegesis if useless when wanting to buy even a piece of candy in the marketplace. He hadn't figured out yet how to say *hello* or *thanks* in Arabic, never mind in Tamazight. Trina clucked her tongue.

"What's bothering you?" Kallum pulled his face away from the carving of the door panel and wrapped his arm around her waist.

"It's nothing." She dismissed his question with a one-shouldered shrug and no intention of voicing her critical thoughts. While on the one hand Kallum lived in rarified air as an academic, on the other he was a true country boy, able to run any machine, fix every household glitch, even live off the land in the wild. She had a lot to learn from him, and he'd pick up from her what he needed, when he needed it. She could be patient.

As she entered the breakfast lounge with Kallum and Bekka, Trina uttered "*Marhaba*" at the other hotel guests sitting before their breakfasts—two couples seemingly nationals given their Mediterranean complexion and garb. She seated herself and opened her linen napkin onto her lap as Kallum boosted Bekka up onto the tall chair. Their tabletop, like the others, was already loaded with food—glasses of orange juice, baskets of breads, and small clay bowls full of honey and ground almonds, of olives and soft white cheese. She began to fill her plate.

Bekka, sounding slightly reproachful, piped up, "Aren't we going to say grace?" She didn't wait for Trina's agreement but folded her hands in front of her and, without reserve, raised her voice so that the other guests turned to stare. "Come, Lord Jesus, be our guest, and let this food to us be blessed. Amen."

Trina sat frozen, stone still. Kallum touched her hand, and it broke the spell. She forced a smile at Bekka—the enthusiastic girl not concerned with the frowns of the surrounding diners—and bobbed her head towards the others in a gesture she trusted came across as conciliatory rather than baldly apologetic. Maybe they wouldn't have understood Bekka's intent or would overlook her childish indiscretion. Youssef hurried towards them with tea and coffee, his complexion flushed red, and everyone returned to their silent eating.

Trina hissed at Kallum, "The mission warned us."

"It'll be fine." Kallum snagged a black olive and offered it to Bekka.

"NCMM told us to keep a low profile here." It was risky enough for them to be making contact with the underground house church in Fez. Trina swallowed her tea, which scalded her throat and set her to coughing, bringing all the more attention to them.

Would Bekka's outspoken invocation of Jesus cause trouble?

Kallum left a ten-*dirham* coin beside his plate and arose with the girls. They had an hour to find the home of Pastor Amastan and, given the maze of the old city's layout, they'd better get moving. Besides, Trina had been too silent for the past half hour.

She did have some reason for shutting down. They'd learned, when agreeing to NCMM's proposal for them to accompany Bekka home to her grandmother, that any form of proselytizing—handing out devotional literature, engaging nationals in religious discussion, publicly sharing personal convictions—could land them in jail or result in their deportation. It was illegal to evangelize, to "shake the faith" of a Moroccan, and Christianity was not formally recognized. The government strictly forbade conversion from Islam, with Muslim families ostracizing relatives and companies firing employees who showed interest in Jesus—the reason for house church secrecy.

As they headed out, Bekka skipping along in front of them, Kallum touched the small of Trina's back. "What's up, doll?"

"Wondering how safe we are here." Her eyebrows bunched adorably.

Kallum slowed down to match her reluctant step. "We're not breaking any laws." Were they? "And the government is unlikely to be alarmed with us as tourists." However, he winced at Bekka ahead, her appearance blending so easily into the milling North African crowd. What would her homeland's officials say of her praying so boldly in the name of Jesus, and what might she say next in her evangelical fervor?

Immediately Kallum castigated himself. He was the missionary here, and that eight-year-old was putting him to shame. A flush burned up his neck and onto his cheeks.

He and Trina hadn't ever run into any significant opposition to their spiritual witness amongst the Indigenous people of northern Canada, despite the widespread entrenchment in pagan ways—the animism and shamanism—perhaps because the MacVicars came bearing NCMM gifts of food, supplies, and service. Kallum also often took the pulpit in rural Canadian churches on his stints to outposts such as Fort Mac and Cold Lake, where he delighted in elucidating his congregations on biblical grammar. But the mission had been clear that their foreign, especially short-term, missionaries in hostile regions like Morocco were to lean upon silent prayer, avoid all dangers, and work within the strictures of the civil and criminal laws.

Kallum gritted his teeth. Why were they missionaries if they wouldn't take a stand, like Bekka in her naïveté had done at breakfast? Hadn't the early church apostles struck against the pharisaical regulations of their day? He took in a deep breath. He wasn't looking for opportunities to challenge the authorities of a foreign culture, but his desire to be true to his beliefs often gave him, too, a boldness that was sometimes hard to quell.

Which was quite a change he'd been noticing in himself since his first international missions endeavor to Bahamas, where his growing doctrinal education had yet left him vulnerable to one young woman's physical charms, teaching him that head knowledge was not synonymous with heart faith. He clucked his tongue, remembering. The following years living in the secluded, family-owned cabin in the foothills of the Canadian Rockies had afforded studying, contemplating, and clarifying of outlook as he applied principles to his heart, keeping his spiritual eyes focused upwards from whence came his help. And these days he'd been using his hands in fulfilling God's command to broadcast the seed of the Word by going into the world to preach the gospel to all creation. Head, heart, hands.

And feet and even wings if he included the geographical and aeronautical aspects of his calling.

Kallum gazed down upon the wild blonde crown of Trina's hair as she and Bekka chatted in animation. What a prize he'd won in marrying her. Dad would have loved her as much as Mom did.

How was Trina serving as a missionary? So different from his own approach, she let her healing practices speak love to her patients. Perhaps he himself should take a page out of her book, simply staying quiet and letting his behavior be his primary testimony. But no. Trina's spiritual gifts through acts of love were not his; he was a teacher through and through.

Anyway, love was not God's sole attribute, was it? His righteousness also demanded full expression. Mercy and justice—*misericordia et justitia*—two sides of the same coin.

As Kallum considered his special charges, both his wife and little Bekka, a wave of sheer affection washed over him. Today, in this season, their safety was his first responsibility. He dug into his jacket pocket for the printout of the directions to Pastor Amastan's house. Complicated questions of faith versus culture and service in the light of marital relationship would be simplified when Bekka wasn't depending on him and Trina anymore. The child would soon become someone else's problem—er, blessing.

Crooked lanes led to a crooked wooden door set within the crooked walls of Fez's old city. Kallum, dragging Bekka's wheeled suitcase over the *medina's* cobbled passageways, stuffed with all the possessions she owned, stopped before the nondescript portal. He checked the number against the map supplied by NCMM and confirmed by Youssef at the *riad's* front desk. He heard a whimper and then Trina's reassuring murmur.

"Does this remind you of your first home?" Trina stroked Bekka's forearm.

Kallum folded the page of directions and returned it to his pocket—needed for finding their way back again—and crouched down beside Trina. Bekka's countenance was stormy with some emotion he couldn't read. "What's the matter, pipsqueak?"

Trina gave her head a slight warning shake, shushing him. He chewed on his thumbnail to stop his words, trusting Trina's intuition, which was much more finely tuned than his.

"Tinkle the bell." Trina pointed to the cord dangling low enough for Bekka to reach. The brassy jangle brought a response soon enough, the door creaking open to a middle-aged man with swarthy skin who wore a loose-fitting robe, tooled red leather slippers, and a broad smile.

"*Azul.* Welcome." He thrust his hand out, his grip firm. "Kallum, no? And Trina. I am Amastan." He addressed them in heavily accented English, and his visage creased in pleasure as he took in the sight of the girl. "Bekhta." He used the guttural ending Kallum couldn't pronounce. "So like your *henna*—your grandmother."

At this, Bekka strained her neck to peer around his flowing, hooded robe. "She's here?"

"No, no. Come in, please. I explain." Amastan threw the door wide and ushered the trio through a foyer lined with blue and white mosaic tiles much like the *riad's.*

He introduced them to his wife, who scuttled off as Amastan seated them before a cedar dining table. She returned with mint tea and a large platter of delicacies—sugar-dusted crescents, honey-drizzled pastry triangles, cookies sprinkled with sesame seeds. Bekka blinked over at their hostess, desire shining on her face, and the pastor's wife motioned towards the goodies.

"*Tenmirt.* Thank you." The girl almost snatched up one of the sweets and then paused as she checked with Trina, her hand in midair.

"Of course," Trina said, stretching for one herself. "I'll bet you remember the taste of these. Right?"

Bekka, mouth full, nodded with vigor.

Kallum turned to the pastor. "Where is her grandmother?" Wasn't the woman supposed to be there, ready and willing to take Bekka back into her culture?

Pastor Amastan hesitated, his vocabulary evidently failing him. "Dihya leaves here in . . . *Tuber.*" His substantial brows—thick caterpillars—arched upwards in resignation at Bekka.

"October," the girl translated, her lips powdered white. She swallowed noisily, tears trembling. "My grandma left here more than a month ago?"

"Why did she leave Fez?" Kallum had understood NCMM had given him the latest info on the family situation, but apparently not.

"She is—How you say?—*tamghart wahid.*"

Bekka moaned. "He says she's old and lonely."

"How old is she?" Kallum calculated mentally when the other man didn't answer. If Bekka's mother had been, say, twenty-five when her daughter was born, then the grandmother could still be in her fifties, right? Maybe Moroccan women dried out young in the arid heat.

Or had the life sucked out of them through the hardships of forced childhood marriage.

The thought soured Kallum's belly. He'd read that, though less prevalent than thirty years ago, child marriage was still widely accepted in this part of the world. He swallowed back a bitter lump and eyed the eight-year-old with new empathy. What exactly would she be getting into? Perhaps this was the reason the grandmother had encouraged her daughter to emigrate with Bekka in the first place—to avoid that particular and popular evil.

Amastan launched into conversation with Bekka, likely realizing she could understand him quite well when he spoke slowly. Even his wife pitched in now and again.

Finally Bekka turned back to her temporary caretakers.

"He says that, when she heard Mommy died, my *henna* went to Äit Anza, her home village in the mountains, where her friends live. He thought she would return to Fez." Bekka contemplated her sneakers a moment. "Maybe she didn't get his messages about me."

Kallum gnawed his knuckle. Internet and cell coverage were very spotty here, it was true—sort of like being off grid at the cabin in the Rockies. Surely Amastan Ohana could have written an old-fashioned letter?

"The pastor is explaining about the secret church meetings in this house," Bekka said as Amastan added another few sentences, pausing while the girl translated. "It's safer for my grandma—and me, too—to live in her Berber village than in Fez."

"Because of the country's history of Christianity?" Kallum had read enough to know the basics before they'd flown out from Canada on such short notice.

The church of North Africa had been established within two hundred years after Christ and, under the influence of such famous Trinitarian theologians as the Roman author Tertullian and Augustine of Hippo, grew to its zenith in the fourth and fifth centuries. Christianity attracted Berber tribes that had wandered the Maghreb region for thousands of years. In the seventh century, Mohammad and his successors conquered the whole area, with only pockets of Christian communities surviving, even those gradually disappearing until an awakening began in the nineteenth century, carried to the Kingdom of Morocco mainly by Protestant missionaries from Europe and America.

Of course, Kallum's understanding was limited when it came to the complicated chronicles of Morocco's story. But he was aware of great societal tensions still existing here.

The pastor's wife said something to Amastan, and he in turn answered simply in his halting English, this time addressing Kallum directly.

"Tomorrow my friend takes you to Äit Anza. He comes to your *riad* at daybreak, when *adhan* begins."

"Tomorrow?" Kallum heard the shrillness of his own voice. Great—another night of honeymoon shared with Bekka. He chastised himself. Where had his so-called maturity gone?

Pastor Amastan, seemingly exhausted of information, sent them to the streets with some napkin-wrapped goodies for Bekka to snack on later. They wended their way back in the direction of their hotel, completely disoriented and not much the wiser for their hours of foot travel. The girl seemed to know a bit more information and filled them in on tomorrow's proposed road trip, explaining that a supply truck on its weekly run would carry the three of them up to the mountainous Berber town in the Middle Atlas and that the driver knew no English whatsoever.

"Allāhu akbar . . . Allāhu akbar . . . "

The haunting Arabic refrain calling Muslim men to mandatory congregational prayer—"Allah is the greatest"—wedged fingers through the wooden lattice of the bedroom windows, nudging Kallum towards consciousness. His sleep-fogged mind in reply swarmed with the words of a different prayer—*Our Father, who art in heaven . . . Forgive us our trespasses . . . Deliver us from evil*—that older prayer not subjected to an obligatory, five-times-daily schedule with a prescribed sequence of standing, bowing, prostrating, with heaped-up phrases rather than worship to be done in secret, in a closet, in a heart without ceasing. That older prayer commanded not by a self-proclaimed prophet, human founder of a false religion, but by the veritable Son of the loving Father God Himself.

Kallum yawned and stretched, then suddenly bolted upright on the velvet sofa.

"We're late!"

At his outcry, Trina and Bekka, too, leapt from the bed to throw on clothing, the three of them running to reach the front desk before the expected truck driver would leave. They followed the portly, bearded man to the city gates and climbed aboard his rickety service van loaded with boxes of dyes and fibers, chicken feed and sugar, tarps and fishing tackle—reminding Kallum of his own delivery runs in his Cessna 206 on the NCMM route. And the ride out of Fez proved as rough as the turbulent northern Canadian skies could be.

Kallum, jammed with Trina between boxes on the floor of the antiquated panel van's benchless back, was jostled and jolted with every pothole. He eagerly sought out the breathtaking scenery through the front windshield. For three hours the truck rattled through agricultural plains and cedar forests, mounting foothill plateaus and skirting crystalline lakes. No desert was to be seen, the mighty dunes of the Sahara much farther east; no ocean was in view, either, left behind when they'd flown their last leg from Casablanca. The winding mountain trails thoroughly tumbled Kallum's inner gyroscope and, had he been in his Cessna, he'd have had the luxury of checking his compass. Here in the truck with his limited view, however, he couldn't find a reference point.

There was a lesson here for him. Kallum, cradling Trina's hand, reclined against a carton. He silently cogitated about his own interior reference point. He might have no mechanical compass, but his internal, spiritual compass was pointing true north. In all that Moroccan wilderness beauty shouting out the presence of the Creator, would the residents of the decaying towns they bypassed or the long-ago inhabitants of the high-walled *kasbah* disintegrating on the hilltop bow to any god other than Allah?

Would the shepherd they passed with his flock clustered on the road or the fellow driving the battered tractor see the thumbprint of the one true God, hear His message of love singing through the skies, encounter the earth-born Living Word presented in the written Word?

Bekka, up front in the passenger seat, was chattering away in a strange mix of languages Kallum couldn't make out over the noise buffeting through the open driver's window, although by her actions he suspected she was treading on dangerous ground. As their chauffeur glanced now and again from the road, Bekka motioned to her ribs and poked a finger in her left palm and then her right, finally spreading out her arms in a caricature of crucifixion.

Trina dug her fingers into Kallum's forearm. "Is she saying what I think she's saying? We should stop her."

"No, let's leave them be." He watched the austere driver bob a nod now and then, possibly with a hint of interest or at least forbearance, and he wasn't shutting Bekka down. "Maybe he's got kids himself."

"He doesn't seem angry." Trina's grip loosened, and she gave out a breathy laugh. "And take a look at that girl. She's positively beaming."

That had caught Kallum's attention, too. Childlike faith was an awe-inspiring quality. He settled back against the boxes and pulled Trina closer so that her head rested on his shoulder.

Might their driver have come into contact with the story of the cross, perhaps in his forays up into the Christianized Berber towns? Was the church alive and well in these hills? For the girl's sake, Kallum hoped so, despite inherent risks—to the body if not the soul.

Äit Anza was a high-altitude village of terraced houses and burnt sienna walls that blended into the reddish clay hillside. Its rickety sign was scrawled in both Roman letters and peculiar squiggles. The townsite sat on a zigzag side road off the beaten track, with goats wandering unconcerned in front of the truck. Kallum could only guess at the number of residents, but certainly no more than a few hundred people lived in the ramshackle hamlet, a scene taken from the pages in his schoolboy memory of *The Arabian Nights*.

The lorry driver dropped off Kallum, Trina, and Bekka near the main square, pointing down a snow-dusted street towards the grandmother's house and making arrangements with Bekka for a late afternoon pickup beside the marble fountain bubbling with thermal spring water. Kallum listened closely to the Tamazight exchange, suddenly hearing a cadence he'd missed in other local conversations—words sounding strangely Hebraic. Hadn't the ancient Berber people in their heyday been influenced by Jewish faith and language? The three of them followed the man's directions, passing by an arched entrance with fragrant steam billowing out, its sign advertising argon oil massage—translated aloud by Bekka.

Trina hummed. "I could go for a *hammam* one of these days."

"A what?" Kallum didn't know that word.

"It's a public bath indulgence of divine proportions. I had one in southern Spain with a friend during a uni break. You remember me telling you about that trip?" He did. "You get scrubbed down with an exfoliating mitt and black soap. Lots of sweating and rinsing."

"Quite unappealing." Kallum stuck his tongue between his teeth.

"Mommy talked about the *hammam*. How when she was little her *henna* took her along with the neighbor ladies to soak and gossip. All bare naked." The girl tittered. "Do you think it was this very place?" She dragged her feet and peeked into the interior.

"You can ask your grandma soon," Kallum said. "Maybe she'll take you." Bekka picked up her pace then, rushing ahead and almost bumping into a black-cloaked figure emerging from a rubble-strewn alleyway, its walls halfway tumbled down, perhaps from a long-ago tremblor. Bekka charged onwards with Trina in close pursuit.

For his part, Kallum paused, then drew closer to the spectacle. He hadn't seen the full *burqa* up close on anyone yet—not in the city and not evident in Äit Anza's small square, either. The woman was likely from a fundamentalist sect mandating the *burqa*. Kallum allowed his focus to travel from the dusty hem of the shroud to the mesh screen almost totally obscuring brown eyes. Did he glimpse a flicker of panic there?

The whole encounter took only an instant, and then he scurried to catch up with Trina and Bekka. He didn't want to miss the family reunion.

"Bekhta! Bekhta!"

The gray-haired woman, appearing indeed to Kallum much older than he'd earlier estimated, had thrown open the door above a rustic cement step. Wiping her hands dry on her bib apron, she enclosed the child within her arms. Kallum hung back, along with Trina. Obviously word of their arrival had reached the woman, but she paid the two of them no mind, fixated as she was on Bekka. She squished the girl to her breast for a long time, fiercely, purring apparent endearments, then pushed back to finger Bekka's hair, to caress her face with gnarled hands. Finally she raised her eyes towards him and Trina, tears tracking her cheeks.

"*Azul. Tenmirt.*"

Bekka wiggled around in her grandmother's grip and grinned at him and Trina. "She says welcome and thank you."

"*Tenmirt,*" Trina responded, and Kallum attempted to echo the word with his atrocious—he admitted in shame—pronunciation.

Dihya waved them into the home, then, and seated them at a table set with mismatched crockery, where a conical clay *tajine* emitted a delicious aroma. Kallum's stomach rumbled a response, reminding him that he'd eaten only an energy bar from Trina's purse since fleeing the *riad* this morning.

Before they dug into the mutton-and-*couscous* casserole or even tore off a piece of flatbread to dip into the oil, Dihya bowed her head silently, hands folded, and above her Kallum noted a tarnished, four-armed Latin *crux* nestled in among a collection of wall photos. It seemed the faith of Augustine still bore testimony here.

Just as her prayer ended, another woman, draped in an intricately embroidered shawl, poked her head into the house, babbling apologetic syllables at the hostess. Bekka translated their exchange.

"This is my grandma's friend, and she's brought another dish to welcome us—*pastilla*."

The friend seated herself and raised the cloth to reveal a small pillow of pastry dusted with icing sugar and cinnamon. She cut open the warm, flaky disk to reveal a stuffing of pigeon—Kallum asked Bekka twice to be sure that was correct—and ground almonds spiced with saffron.

The feast commenced with lots of chatter between the women and aimed mostly at the girl, who was listening intensely, her brow furrowed in concentration. Every now and then Bekka passed along a bit of information to Kallum and Trina.

Kallum learned, for example, about Bekka's mother growing up in this very house, then marrying her soldier in Äit Anza. Mother and grandmother, once they were both widowed, had moved to Fez to practice their craft as weavers, apparently no government pension available to sustain them. When an opportunity presented itself, Dihya strongly encouraged her daughter to move with baby Bekhta to Canada.

"My *henna* is so happy to be back in her village, especially because I'm here." Bekka kissed Dihya's cheek and lifted the long-spouted brass pot all by herself to pour the tea, stepping so easily into the role of tiny hostess. She added, "I'll be going to the school just up the road. There's no church here like at home—I mean, in Alberta." She paused to glance at Dihya's friend, then added, "The town's mosque was destroyed in an earthquake when Mommy was small. Grandma is holding Bible classes in her house. Maybe I can invite some of the other children."

Through the steam rising from his cup, Kallum regarded the two women fawning over Bekka. The neighbor lady petted her hair.

The misplaced orphan would do well here in her real home. At least, Kallum prayed she would. How else would he find peace about leaving Bekka in this strange culture with its inherent dangers?

Then again, didn't God's love supersede all cultures, offer all people Himself as home?

When dinner was over and the other guest had left with a brief "*Beslama*," Dihya insisted on showing Kallum, Trina, and Bekka her loom—a simple wooden frame she carried with her to the local weaving group. She explained through Bekka that Berber women were guardians of their language and culture, continuing the venerable practice of storytelling as they wove traditional patterns into useful items—cushions and carpets and capes. The van driver—the same one who'd dropped them off—would then collect the pieces for distribution to *souks* in Fez.

Bekka leaned toward Trina. "Maybe the *cheche*, the scarf you bought yesterday, was made by my grandma."

"Good thought." Trina retrieved her wallet from her bag. "Please ask Dihya how much she charges. I want to buy a couple of gifts from the artisan herself."

The older woman readily presented a selection from her stash, and the transaction was made, with Bekka's grandma insisting on tossing in a free tea towel—checkered green and white for prosperity and fertility, she explained.

Then the grandmother-granddaughter pair settled down close together on a low couch, carding paddles in hand and a pile of raw wool before them. Trina rubbed her belly, complaining of slight nausea she hoped wasn't from the mutton. So Kallum ushered her outside to sit in the cooling mountain air, the two of them swathed in handwoven blankets beneath the overhang of the flat roof. Bekka and Dihya needed bonding time without their interference.

Kallum checked his watch. "We'll have to get to the fountain soon to catch our ride back to Fez. Long trip." He cozied up closer to Trina without actually touching this time, suspecting public displays of affection weren't acceptable here, so far out of the city. Indeed, several faces peeped out of nearby windows, curtains dropping in what might have been sudden shyness or scandalized judgment.

"Don't stare," Kallum muttered, "but it seems we've made a friend." The *burqa*-wearing woman from earlier in the day had made her way up the street to Dihya's corner, sagging now in the shadow against an exterior wall.

"Where?" Trina's slid her eyes to the right, her brows rising. "Hmm."

"What?" Kallum straightened, knowing that tone—half surmising, almost suspicious. Diagnosing.

"She's standing sort of hunched—"

A moan just loud enough for them to hear writhed towards them. Trina leapt up and, in three long strides, reached the woman's side. "Are you in pain?"

A ragged voice uttered something unintelligible to Kallum, and then the figure collapsed onto Trina.

"Help me here, Kallum!"

He dashed to his wife's side and encircled them both with his long arms, in the process his hand inadvertently brushing the other woman's abdomen. A very round and rigid abdomen hidden beneath her *burqa*.

Kallum gaped at Trina, who nodded in affirmation.

Trina staggered under the weight of the laboring woman as she and Kallum half carried her to the stoop they'd deserted, forced to halt for another contraction along the short way. How in the world was Trina to help? Sure, she'd had some experience in a city maternity clinic during her ob-gyn rotation and had attended three home births alongside a midwife in Peace River country. Yet she wasn't at all prepared for an emergency delivery.

"Bekka!" Trina yelled it aloud, taking charge. The girl threw the door open, Dihya close behind her, and both stood rooted to the spot.

"Where is the hospital?" Trina shot the words like bullets. "Ask your grandmother."

Bekka fumbled with her translation, and finally the older woman shook her head.

No hospital? Of course not, as remote as the village was. Almost certainly no other doctor around, either.

Trina appealed to Dihya, assuming Bekka would translate: "Let's get her into the house." The birthing bedside would be no place for a prepubescent girl, but what choice did they have? Between the four of them, they moved the distressed woman through the doorway, where Kallum stopped. He was likely unsure of getting any closer, so Trina added, "Kallum, you stay outside."

Trina flung up the wet hem of the *burqa*, exposing stretched-out leggings and T-shirt as well as the soon-to-be mother's full face. Another labor pang elicited a near scream from the tormented teen—she was without doubt still a minor.

Dihya hesitated, maybe shocked at the turn of events, or at the advanced condition of the young woman's travail, or at the evidence of Islam appearing in her own house where the cross of Christ guarded them from its place on the wall. Then she pitched into action. Fatimata—that was how Dihya addressed the young woman after a few words of query—soon lay on the towel-covered couch, knees bent and stripped bare below the waist. She was straining already, her face crimson with exertion. Bekka fetched water under Dihya's instructions, and Trina pulled a stool up to the end of the divan for an initial assessment. She gasped at what she saw.

"What's wrong?" Bekka called from the kitchen sink. Trina shifted her body to block the girl's view.

"You stay over there." Trina made her tone all calm business. "I need you to make sure we have what I need." What she needed was unlikely to be found in a primitive cottage in the middle of the Moroccan wilderness. If only she'd carried along her trauma kit with sterile gloves and stethoscope, clamp, bulb syringe. And, especially, scalpel.

Dihya bent down alongside her, assessing the situation through slatted eyes, unruffled, as though in confirmation of her own suspicions. She closed her eyelids briefly, as she had at the table, breathing out a silent word or two.

Fatimata, eyes and mouth screwed up in agony, lamented again, and Trina palpated the young woman's abdomen to feel the clenching of a strong spasm.

"Lord, have mercy," Trina whispered. She leaned across the girl's body to cup Fatimata's cheek in one palm. Anguished lids opened, tears spilling. Trina captured Fatimata's full attention by peering deep into her brown irises. "It will be okay." She patted the bulging tummy. "You and baby will be okay."

"Okay." Fatimata repeated that singular international word, and her head relaxed back onto the cushion. Notwithstanding Trina's limited acquaintance with labor parturition, she knew intuitively that the teen's soul was of utmost importance. She stifled an urge to hug Fatimata in comfort. Poor girl.

Trina motioned for Dihya to soothe the beaded forehead with a moistened cloth and crouched again to visually inspect the bulging pelvic floor. But Trina couldn't check dilation as there was hardly an opening, the scarred flesh having been stitched nearly closed. *Closed!*

Medical texts dealt with female genital mutilation, of course, and Trina had read about the prevalence of FGM in this region. She knew of the religious and societal excuses for the "cutting" of female children. She'd learned that hospitalized FGM was rare compared to the much more usual, barbaric practice by community elders in unsanitary conditions using old scissors or shards of shattered glass, leading to a high incidence of stillbirth or maternal death.

However, reading it on a glossy page in a Canadian medical book and understanding it at the side of a laboring teen were two very different things, and Trina gagged at the sheer butchery of so desecrating one made perfect in the image of God.

"*Abba*, Father," Trina exhaled, "be with this child and her child. Guide my hands." She carried out as thorough an examination as possible, given the constraints, and knew that infibulation reversal was the only solution. Last spring she had indeed witnessed—if not performed herself—an emergency episiotomy on a Métis mom in a settlement north of Edmonton, training that would have to do for the moment.

This baby had to come out now!

Kallum paced outside Dihya's house as though himself a father-to-be in a Western hospital ward, worrying at his thumbnail with his front teeth. He recalled the pregnant runaway beauty who'd appeared on his doorstep and gotten stuck with him in a snowstorm back when he was living in the MacVicar cabin full time. What if she had gone into labor when they were alone out in the sticks? A drop of nervous sweat trickled down his temple.

Activity was definitely going on behind that door in Äit Anza. Kallum could hear groaning, and Bekka's excited tones, and Dihya's gentle crooning—but no clear words. What was happening in there? Apparently neighboring women were curious as well. Lacy curtains again moved at the window of the closest house, though no one approached. Perhaps the *burqa* had put them off.

Then, with clear and shrill urgency, Trina called out to him. "Kallum, get me a razor blade!"

He grasped the door handle but at the last second didn't turn it, instead jutting his face close to the jamb and rasping, "Why?" before realizing the only possible answer. "Isn't there a razor blade in the house?"

Trina opened the door a crack. "Only this." She held up a pair of crafting shears and a serrated bread knife. "Hurry."

Kallum threw glances around and bounded over to the dwelling with the lace drapery, then hammered at the door before he had time to think up a conversational plan. He stuttered when the homemaker, sadly not the one he'd eaten with, opened to him. Her sun-weathered complexion was full of doubting wrinkles.

"Hi. Um"—Kallum swallowed—"we need help."

The woman stood, arms crossed and silent.

"Do you have a sharp blade, by chance?" Kallum berated himself. Stupid question she obviously wouldn't understand. He tried again. "*Ta'ar?*" It was the Hebrew for "razor" and possibly shared meaning with the Judeo-Berber tongue evident in the region. "*Karat?*" The Hebrew verb meant "to cut" as in cutting a covenant. "*Palach?*" This second verb translated as "to cleave." His attempts only drew a blank stare from the woman, who then called the nearby residents outside, and the herd of women gawked at Kallum as he dug his fingers into his hair.

A picture of wee Bekka singing her lullaby on the flight flashed into his mind along with the lyrics, and he blurted, "*Yemma.*" He pointed to Dihya's house. "There's a new mother trying to have a baby. *Tinok.*" He fairly shouted that last word, cradling an imaginary infant, following Bekka's example of pantomime. He snipped at the air with two fingers as the bemused women scrutinized him. He acted out scraping at his chin, finally bellowing in frustration, "Razor!"

Finally the light dawned on one face.

"*Zeezwaar?*" The woman's eyebrows rose, and she repeated to the lady next to her, "*Zeezwaar.*" A flurry broke out as several dashed into their homes, one returning with a folding stainless razor, the kind to be found in a professional shaving kit.

Kallum snatched it from her with a nod of his head and a quick "*Tenmirt.*" He yelled out to Trina—"Got it!"—and raced back to his capable and caring doctor-wife, who nabbed the implement and slammed the door in his face again.

He resumed his pacing.

The intensity of Fatimata's deep groans and panting gave way at last to a baby's lusty scream. Kallum exhaled in noisy relief and pounded again on the door.

"Trina, can I come in?"

"Give us another minute."

When they finally opened to him, leaving the crowd of ladies milling outside, the tiny baby bundled in a blanket lay tucked beside Fatimata, who was now swathed in a quilt and smiling without shy reserve or the covering of the *burqa.* Dihya was gathering up towels Kallum tried not to stare at in case they were bloody. Bekka bounced up and down on her toes.

"She had a baby, Kallum! A boy!" Bekka's face shone. How much had she seen of the process? The eight-year-old seemed no worse for wear, that was for sure.

"What about the husband . . ." Kallum's voice trailed off. Maybe there was no husband.

Trina squeezed his hand. "From what I've gathered, Fatimata is the youngest of three wives married to a wealthy Algerian businessman who has meetings in Casablanca. Apparently he sent his family to the countryside for a couple of days on a tour bus. Fatimata slipped from the entourage, and her absence wasn't immediately noted." Trina's forehead bunched up. "Or maybe it was deliberately overlooked. Makes you wonder about her personal happiness, right?"

Did it ever. But Fatimata's besotted expression as she gazed upon her baby left little doubt about her current emotions. Bekka horned in between Kallum and Trina to coo at the newborn. What was it about females—even this young—that made them so nurturing? Then again, even he had to admit the newborn was riveting—crinkled red skin, teeny fingers, so utterly dependent.

"Anyway," Trina continued, "the husband texted that he'll pick Fatimata up on his return through the area later in the week to take her home with them. Did I get that right, Bekka?"

"Yep." Bekka chewed on her lip before adding, "Maybe I'll have time to tell her about Jesus."

Kallum chuckled—the child was an unstoppable force—but sobered immediately. How could he laugh considering the new mother's situation? Sending Fatimata back into polygamy seemed abuse by any standards. By Western, Christian standards, at least. He scrubbed the palm of his hand over his forehead, nose, chin.

Truly *rescuing* her was not a geographical or cultural issue; it was a spiritual matter, a matter of the heart. So maybe Bekka, under her grandmother's guidance, was the very one who had the answer.

Fatimata murmured something more, and Bekka listened closely, asking a question or two. She turned to Dihya, who pitched into the conversation. Finally Bekka included Kallum and Trina.

"So . . . my grandmother is surprised because usually it's the father who gets to do this." She shrugged. "Fatimata says she wants to name her baby after you."

"Me?" Kallum snorted, and Fatimata leveled a piercing glare at him.

"I think you offended her." Trina's whisper held censure.

Kallum blinked away his jollity. He hadn't intended that. He bent closer to Fatimata and said, "Sorry."

Bekka translated his apology, and Fatimata inclined her head, lips still sulky.

"My name is Kallum." He pronounced it clearly.

Fatimata's eyes widened. "Kaleem?"

"Close enough," Kallum said, but Dihya interrupted with a message aimed at Bekka.

The girl translated again. "Grandma says Kaleem is the Arabic title of Moses—'the one who spoke with God.' It's a very honorable name."

"Kaleem." Fatimata's facial expression was full of wonder. She touched her son's cheek with an index finger. "Kaleem."

If Trina ever had a baby—well, if the two of them did—what moniker would they bestow? He'd never given thought to that until now.

"So what does Kallum mean in English?" Curious Bekka.

"It's from the Latin *Columba*, meaning 'dove.'" Kallum's mom must have expected him to be gentle and peace filled like his father had been. Like his contented older brother, Jonah. Yet Kallum was only now, in his third decade, coming to terms with his mad craving for scholastic achievement. Maybe he'd eventually apply enough Greek *sophia* to his *episteme*—enough "wisdom" to his "knowledge"—to grow into the meaning of his name.

"Dove?" Bekka set her mouth. "I'm going to tell her stories about the dove, then." She pitched into an animated narrative incorporating physical gestures of the flood waves heaving around Noah's rocking boat and of the messenger bird's wings as it returned with a fresh olive leaf, of Jesus plunging beneath the baptismal waters and rising to the fluttering of the Holy Spirit resting upon him, of overturned Temple tables scattering coins and opening the cages of the sacrificial doves.

Bekka was a dynamo. Full of *dynamis*, as Kallum's expository dictionary taught him. She'd be a joy to her grandmother and the whole town, he was sure. She was a joy to *him*, he admitted as he watched her acting out stories from the Holy Writ—this slip of a girl he barely knew.

Just then, the women of the community filtered in with food and chatter, as women all over the world seemed to do on the birth of a baby. One of the neighbors brought news that the van driver, their ride back to Fez, was waiting at the town fountain. Kallum and Trina bid hasty farewells to Bekka and Dihya with promises to keep in touch.

Over the next three days, Kallum cheerfully followed Trina around Fez, sightseeing spots of historic interest along with throngs of other tourists—visiting the tanneries, exploring the Jewish Quarter, ogling the Islamic architecture of university and palace, of courtyard and museum. He scouted out the world's oldest working library; she soaked in a *hammam*. And five times a day, the beguiling *adhan* sounded from the skies above, from the minaret, from the mouth of the *muezzin* and the heart of Islam itself. And five times a day Kallum found himself praying instead to the God of the Bible on behalf of the residents of Fez, of the mother and newborn in Äit Anza, of Muslim people globally.

But their evenings—ah, their evenings! Those Kallum cherished all alone in the *riad* with his bride, the one he'd chosen as his forever love. A true honeymoon with nightly bed turndown service and a heart-shaped chocolate on each pillow, no Bekka in sight.

Although Trina *did* bring up the girl's name often enough.

"Do you think she'll be okay?" Trina might ask him upon their return from supper at night. "She must miss her mom something fierce." Or "I wonder if she's explained yet to Fatimata how Jesus saves." Or "Dihya will give Bekka the motherly love she needs."

"Yes, we've done our job," Kallum would reassure her. "Now we leave the pipsqueak to prayer." And Trina would nod.

On their final morning before leaving their exotic surroundings to climb onto the plane for the long journey home, Kallum let

Trina—still madly packing—push him out of the room to start the checkout procedure. They planned to eat breakfast together at the airport before boarding, nothing set out on the *riad* tables this early. He'd just punched in his credit card PIN when Youssef made a suggestion.

"May I offer you a farewell cup of tea, sir?" He indicated the fresh pot at his elbow.

"It's Kallum to you." No harm suggesting rapport at this late date, not that he expected Youssef to reciprocate. Trina hadn't made her appearance yet, so Kallum had time for a cuppa. "You're not too busy?"

Youssef, about the same age as Kallum himself, let his sardonic gaze, one brow lifted, flit wryly over the empty lounge. The guy had a sense of humor.

Kallum sat down on the blue leather ottoman, and Youssef performed the elaborate ritual of the pour, then remained standing at Kallum's side, white towel over one forearm. When Youssef cleared his throat, Kallum cranked his neck up at him.

"Sir, er, Kallum," Youssef began.

Interesting. The guy who hadn't shown this much informality since he and Trina first arrived seemed to be accepting his bid for connection.

"Please join me." Kallum indicated the empty seat across the low table from him. Youssef likely wanted to know how he might immigrate to Canada, something Kallum had been asked a couple of times by merchants in the *souks*.

Youssef threw another gander over the empty lounge. He sat but didn't speak right away, his lips jittering as though words were about to creep out. Kallum waited, taking a sip of the minty brew.

"Could you, um, tell me about *Isa*?" Youssef barely whispered. "About Jesus?"

Kallum burnt his tongue on that one. He set the cup down and breathed a spontaneous prayer to the loving Father who delivers from evil. He reached into his jacket pocket for the travel Bible—his spiritual compass—which he might well end up leaving behind for his new friend.

"Yes, Youssef, we can talk about Jesus. What would you like to know?"

After Trina had sent Kallum out of the *riad* room amidst her whirlwind of showering and dressing and packing souvenir purchases into her too-small suitcase, she allowed her mind to unpack the emotional mishmash of the past week.

The pleasure of their jaunt through Fez, with all its splash and charm, would satisfy her wanderlust for a long time to come. Her euphoria from Kaleem's emergency birth was finally moderating and was certainly something to write home about—or verbally tell to Mom and Dad and the siblings she missed. Witnessing the grandmother-granddaughter reunion had sparked a lingering nostalgia; maybe it was time for a visit to Rosenwalde, her home town full of relatives, though some there seemed as rigid in their religious rituals as here in Northern Africa.

From the start, Trina had felt singularly out of place in Morocco with her blonde hair and complexion, though not so much in touristy Fez as in the rural village of Äit Anza. Yet hadn't she also sensed the warm fellowship of the pastor and his wife, of Dihya? Trina belonged to the worldwide church if not the culture of the foreign setting, despite the constant, external demand of the *adhan*—nothing like the gentle wooing of the Holy Spirit within.

Trina had come to love young Bekka—a love that dispelled her original fear over the girl's bold testifying. Most moving of all, Trina's affections had been further aroused towards Kallum, who was proving his stuff to her over and over. Imagine his using obsolete languages—and miming gestures—to procure the razor that surely saved two lives!

Trina jammed the last scarf fringe into her bag, edging the zipper closed. She'd successfully delivered a baby, she and Kallum had delivered a granddaughter to the womb of her family, and she'd witnessed Bekka deliver the gospel in her own unique fashion. Trina sighed with deep gratification. It was time to go, and she was ready to settle back into the airplane seat beside her husband to wing their way home through the heavens.

And Trina, patting her belly, knew what her first stop would be, once they'd landed at Edmonton's airport—a pharmacy to buy a pregnancy test. She had a feeling she knew what the results would be.

A Note from the Author

Dear Reader,

My most recent international trip with my husband included a stay in Morocco. What an ancient and foreign culture, especially with the ubiquitous Muslim call to prayer echoing five times a day, beginning with that increasingly familiar-to-us phrase, *Allāhu akbar*.

I walked the shadowy, crooked streets of Fez in the millennium-old *medina* behind a woman clad in a full *burqa* (and captured her image for my story cover). The marketplace *souks* were stocked to overflowing with leather goods, spices, pottery, and carpets galore. On a wooden post at a meat counter, a camel's head with tongue lolling hung above its own butchered roasts. I negotiated the price of silver earrings a jewelry merchant declared to be of Berber (or, to use the more acceptable term, Amazigh) design, crafted by the descendants of that nomadic Judaized and Christianized group, the aboriginal people of Morocco. The church has deep roots in Northern Africa beginning back in the earliest centuries, long before Arabic immigration, and my learning about the remnant Berber society was the inception point for this story.

Perhaps you've read my first two instalments of the Kallum MacVicar trilogy, "Adrift" and "Aloft." In the current story, "Abroad," a slightly older Kallum has another chance to put his evangelical faith into action, this time alongside a loving wife. (For all three of these stories, I acknowledge the wonderful support of my Mosaic sisters.) In stark contradiction to my fiction stands the nonfiction reality of childhood Muslim marriage—Mohammed himself having taken a bride of only six years of age—and the widely practiced Islamic ritual of female genital mutilation affecting untold millions of girls and women. (I've written an allegory of FGM, "Taste Budding," included in my collection *Vagabond Come Home*; you can research the ugly, real-life details on your own.) However, I don't mean "Abroad" as a political statement but rather as an observation of the very complex polarization between cultures that is largely dependent upon how people pray, and to whom, and to what result.

How do *you* pray?

Deb

ABOUT THE AUTHOR

Deb Elkink writes from a cottage beside a babbling creek in southern Alberta, Canada, a stone's throw from the Montana border and home base for exotic travels with her husband of half a century. She published her first bits of writing after graduating university (BA Communications), then married and spent twenty years as a homeschooling mom and ranch wife—rounding up cattle, earning her private pilot's license, and cooking for huge branding crews. A second degree (MA Theology, *summa cum laude*) led to publication of a literary study on the fiction of G.K. Chesterton (*Roots and Branches*), prepared her as an academic editor, and jettisoned her into her long-held dream of writing literary fiction with a theological twist. Her publications so far—incorporating travel and taste buds and tumults of the heart—include two award-winning novels (*The Third Grace* and *The Red Journal*) and a collection of short stories (*Vagabond Come Home*).

Get to know Deb better at https://debelkink.com, or find her on Amazon, BookBub, Goodreads, and Facebook.

TITLES BY DEB ELKINK

THE MOSAIC COLLECTION: NOVELS

The Third Grace
The Red Journal
Vagabond Come Home: Collected Stories of the Wayfarer's Return

THE MOSAIC COLLECTION: ANTHOLOGY STORIES

"Ever Greening" in *Hope is Born*
"Blue Genes" in *Before Summer's End*
"Reconstituted" in *Song of Grace*
"Taste Budding" in *All Things New*
"Clanging Symbols" in *Dancing in the Rain*
"Scrabbling" in *A Thrill in the Air*
"Aloft" in *BirdSong*
"Adrift" in *Skipping Winter*

THE GRIFTER CHRONICLES

Thief, Interrupted

JOHNNIE ALEXANDER

Thief, Interrupted

Johnnie Alexander

She can steal a wallet without being noticed—but can she walk away from the only family she's ever known?

Chaney Rose and her cousin Marsh Jacobsen were raised in their grandfather's school of cons and petty crime. When the Old Man frames them as the scapegoats in his latest scheme, they hide out in a small Montana town crowded with summer tourists and easy marks. But as they try to outrun the Old Man's reach, Chaney realizes the person she trusts most may be playing his own game. As the once-unbreakable bond between Chaney and Marsh begins to fracture, she must decide which code she will follow and which one she will leave behind.
Because sometimes the bravest thing a thief can do is walk away.

A story of redemption, second chances, and discovering that the greatest risk isn't getting caught—but choosing a different path.

Whether you turn to the right or to the left,
your ears will hear a voice behind you, saying,
"This is the way; walk in it."
~ Isaiah 30:21 (NIV)

For Stacy
Because traveling to Montana was
an experience I'll never forget.
And because our trip inspired new stories!
("Bear ... Bear ... Bear!")

Chapter One

Better to be a live guppy in a big pond
than a dead barracuda in a small pond.
~ The Family Code ~

Chaney Rose's back and shoulders ached from straddling the Harley Davidson for long hours behind her cousin. They'd ditched Marshall Jacobsen's hand-me-down Ford Explorer after borrowing the all-black motorcycle from LAX long-term parking. As a precaution, they swapped out license plates within fifty miles of crossing each state line on their reckless escape from Los Angeles. Except for that and brief rest stops, they zipped along a zig-zag route of interstates and rural roads. Achy muscles and tired bodies couldn't be coddled.

Not after they'd committed the unforgiveable sin of running out on the Old Man.

Blood might be thicker than water, but that adage only worsened their betrayal.

Bone weary, their souls dying from a thousand cuts, they rode toward an uncertain future with only a couple hundred pilfered dollars in their pockets and nowhere to call home.

Chaney leaned with Marsh as he maneuvered another S-curve. Once the road straightened, he pulled to the shoulder and dropped the kickstand. Chaney slid off the saddle and removed her helmet as she approached the bluff. The mid-afternoon sun cast lengthening shadows across the pastel houses and brick buildings in the valley below. Its rays cast sunpennies upon the sparkling river flowing along the town's southern edge. Houses of stone and brick dotted the opposite mountain, where a handful of horses grazed in a grassy meadow.

An upward draft ruffled Marsh's honey-brown hair as he stepped beside her. "From up here, Hartwell looks like any other sleepy mountain town. Whispered secrets. Fake friendships. Petty intrigue."

"In a place where everyone knows their neighbor," Chaney warned, "they know who belongs and who doesn't."

"Not always."

She slid her eyes toward him. What could he know about this place that she didn't? "Care to share?"

"You must have missed the poster at that gas station outside Absarokee." Marsh tapped his helmet against his leg. "We're just in time for the annual Huckleberry Jubilee."

"Tourists." She curved her lips into a knowing smile. "We'll blend right in."

"We'll do more than that."

Chaney flexed her fingers, an almost unconscious gesture, to loosen the joints and lighten her touch. Beside her, she sensed Marsh doing the same with his free hand.

"I don't think I've ever had a huckleberry," he said. "Maybe it's time to try one."

"Are you sure stopping here is worth the risk?"

"We need enough money to get as far from the Old Man as possible." He pointed his helmet toward the town. "Those charitable folks don't know it, but their generosity will get us across the Mississippi. Even farther if we keep roughing it."

Another reason for Chaney's sore muscles. With their backpacks stuffed into the motorcycle's saddlebags, there was no room for camping gear. They'd already spent more than one night sleeping on the ground.

"For all we know, he could be right behind us," she said.

"Maybe." Marsh's grim tone sent a shiver up her spine. Apparently sensing her tension, he gently elbowed her arm. "Remember what Doc Holliday said in *Wyatt Earp*?"

Only one of his favorite movies. She'd watched it with him two or three times over the years but not recently enough to recall any of the lines.

"Stay away from the O.K. Corral?"

He let out a good-natured grunt. "'I'm your huckleberry,'" he drawled in a passable imitation of the actor. "We'll get through this. I promise."

"As long as we keep running." As long as they stayed together.

Born the same day to twin sisters, the only times they'd been apart were their off-and-on stints in foster homes. Only rarely did a family take in the two of them. Those placements never lasted long.

"With the occasional stop, like now, to do what we do best," Marsh continued. "Take from the haves and give to the have-nots. Us."

Despite her misgivings about staying more than an hour—if even that—in one place, Chaney understood the Jubilee's appeal.

If they didn't take advantage of this opportunity, they might have to resort to a riskier theft. "What's the plan?"

"Stick around a day or two and enjoy the festival." Marsh tapped his helmet against his leg again. "Shear a few sheep and hightail it out of town."

And then where would they go?

Chaney slid the heavy helmet over her head as she followed Marsh to the motorcycle. How far could they run before the Old Man caught up with them?

Chaney studied the L-shaped corner building while Marsh retrieved her crossbody bag and his wallet from their backpacks. A railed porch furnished with rockers, chairs, and gliders ran along both sides of the historic inn. Three sets of steps—one facing the side street, another angled at the corner where the two legs of the L met, and the third across from the river—led to openings in the rails. The sign above the angled entrance read *The Larkspur Lodge* in large bold letters.

"If this doesn't work out, we can head to Cody." Marsh handed Chaney the crossbody bag, and she slipped the strap over her head and shoulder. "Find a sucker who'll give us cash for our 'troubles.' Preferably enough for a decent meal and a roof over our heads."

"Only as a last resort." Chaney shifted her gaze toward the variety of people meandering among the temporary booths blocking the street from thru traffic. While the potential marks scanned the various arts and crafts on display, she gauged which of them was most likely to carry cash. And lots of it.

From her light-fingered experience at other festivals, she knew amateur vendors often preferred cash-only transactions. Experienced shoppers knew to bring money. She adjusted the shoulder strap of her bag and waved her hand toward the crowded street. "Besides, there's gold in them thar pockets."

Marsh grinned at her feigned accent as he scanned their potential pigeons. "You got that right, pardner."

Chaney took a long, cleansing breath and led the way through the double doors into the inn's spacious lobby. A huge stone fireplace with shelves on either side dominated the wall next to a broad staircase leading to a mezzanine. Tables and shelves displaying a variety of antiques and vintage items were interspersed between comfortable seating areas. Her fingers brushed the top of an upholstered wingback as she approached the long wooden bar at the opposite side of the room. Gold lettering on a huge, mottled mirror read *Larkspur Saloon*.

A slender woman with warm brown eyes and an engaging smile emerged from a door at one end of the bar. Her thick, chestnut hair fell to her shoulders in soft waves held back on one side with an ornate silver clasp. A white wirehaired terrier with brown markings, including a large brown patch over one eye, ran around the bar and politely sat in front of Chaney. She immediately dropped to her knees, and the dog wriggled into her arms and kissed her chin.

"Welcome to The Larkspur," the woman said with a lilt in her voice. "Looks like Bramble has found another kindred spirit. He usually has better manners."

"He's adorable." Chaney had always wanted a dog, but the Old Man didn't allow pets. The closest she'd ever come was a goofy St. Bernard owned by an early foster family. She remembered little about them except for the giant teddy bear of a dog who'd eased the hole in her heart left by Marsh's absence. And how the foster mom's tears dampened Chaney's cheek when social services took her away from them.

Bramble's owner nodded toward their helmets. "Are you on your way to or from Sturgis?"

Chaney and Marsh had considered going to the popular motorcycle rally, held about six hours away in South Dakota, but decided against it. Sure, they might have gotten lost in the crowd as they pickpocketed their way through it, but that crowd wouldn't give a second thought to handing out its own version of justice to a thief. As confident as the cousins were in their abilities, some risks weren't worth taking.

"We enjoy riding the highways and byways." Marsh's warm smile never wavered as he leaned one arm on the bar. "But bike culture isn't our thing."

"And a Huckleberry Jubilee is?" A small tone of doubt edged the woman's voice.

"We've never had huckleberries." Chaney stroked Bramble's soft ears, then met the woman's gaze with her own winsome smile. "By the way, I'm Carrie Robbins. That's my cousin, Mark Johnson."

"I'd have guessed you were siblings."

Chaney rose to her feet. "We hear that a lot. Our mothers were twins."

Sympathy, triggered by Chaney's slight and purposeful emphasis on "were," momentarily flickered in the woman's dark eyes. If Chaney read her right, which long experience assured her she had, the woman would suppress the urge to ask about their loss while feeling a maternal obligation to help.

"I'm Amelia Boone and, yes, I'm a distant relation of Daniel's, though not a direct descendant." The lilt in her voice had returned, and her playful expression indicated she'd recited that little tidbit a gazillion times. "As pleased as I am to meet you both, I'm sorry to say I don't have any vacancies."

"No one does," Marsh said. "But we stopped at a place down the street—"

"The Copper Hart," Chaney chimed in. "The owner there . . . I believe her name was Liz Stiller?"

"That's right. I know Liz."

"She spoke very highly of you." Marsh gazed straight into Amelia's eyes and added a slight flirtatious tone to his voice. "She said there's not a room to be had around here, but if anyone knew where two tired travelers could find a place to lay their weary heads, it'd be you."

Amelia stared at Marsh and laughed. Her gaze shifted to Chaney as she pointed a finger his way. "Does that usually work for him?"

"More often than you'd believe." Chaney grinned, though her nerves tingled. Amelia had a no-nonsense side beneath her hospitable exterior. "Though it's true Ms. Stiller suggested we talk to you."

Amelia seemed to study them in turn, gauging them as Chaney had gauged individuals in the crowd outside. Then she closed her eyes for a moment.

Was she . . . *praying?*

Chaney exchanged a quick glance with Marsh, who twitched the corner of his mouth.

Amelia's pleasant smile returned as she opened her eyes. "I may have an option for you, though it's not ideal. One tiny bedroom with a pull-out sofa in a separate seating area. My brother calls it the Hideout. He stays there when he's in town."

"It sounds perfect," Marsh assured her.

Amelia held up a warning finger. "The biggest drawback is the bathroom. It's across the hall, but I can give you the key so you're the only two with access."

"We can live with that," Chaney said. "What's the rate?"

Amelia thought a moment then responded with an amount lower than they'd expected. They paid for one night, though Amelia agreed they could spend a second night if they wished.

"We'll take it a day at a time. I won't be renting it to anyone else." A guarded look came into her eyes. "If Bramble hadn't liked you so much, I wouldn't be renting it to you."

"We appreciate it." Chaney pressed her lips together as she tried to shake off the feeling that this woman could see right through them and then honestly added, "More than you know."

The Old Man, a believer in "hiding in plain sight" when possible, might suspect they'd go to the crowded rally in Sturgis. They were safe here.

As long as they didn't end up in jail.

CHAPTER TWO

Chaney and Marsh handed over their fake IDs for Amelia to copy. Once the transaction was complete, she gave them a brochure detailing the Jubilee's events and asked them to wait in the lobby while she changed linens and set out towels in the Hideout. She called Bramble, who was once again engaging Chaney's attention, to go with her.

Once they'd crossed the mezzanine and disappeared into the corridor, Chaney scanned the brochure. "Tomorrow seems to be the big day. A parade in the morning. A huckleberry-pie-eating contest in the afternoon. You should enter. The winner gets fifty dollars."

"I can think of easier ways to get a flat fifty." Marsh sauntered to a display cabinet and gestured toward the framed parchment next to it. "This says we're standing in one of the oldest buildings in Hartwell. 'The Larkspur Saloon & Boarding House was built in 1884.' That's close to 150 years ago." He continued reading. "'The saloon was shut down in 1920 because of Prohibition.'"

"Shut down or moved elsewhere?" Chaney didn't know if speakeasies were as popular in the west as they were in places such as New York and Chicago. But she found it hard to believe that the saloon's customers no longer indulged their thirst for whiskey. She gazed at the giant mirror behind the bar, guessing it was part of the saloon's original décor. If so, how many gunslingers and cowboys had stared into that mottled glass over the decades?

"This place is like a miniature history museum." Marsh's voice dropped to a stage whisper. "Come look at this."

She joined him at a weathered secretary desk with folded quilts spilling from half-open drawers. The oldest typewriter she'd ever seen perched on the desk's lowered lid beside an old-fashioned pedestal telephone. Various antique items were showcased behind the glass of the hutch's closed upper doors. The bottom shelf held a porcelain tea set. An inkstand with a feathered quill pen and a parchment scroll flanked a large, open compass perched on an acrylic stand.

He looked around to ensure they were still alone, then opened the doors.

"What are you doing?" Chaney's gaze darted toward the mezzanine at the top of the stairs. "Amelia will be back any moment."

"Only checking a hunch." He removed the compass from its acrylic stand, closed the lid, and hefted it in his hand. "Solid brass. And look at this design. I'd bet you anything this is an old surveyor's compass."

Chaney ran her finger across the raised locomotive against a jagged mountain skyline. "It's die-struck, right?"

He nodded and examined the back of the compass for the manufacturer's mark. "I knew it. A Monticello. Just like the one my dad had."

Marsh's great-grandfather Jacobsen had been a railroad surveyor who'd left his custom-made compass and assorted implements of his trade to the family. Uncle Drake had promised the compass to Marsh but pawned it instead. Marsh had never quite forgiven his dad for that.

"Do you have any idea how much this could be worth?" His whispered tone was filled with awe over his discovery.

"Don't care and don't want to know." The Family Code was clear—no stealing from the host. "Now put it back."

Chaney walked away and settled in the chair farthest away from the secretary desk. She found a large book called *The Photography of Yellowstone* on the table next to her and flipped through the pages. Amelia might catch Marsh with the compass, but he could talk himself out of any trouble. She'd find Chaney engrossed in the book's photographs.

Maybe she and Marsh should go to Yellowstone after they left here. They'd never been to the national park before, and she'd like to see the wildlife in their natural habitat. Especially the wolves and maybe even a bear. A large map in the front showed a route that crested at Beartooth Pass. Making that adventurous drive on the Harley would be an experience they'd never forget.

Hearing footsteps, she darted a glance toward Marsh, who now sat on the large hearth, elbows on his knees, and stared at his phone. Exactly what Amelia would expect a young man of his age to be doing while killing time.

Except that the phone was a burner with no access to the internet. It couldn't even take a photo. They'd smashed their smartphones and slipped the broken pieces into the bed of a battered pickup at an LA gas station near the I-405 on-ramp.

Their burner phones contained each other's new numbers and nothing else.

Numbers the Old Man had no way of knowing.

Even with the mediocre water pressure, the long shower eased the aches in Chaney's legs and shoulders from the long days of riding on the Harley and short nights sleeping under the stars. After pulling on a pair of khaki shorts and a pale green T-shirt, she peered in the steam-dampened mirror and frowned.

A hairdryer was a luxury for anyone living out of a backpack. Apparently, it was a luxury for anyone using this bathroom, too. The cabinet beneath the sink held extra toilet paper, a small first aid kit, and a few cleaning supplies. Nothing else.

She scrunched the short layers of her blonde hair, thankful for a cut that dried *au naturel* without too much fuss or bother. Her simple makeup routine took only a few minutes. A little powder, blush, eye shadow, and mascara were all she needed for that all-important girl-next-door look.

Anything dramatic risked standing out. Standing out risked being remembered. Being remembered risked . . . everything. While in this festive little town, both she and Marsh needed to blend in. To interact with as few people as possible and to do nothing to bring attention to themselves.

Maybe they'd already gone too far with Amelia Boone.

The woman's thick hair and youthful features had made her appear younger than her years at first glance. A casual observer, responding to the cheerful warmth in Amelia's brown eyes, might not notice the telltale signs. The tiny lines, not wrinkles, that appear then fade. The slight heaviness of the eyelids. The softening of the jawline.

Chaney was *not* a casual observer. Their hospitable landlady was at least forty-two or forty-three, a non-smoker who rarely, if ever, drank alcohol, and somewhat perceptive behind her welcoming demeanor.

Not that she was a threat. Or a potential mark once she provided them shelter. The lobby's antiques and collectibles were safe from Chaney's nimble fingers. The contents of the money drawer, located beneath the bar, would still be there when she and Marsh rode out of town.

They'd get their haul, hopefully enough to get them to the Mississippi if not beyond it, by other means.

When Chaney returned to the tiny, two-room Hideout, she found Marsh sprawled on the sofa while a true crime re-enactment played on a decent-sized television. His eyes were half-closed, and his hands were folded on his chest.

She stood over him, her laundry and makeup bag tucked in her arm. "Your turn."

"Did you leave me any hot water?"

"Enough to get your hair wet."

He planted his feet on the floor and groaned as he rolled his shoulders. The toll of riding day after day must be getting to him, too.

"Since we're sure to line our pockets this weekend, how about we splurge on dinner tonight? I noticed a steakhouse a few doors down from the Copper Hart." He dug into his backpack for a pair of tightly rolled jeans and a clean shirt, then squinted at Chaney. "This is beef country," he drawled, channeling his inner Clint Eastwood, as he shook out the shirt. "Steaks oughta be mighty fine."

"All you need is a Stetson," she teased, "and you'd fit right in on a cattle drive."

"Maybe I'll pick up one while we're here. Authentic boots, too."

"Only if you pay for them. No shoplifting allowed." They were too desperate for cash to risk stealing merchandise. Or to buy anything beyond the necessities. "Not even tokens."

Chaney herself had coined the term for valuable items that were easily palmed and easily pocketed when she and Marsh were about six. Back then, a token meant a candy bar or a small toy. On their fifteenth birthdays, Grandpa sent the two of them to a shopping mall to "purchase" their presents. Chaney returned with the birthstone ring she still wore hidden in her pocket and Marsh with a sturdy pocket knife hidden in his. He still carried it.

Unless, in the rush to leave, he'd left it behind.

She idly glanced at his backpack, her mind skittering over the last minutes she'd spent in her room at The Station. The ever-ready go bag, a heavy-duty backpack identical to Marsh's, always held a change of clothes, travel-sized toiletries, and a few essentials for a quick getaway. In her mad dash, she'd tossed a few more items inside, knowing that anything she left behind was lost to her forever. The Old Man would see to that.

"How about one token each?" Marsh grinned as he headed for the door with his change of clothes and travel kit. "A souvenir."

"Take a picture."

Marsh hmphed. "Yeah, right."

After the door clicked behind him, Chaney started to arrange the clothes she'd been wearing in her backpack. Maybe they could take time tomorrow to visit a laundromat. Before their light-fingered spree.

Suddenly the door opened and Marsh stuck his head through the narrow opening. "About the steakhouse. I already made the reservation." He disappeared before Chaney could respond.

Not that she objected. Just the thought of a fresh garden salad and medium-rare steak got her stomach rumbling and her mouth watering. Sitting down to a scrumptious meal, being waited on—how could she argue with such a luxury? Especially when potential pigeons would be dining there, too. While enjoying their dinner, Chaney and Marsh could scout the diners to spot those who preferred cash to cards. Though they'd steal nothing this evening. Only observe.

While she waited for Marsh to return, Chaney double-checked the amount of money in the small crossbody bag that held her burner phone and driver's licenses under three different names from three different states. She returned everything else to her backpack and set it beside the door—ready to grab at a moment's notice.

Marsh's open backpack sprawled in the middle of the couch. Chaney tried to move it to one end so she could curl up in the other, but the bag was heavier than she'd expected. She shoved it again and this time the bag rolled off the couch, spilling already-worn socks, folded shirts, and a flashlight.

With a groan, Chaney slid to the floor and set the bag upright. She might as well repack it, too. Hopefully nothing would keep them from staying the night, maybe even two, here at the Larkspur. But at the first sign of trouble, they'd grab their bags and race away.

She rolled the grungy socks into one another and tried to slide them deep into the pack. Beneath a pair of folded jeans, something hard and stiff covered in a soft fabric obstructed her effort. She released the socks and wrangled the wrapped object from the bag.

The fabric turned out to be a worn and torn, faded gray UCLA sweatshirt Marsh's mom sent him when he got his GED certificate. No surprise he'd brought it along. Noting the hidden object appeared to be a book, Chaney paused to guess which of his hardback editions he'd brought along. *Shane? The Count of Monte Cristo? The Call of the Wild?*

Eager to see if she'd made a correct guess, she unwrapped the book and stared in disbelief. Bile rose in her stomach as her esophagus closed, making it difficult for her to breathe. Her body shivered while the worn leather journal seemed to burn her hands.

"No," she muttered. A heaving sob wracked her frame. "No, no, no."

She laid the journal on the sweatshirt and pushed them away from her. While hugging her legs to her chest, she pressed her face into her knees.

How could Marsh have done anything so stupid? Weren't they in enough trouble with the Old Man without stealing his ledger?

Chapter Three

At the click of the door opening, Chaney raised her eyes to Marsh's in time to see his good-natured expression turn grim when he spied the unwrapped journal. He locked the door behind him and then lowered himself to the floor beside her. He rested his elbows on his knees and stared at the opposite wall.

Chaney blinked back the tears she'd been struggling to keep at bay while taking long, slow breaths to control the nausea roiling within her.

After a long and heavy silence, Marsh cleared his throat. "I was going to tell you after we settled somewhere. Once we were safe."

Chaney squeezed her eyes shut. She refused to be distracted by their childish daydream of a home apart from the family. That dream was nothing more than a high-flying kite held by a slender, fraying string.

"When he finds out that's missing, he'll . . ." The horrible words caught in her throat and the nausea roiled again.

"He'll leave us alone."

"He never will."

"Don't you see?" Marsh reached for the journal and pressed his fingertips on the embossed cover. "This is our insurance policy. If he threatens us, we give it to the FBI. The attorneys general in every state mentioned in these pages. Maybe even the IRS. They'll go after him even if no one else does."

For the first time since he'd sat beside her, Chaney met his gaze. "We'll go down with him. He'll make sure of that."

"He has to find us first." Marsh's eyes narrowed and his jawline tightened as he thrust the book into her hands. "I promise you, that will never happen."

Chaney lowered her eyes to stare at the journal. Time had lessened the depth of the words embossed into the cover, though the title's block lettering with its serif flourishes remained easy to decipher: *Grifters Guild*. In the lower right corner was a worn image of an eight-pointed star embedded in a wax seal.

She fanned the pages of what the Old Man called his ledger, getting glimpses of their grandfather's scratchy penmanship in shades of blue and black ink. The well-worn book was an incomplete record of his cons, his grudges, the philosophies he preached but didn't always practice.

Like now.

How many times had she heard him say things like "We don't turn on our own" and "Family is the one rule you don't bend"? Then there was his all-time favorite: "Cheat the world but never family."

Yet he'd been more than willing to offer Chaney and Marshall as sacrificial lambs to law enforcement the minute his latest fraudulent scheme came to light. Not only had he been willing, he'd *planned* for them to take the fall if the job went sideways.

Worst of all, he'd been certain they'd never betray him, even if it meant they spent years behind bars in his place.

Because "family never forgave a traitor."

A simmering anger stirred within her. Anger at the Old Man, who expected all their loyalty while giving none in return. Anger at Marshall for stealing the journal, which only added to their danger. Anger at herself because this was who she was—a pickpocket and a thief and her grandfather's pigeon.

The time for their steakhouse reservation came and went. Marsh wrapped the menacing journal in his sweatshirt, dumped everything out of his backpack, and placed the book at the bottom. While he repacked, Chaney retreated to the restroom to wash her tear-streaked face. At least her waterproof mascara had lived up to its name.

When she returned to the room, Marsh's bag rested beside hers. He sat at the table shuffling a deck of cards—his way of nimbling his fingers for any unexpected opportunities that might arise. She took the seat across from him while he spread the deck face down and then, with the expertise of a casino dealer, reversed the spread so the cards were face up.

Just one of the many skills the Old Man insisted they learn from an early age. After shuffling the cards again, Marsh cut the deck to the ace of spades.

Shuffle. Cut. Ace of hearts.

Shuffle. Cut. Ace of clubs.

Shuffle. Cut. Ace of diamonds.

"Your turn." He slid the deck across the table, a hard glint in his eyes. "I'm not sorry."

She lowered her gaze and focused on her shuffling. Though she didn't have his dexterity, she managed her own impressive set of cuts that revealed the jack of each suit. She slid the deck back to him.

"We needed leverage." This time, he avoided looking at her as he returned the cards to their plastic container. "And now we've got it."

"What we've got is a price on our heads." She traced a burn mark that marred the table's surface. If not for her lingering anger, she'd be imagining a story about who put it there and why. "Too bad for us, what's done is done."

"Where have I heard that before?"

The rhetorical question didn't need an answer, and Chaney didn't give one. Their moms recited the words as a flippant excuse any time she and Marsh confronted them with their maternal shortcomings. The cousins had long ago turned it into their own private joke, reciting the phrase as lighthearted encouragement when a plan went awry or one of them did something foolish.

This time, it carried a weight heavier than ever before and did nothing to ease the tension between them.

Marsh pushed back from the table. "It's getting late. We need to scout around town and find something to eat."

"I'm ready when you are."

After leaving the lodge without seeing any sign of Amanda, they wandered among the vendor booths and exhibits set up along the closed-off streets. The unfamiliar friction stayed with them as they entered the Pony Express Pizzeria, a restaurant located in what had been a post office in the early decades of the last century.

The hostess stand was a narrow bank of antique mailboxes with glass fronts and brass locking mechanisms. An enthusiastic teen with a shock of red hair and faint stubble above his lip led them to a booth near a coin-operated bull-riding machine. Any other time, Chaney would have insisted Marsh give it a go. Any other time, he would have.

The double-sided menu featured the usual pizza sizes and toppings and a variety of other items such as appetizers, calzones, and stromboli. The specialty pizzas had names reminiscent of the Old West.

"Are we sharing or getting our own?" Marsh asked without making eye contact.

Even a small pizza was too large for Chaney to eat by herself, as he well knew. "Sharing. Plus a salad."

"Which do you prefer, the Wild Bill Hickok—pepperoni, bacon, sausage, and jalapeños—or the Jesse James meat combo?"

"You choose." Chaney returned her menu to the holder behind the napkin dispenser and gazed around at the décor.

A mural-sized map across the back wall detailed Pony Express stops across several states. Even though Hartwell wasn't one of the stops, the pizzeria seemed proud of their history. Poster-sized prints of the original post office were also on display. Old mailbags, additional banks of the vintage mailboxes, and other western décor added to the sense of stepping back in time.

When the teen returned with their soft drinks, Marsh placed the order for a large Hickok and two garden salads. Chaney opted for balsamic vinaigrette dressing, while he chose peppercorn ranch.

The tense silence stretched between them, a silence that seemed impossible to break.

As much as Marsh's theft of the ledger frightened Chaney, what hurt most was that he kept it a secret. They never kept secrets from each other. Not only that but, a few hours ago, he'd said she was his huckleberry. His best friend. His Doc Holliday to her Wyatt Earp.

Or should that be the other way around?

She didn't remember enough of the movie to know, and it didn't matter anyway. The quip had eased her misgivings when they stood above the town, evaluating its risks, and now it seemed a lie.

All their lives, Marsh had been the only person she could fully, completely trust. Without him, she was totally alone.

Chapter Four

Only a fool carries baggage that does him no good.
~ Family Code ~

To draw as little attention to herself as possible, Chaney wore a ball cap, sunglasses, and a lightweight gray pullover with denim shorts. By the time she'd made her third circuit of the festival's booths, she'd savored a huckleberry scone and sipped a huckleberry milkshake. The plump purple berry was definitely a new fave. By early afternoon, she'd browsed the bookstore, the candy store, three clothing stores, and a gift shop.

Without once crossing paths with Marsh.

He'd been gone when she got up that morning, and he hadn't answered her call to his burner phone. The panic knotting her stomach eased when she found his backpack tucked beside the couch, and she'd breathed a sigh of relief at the sight of the motorcycle still parked in the lodge's courtyard.

Even without his assistance as a distraction or backup, she'd had a profitable morning.

The second wallet she lifted, from an all-hat-and-no-cattle wannabe cowman, yielded around three hundred dollars and change, slightly less than the total from the three others she'd taken. She'd stashed the wallets, wiped clean of prints, in separate trash cans set out especially for the festival.

The aroma of grilled meat drew Chaney to check out the menu board at the Chamber of Commerce's food tent. Cheeseburgers, hotdogs, and brats. Pulled pork. Fries and onion rings.

Before she could decide, her last pigeon approached the tent. The thirty-something woman had been too engrossed in sniffing the candles at one of the booths to notice the nimble fingers slipping into her open bag. Though she doubted the woman recognized her, Chaney immediately crossed the street.

And found herself outside the Copper Hart Café.

She removed her sunglasses and entered the coffee shop. Less than a third of the tables were unoccupied, and she quickly claimed one that allowed her a view of the room plus a clear path to the rear exit. She placed the book on Montana's myths and mysteries she'd purchased in her role as tourist on the table and joined the short line at the counter. Instead of Liz Stiller, whom Chaney and Marsh had met yesterday afternoon, a thirty-ish woman with dark, curly hair was taking the orders.

When it was her turn, Chaney ordered a lettuce wrap and homemade chips from the limited menu, plus lemonade with lavender syrup.

"How about a huckleberry tartlet for dessert?" The woman gestured toward a nearby tray of tiny pastries with a rich, purple filling. They were identical to the tartlets available on the lodge's morning buffet. "I baked them myself."

Chaney widened her eyes. "I had one for breakfast. It was delicious."

"You must be staying at the Larkspur. Amelia is one of my favorite customers." The woman eased into a conspiratorial smile, and she lowered her voice. "Though don't let my other customers know that."

"Your secret is safe with me." Chaney glanced at the woman's name tag. "Your name is Delaney?"

"That's right. Delaney Hutchins."

"It's an unusual name. A pretty one," she hastened to add. She kept to herself that Delaney was also her middle name. *Chaney Delaney Rose.* How she'd hated the sing-song rhyme as a child. Now it appeared as a surname on one of her fake IDs.

She gestured toward the tartlets. "I'll take two of those, please. Could I have them to go?"

"Absolutely." Delaney totaled the order and Chaney handed over a pilfered twenty. "Are you enjoying the festival?"

"Very much."

"Glad to hear it." She handed Chaney her change and then fixed her beverage. After adding the lavender syrup to the lemonade, she garnished the drink with a rosemary sprig and a thin lemon wheel. "Here you go. Your order will be out soon."

Chaney thanked her and returned to her table. After settling in the padded seat, she savored the refreshing beverage. She'd enjoyed the huckleberry shake, but this lemonade and lavender concoction tasted even better.

While she waited, she opened the paperback and skimmed the table of contents. She'd almost finished reading the introduction when a teen wearing a burgundy polo shirt with the Copper Hart logo arrived with her wrap and chips.

She tried to focus on the first myth in the book, a story about gold stolen from a stagecoach, while eating her meal. Though she sometimes read the same paragraph three or more times, she needed the book as a shield, a way to protect herself from being noticed by the other diners even as she took a furtive read on them.

The teens in the corner, who only had eyes for each other. Three women sharing laughs and gossip in the comfy leather chairs near the front window.

On the opposite wall beneath several framed landscapes, two tables were pushed together to accommodate what appeared to be indulgent grandparents, loving parents, two young sons, and a toddler in a high chair. She wore a pink-and-white polka dot bow clipped to her fine, downy hair.

The toddler giggled, flashing deep dimples, as her dad gently dabbed her chin with a napkin. A physical ache pressed against Chaney's heart, a deep longing for what she wanted so much but never had.

Chaney finished the first chapter of the book at about the same time she finished the delicious wrap. As she considered eating one of the tartlets, Marsh entered the café. He scanned the room, smiled as he met Chaney's gaze, and sauntered to the table. She closed the book as he sat in the chair nearest her own.

He gestured at the folded brown paper holding the last of the chips. "May I?"

She slid them toward him. "Since when do you ask first?"

"Since you zagged when I zigged." He held her gaze, his own nearly inscrutable, as he popped a chip into his mouth. "Umm. That's good."

"Real potatoes. You can finish them." She played with the rosemary sprig, gently stirring the ice in her glass. Apologies weren't forbidden within the family, but woe to the weakling who offered one. Marsh wasn't about to say he regretted taking the ledger. She couldn't forgive him for placing them in even greater danger.

No matter how deep the cut, saying "I'm sorry" was never going to happen. Not on either side.

Marsh folded his arms on the table "Good book?"

"Good enough."

He pressed his lips together and averted his gaze. The uncomfortable silence pressed between them. He was close enough for Chaney to touch his arm, but he might as well have been on the opposite side of the room. She turned her attention back to the little girl in the high chair.

A moment later, a fortyish man wearing a county sheriff's uniform entered the café. He removed his tan Stetson, his gaze sweeping the room, as he approached the counter. Probably a star football player back in the day, Chaney deduced, judging by his muscular build, still-handsome looks, and confident gait.

She consciously relaxed her shoulders and sat back in her chair, the posture of a self-assured young woman with nothing to hide. Marsh popped the last chip in his mouth and brushed his hands on a napkin.

"Enjoying the Jubilee?" he asked, pretending to ignore the sheriff, who was now talking to Liz Stiller. She'd joined Delaney at the counter a few minutes before. Like the day before, the café owner wore her thick, red hair in a long braid.

"I've had a good time," Chaney replied. In other words, she'd made a respectable score.

"Me, too. Tons of fun, in fact." He stretched to pull something from his pocket when Liz stepped out from behind the counter. "I got you a souvenir."

A bell rang and Marsh stopped reaching into his pocket.

"Hey, everyone," Liz called out. "Could I have your attention please? Sheriff Chandler has something important to share."

The sheriff positioned himself so he could see most of the diners. "Afternoon, folks. Sorry to interrupt your delicious meals, and I promise this will only take a minute. We've had a few reports of lost wallets and disappearing cash. A couple of smart phones, too. It's sad to think we have thieves in our midst, but an event like this can be too great a temptation for those without a conscience. So keep an eye on your valuables and, if you see anything suspicious, let the sheriff's office know about it."

"You got any suspects, Sheriff?" asked a balding man with a middle-aged paunch. He wore a gaudy gold watch and a ruby pinkie ring. Chaney's fingers flexed as if itching to possess his wallet.

The sheriff paused and looked straight at the man while maintaining a non-threatening expression. "We wouldn't want 'em to know we did if we do, now would we, Carlton? That wouldn't be too smart."

Chaney suppressed a grin. Interesting how Sheriff Chandler's accent had broadened and his vocabulary changed when he replied to the man. He obviously didn't have much respect for the guy.

Even though it was a fair question, the sheriff's "I'm just a dumb cop" ploy made Carlton appear foolish for asking.

Though that ploy meant the sheriff was sharp. Chaney hoped she and Marsh wouldn't have any personal encounters with him before they left town tomorrow.

"Only asking," Carlton said. "I heard tell someone took off with the cash box from the   Big Sky Children's Foundation face-painting booth."

Chaney's stomach clenched at that news. The Old Man wouldn't care if they'd stolen from the group. He'd probably applaud them for doing so. But she and Marsh had a code of their own separate from the family code. After their foster care experiences, they'd vowed that children and any charities catering to them were off limits.

If Marsh's "tons of fun" included robbing the organization . . .

She took a deep breath and met his gaze for an almost telepathic conversation, the kind often attributed to twins or long-married couples. His eyes denied any involvement. Hers said she didn't trust him. How could she, after she'd found the ledger? He blinked and turned away.

"Be assured we're investigating that theft, and we will find the perpetrator." Sheriff Chandler's expression was grave as he scanned the diners. When his gaze lingered on Marsh, Chaney pressed the side of her foot against his as a silent warning. He casually opened the to-go box holding the tartlets and bit into one as if he didn't have a care in the world.

"Like I said, folks," the sheriff continued, holding out his hands as if to extend a hospitable welcome, "enjoy yourselves, but don't be careless." With that, he returned to the counter.

Trained all their lives not to draw attention to themselves, Chaney and Marsh stayed in their seats as the hum of conversation grew around them. When the trio of women gathered their things to leave, Chaney did the same. After she returned the book to its bag, along with the tartlets, Marsh tossed their trash and followed her out the door.

Neither spoke a word as they mingled among the festivalgoers and kept their fingers out of the pockets of strangers.

The crowds thinned as Chaney and Marsh approached the Larkspur Lodge. As they climbed the front steps, he gestured toward the end of the verandah, where a cushioned swing hung from the porch rafters. "We need to talk."

"Agreed."

She sensed him darting a glance her way but didn't acknowledge it. They rarely disagreed on anything more important than what to fix for supper and never engaged in a no-holds-barred argument. They'd witnessed too many to exult in drama overload.

Everything was different now.

They were different now. Paranoid. On edge. Suspicious.

Weaknesses that needed to be squashed before one of them made an irreversible mistake.

Marsh plopped onto the swing and then planted his feet to keep it steady until Chaney settled in the corner. She tucked her legs beneath her and hugged a denim pillow to her chest as a balm to ease her troubled heart.

"I could've taken that face-painting money." Marsh pushed the swing back and forth with his foot. "Can't say I wasn't tempted, especially since all the adults there were more focused on the kids than the cash. But I didn't do it."

"I want to believe that."

"You can. I got my score the same way you got yours. One situationally unaware pigeon at a time. I tapped out at three."

Chaney held up four fingers and let out a resigned sigh. "Maybe we should get out while the getting's good."

Instead of answering, he unbuttoned the side pocket on his cargo pants and held out a gold-plated object. "I found this at that antique store across from the Pony Express."

"We agreed no tokens."

"It was an easy lift," he said dismissively. "What's done is done."

At first, the object appeared to be an oversized pocket watch. But when Chaney snapped open the lid, she found a cheap compass inside. With his detailed knowledge of such items, Marsh had to know it was practically worthless.

"What was the price tag on this thing?"

"Five times what it should have been." His lighthearted tone was edged with smugness. "You could say I kept the proprietor of that sham establishment from taking advantage of a naïve customer."

"Why take the risk?" As soon as Chaney asked the question, she intuited the answer. Her heart dropped to her stomach. "You're planning a fraud swap."

Irritation hardened his features. "What if I am? We need more than a pickpocket's pittance to survive."

First the journal and now a blatant disregard of their code? "We can't do it. Not to Amelia. We have a roof over our heads thanks to her taking a chance on us."

Marsh's lips pressed into a thin line, and his jaw was set in that familiar expression Chaney knew all too well. "I spent time on a computer at the library this morning. Her compass is worth a small fortune."

"You already have a buyer." A statement, not a question.

He shrugged. "Maybe two."

Chaney resisted the urge to smack him with the pillow. A feeling of helplessness washed over her, a sensation she hated with every fiber of her being. How dare he be so callous? So stubborn?

She met his gaze and searched his eyes. Her frustration with him melted into dread at the anxiety she detected beyond his harsh bravado.

Marsh must be more concerned about their future than he wanted her to know. Why else would he risk researching the compass on a public computer? Once Amelia discovered the switch, would Sheriff Chandler think to check those computers? If so, would he be able to recover the research history? To discover who was looking up the info?

Surely not. And even if, by the slimmest chance, he did, would it matter?

Amelia knew them under different names and had copies of their false IDs in her records. They'd be far, far away before the local authorities found out their true identities—if they ever did.

Every member of the Old Man's family knew how to hide and disappear.

A shiver ran up her spine.

Except from him.

"I'm talking five figures," Marsh said quietly. "Once I close a deal, we can go wherever we want. North Pole. South Pole. Anywhere in between."

Chaney stared at the compass in her hand. It resembled Amelia's antique compass in size and shape. Even the shallow relief struck into the lid, a mountain range and locomotive, was similar though not nearly as finely crafted. A cheap replica of the genuine article, for sure.

Yet the eight-pointed star design of the compass itself, identical to the antique one, pointed them to freedom.

Marsh tapped the compass with his finger. "Will you do it?"

"Me?" She stared at him for a long minute. Of course, he expected her to make the swap. She was the Old Man's little sprite. His nimble one.

Marsh's eyes pleaded with her to say yes. The code they'd held to for so long insisted she say no.

Chaney clutched the gold-plated compass to her chest as she stood before the secretary desk in the wee hours of the morning. The security lights above the bar and a few dimly lit lamps cast strange shadows in the spacious lobby but also provided enough light to avoid bumping into the furniture.

Their disagreement on the porch had ended when Marsh insisted he'd make the swap if she didn't. In that heated moment, she'd told him to go for it. But when he started to leave their room, she snatched the compass from him. If he got caught, she'd never forgive herself.

Now he stood guard in the hall next to the mezzanine, poised to grab their bags and run if the swap went sideways. Otherwise, they'd get a few hours of sleep before hitting the road at dawn.

Chaney released a quiet breath then slowly opened the doors of the hutch. Thankfully, the hinges didn't squeak even a little bit. She hesitated, her focus on the brass compass as she bit the inside of her lip. A slow exhale and she deftly removed the antique, then slipped it into her pocket. As soon as the fake compass, its lid wide open as the other had been, was secure on the stand, she closed and latched the hutch's doors.

When she turned around, a shadow moved along the stone hearth. She clapped her hand over her mouth and froze.

As the shadow came toward her, it moved into the circle of light from a nearby floor lamp.

Bramble!

Chaney dropped to her knees as the terrier bounced into her arms. He whimpered while giving sweet puppy kisses. She shifted to sit on the pine floor, and Bramble leaned his body against her chest. While holding him close, she scanned the lobby's shadows for Amelia and held her breath to listen for any sound beyond the ticking of the mantel clock.

Nothing.

Though if Amelia showed up now, Chaney had a ready excuse. Insomnia had sent her downstairs to raid the refrigerator but, before she reached the kitchen, she'd stumbled onto Bramble.

Who wouldn't like her so much if he knew what she'd done.

"I didn't want to," she said, keeping her voice low. "Someone's after us, Marsh and me. He's very dangerous, and we have to get as far away from him as we can."

She paused to swallow the growing lump in her throat. "If he finds us, I'm not sure what he'll do."

Bramble peered at her with his large brown eyes and snuggled even closer as if trying to get inside her skin. Chaney caressed his wiry fur and bent her head over his.

"Please don't tell on me." She slowly rose to her feet as the burden of the compass weighed heavy against her thigh. Despite the risk, she pulled it out and examined it under the light of the floor lamp while Bramble leaned against her leg.

Like other valued objects Chaney had examined as part of her education, the compass exuded authenticity and quality. The minute scratches and tiny signs of wear added to its value. This compass had been *used* by someone, most likely a surveyor, as Marsh believed, when this western region opened up to settlers.

She opened the lid and studied the compass's eight-pointed star. No matter how she rotated the compass, the needle insisted on pointing true north. As she started to close the lid, the lamp light revealed deep scratches along the lid's lower lip. By moving the compass first one way and then another, she finally deciphered the engraving.

"'The Way,'" she read aloud to Bramble. "'Jn 14:6.' I think that means John in the Bible. But I have no idea what that verse says, do you?"

Bramble responded by lying on her feet.

An engraved Bible verse on the compass made sense, Chaney supposed. People back then were more religious than today. She had a vague notion of who John might be because of the few times she'd attended church while in foster care. If she remembered right, he lived alone and ate grasshoppers until Jesus came along. Wasn't there something about tying shoes?

With a *who cares* shrug, she shut the lid. A nineteenth-century surveyor might find comfort from the inscription. But without knowing the meaning of "The Way," it had nothing to do with her. Or her choices.

A burning sensation brushed against her fingertips as she shoved the compass into her pocket.

Chaney preceded Marsh into the Hideout and stood in the center of the room, her arms crossed, while he locked the door.

"Took you long enough," he grumbled. "I was about to come after you."

Those were the first words either of them had spoken since she joined him at the top of the stairs.

He held out his hand. "Let me have it."

"Give me the ledger."

"What are you going to do? Mail it back with an apology?" He shifted to a high-pitched mimicking tone. "'Sorry, Grandpa. Didn't mean to run off with this.' Do you think he'd welcome you back? Let bygones be bygones?"

Good-humored teasing she could take. But not this cruel condescension. Not from Marsh.

"You've changed."

"I've gotten smarter. You need to do the same."

She glared at him as she smacked the compass against his palm.

He glanced at it, then returned her glare, his eyes dark with anger. "You chickened out?"

"I made the swap." She straightened her posture and lifted her chin. Though her insides were as squishy as gelatin, she refused to be intimidated. Or to allow him to bully her into tarnishing her conscience any more than it already was. Their code, unconventional as it was, at least gave them guidance. Some might even say a moral compass—their own version of true north.

While downstairs in the lobby, she'd determined to stick to it. If the Old Man had done the same, she and Marsh would still be in LA instead of shearing sheep in a sleepy little town.

Instead of arguing, they'd still be each other's huckleberry.

She averted her gaze. Despite her momentary bravado, she couldn't endure the pain of betrayal lurking behind the outrage in his eyes. "Then I swapped them again. It was the right thing to do."

Marsh's jaw clenched and he slammed the gold-plated compass to the floor. It landed at Chaney's feet with a clatter as the lid and the glass protecting the compass broke into separate pieces.

She looked up in time to see his expression flicker with regret but, an instant later, tension hardened his features again.

He jerked his backpack from the floor and slipped his arms through the straps. When Chaney started toward her bag, he placed a hand on it to stop her and shook his head. "I can't trust you anymore," he said, his voice soft but firm.

"You can't trust *me*? How can I trust *you*?"

"Because I took that ledger?" He sucked in air. "I took it to protect us."

"And now you're leaving without me?"

"That's exactly what I'm doing." His eyes softened. "As much as the Old Man wants to find us, he wants the ledger even more. As long as I have it, you're better off without me."

"You don't believe that. You can't."

Marsh's mouth quirked into a half frown, half smile as he visibly relaxed his shoulders. "Maybe I'm better off without you."

Chaney couldn't have been more surprised if he'd slapped her. Hot tears stung, but she refused to cry. She hated that he had the power to make her feel so vulnerable and small. That he could so easily walk away. Apparently their close-as-siblings bond was nothing more than a façade. As inauthentic as the pieces of the broken compass scattered along the floor.

"Then go," she said as if she no longer cared what he did and despising the quiver in her voice that gave her away.

Without saying another word, Marsh slipped into the hallway. Chaney stared at the closed door, half expecting it to open again. For Marsh to stick his head around the door and tell her to come on. They were burning daylight. Another movie quote, this time from John Wayne's *The Cowboys*.

But the seconds ticked by, and the door stayed shut.

Chapter Five

What's done is done.
~ The Family Code ~

Chaney eventually fell into a fitful sleep on the couch, where she faced sweat-inducing, claustrophobic nightmares. Only a few hours later, the morning light intruding through the slender crack in the window curtains awakened her. Groggy from tossing and turning, it took a moment for her to get her bearings. To accept that the hurtful scene with Marsh hadn't been a bad dream.

She crossed to the bedroom door and rested her hand on the knob.

Please let him be inside.

He wasn't.

He'd left her, and she needed to leave, too, even though she had no idea where to go. Not that the destination mattered. She couldn't think about *where* and she couldn't think about Marshall. Right now, her sole focus needed to be on finding a suitable vehicle to hot-wire. Something ordinary that wouldn't be missed for a while.

Since Marsh had already paid for their second night and told Amelia they'd be checking out today, Chaney slipped down the back stairs and out the courtyard exit. Just in case the motorcycle was where they'd left it.

It wasn't.

Blinking back tears, Chaney hoisted her backpack onto her shoulders and stared across the street at the river. Maybe instead of a car, she could borrow a boat. The Old Man wouldn't likely think to look for her on a river. Nor would he expect she and Marsh had separated. After all, loyalty to family came first.

Except when it didn't.

Chaney swiped at her cheek as another of the Old Man's infamous quotes resounded in her brain: *You don't need to outrun the bear. Only your partner.*

Marsh's words quickly followed: *You're better off without me.* Was that him giving her the chance to outrun him? Except he'd also said he was better off without her. How could that ever be true?

"Good morning, Carrie."

Chaney startled and quickly turned at Amelia's unexpected greeting. She stood near the courtyard door with a watering can in her hand and sympathy in her eyes. As she stepped closer, her lips pressed into a sad smile.

"Though that's not your name, is it?" Her steady gaze seemed to pierce into Chaney's soul. "I know fake IDs when I see them. I also know the look of someone on the run. Until a few years ago, I saw it every time I looked in the mirror."

Chaney stiffened her shoulders and lifted her chin. "I don't know what you're talking about."

"Mark—or should I say Marsh?—is gone."

For one of the rare times in her life, Chaney couldn't hide her surprise or feign ignorance. Amelia must have overheard her talking to Bramble.

Amelia set the watering can on a nearby table, then stood beside Chaney while staring toward the river. "He left before sunrise. Did he know someone saw him hanging around the face-painting booth and gave his description to the sheriff?"

"He didn't take that cash box."

"I know. The thief turned out to be one of the high school volunteers. He took it when his shift was over. But Marsh didn't know that. Did he?"

Whether he did or not didn't matter. The news that he'd told her the truth lifted a weight from Chaney's heart that was heavier than she'd realized. As much as she'd wanted to believe his claim of innocence, she'd still doubted him. And he'd known it. Maybe that's why he'd abandoned her.

Amelia shifted to face Chaney and waited to speak until their eyes met. "That surveyor's compass doesn't belong to me. It's an heirloom in the proper meaning of the word, just like the mirror behind the bar, and even the bar itself. They belong to the Larkspur, not to the owner of the lodge. Thank you for not taking it."

Heat burned Chaney's cheeks. From their initial meeting, she'd suspected Amelia of being perceptive. But nothing had prepared her for this feeling of being turned inside out and completely exposed. She opened her mouth to speak, but what could she say? "You're welcome" hardly seemed appropriate.

"You made the right choice." Amelia's kind smile exuded compassion. "Now you need to make another. The Hideout is yours as long as you need it. But if, for whatever reason, you can't stay"—sudden tears shimmered in Amelia's eyes—"then I'll get you a bus ticket to wherever you want to go."

Chaney's eyes widened at the unexpected offer. Shifting her focus to the lodge, she fingered the pieces of the broken compass she'd stuffed in her pocket before leaving the Hideout.

What would it be like to live in the Larkspur? To have her own tiny apartment as her home? She could help Amelia around the lodge. Bake huckleberry tartlets with Delaney. Maybe even get a job at the Pony Express Pizzeria. Better yet, the bookstore.

A cold shiver wracked her body, and she adjusted the backpack weighing down her shoulders. The compass's black needle, bent by the impact with the floor, could no longer point north. It couldn't tell her the way she should go. But in the depths of her heart, she knew the choice she had to make.

Though touched to her core by Amelia's generous offer, staying at the lodge could be dangerous. If the Old Man traced Chaney to Hartwell, he'd be merciless to anyone who tried to help her.

She cleared her throat as she turned back to Amelia and willed her voice to stay strong. "I have to go."

Amelia held her gaze for a few seconds and then nodded. "The inscription on the compass refers to Jesus. He is the Way, the only True North. You can trust Him to guide you."

Chaney turned to stare at the sunpennies sparkling on the river. "I can't trust anyone."

After settling into her seat on the surprisingly clean bus, Chaney half wished she'd had the courage to stay in the Montana town. What was it Marsh had said? A place of whispered secrets, fake friendships, and petty intrigue. In a weird way, that sounded appealing.

But when a gal spends most of her life on the run, running becomes a way of life. She doubted she'd ever settle anywhere.

Especially not when her huckleberry friend was no longer at her side.

She blinked away tears as the bus left the boarding area and waved goodbye to Amelia, who'd driven her to the station. Before they parted, she'd hugged Chaney and whispered, "You always have a home here. And you'll always be in my prayers."

As the bus rumbled away from the Huckleberry Jubilee festivities, Chaney rested her forehead against the window. That long-ago foster family with the Saint Bernard, who'd taken her to church, had promised to pray for her, too. Did they still, after all these years? Would Amelia keep her promise? Even if she did, would it make a difference?

When the bus stopped at a traffic light, the gunning of an engine caught Chaney's attention. On the side street, Marsh sat astride the Harley, his expression hidden within the dark helmet.

Her hand pressed against the window, her first impulse willing him to wait for her. An impulse she squashed as she drew back her hand and then waved goodbye.

In response, Marsh gunned the engine again, made a U-turn, and sped away.

Chaney slumped back in her seat and pulled the broken compass from her pocket. No matter how she rotated it, the needle didn't move.

Amelia's words whispered in her heart: *You can trust Him to guide you.*

Chaney wasn't sure she could. At least not on her own, and not when everyone she'd ever trusted had either betrayed or abandoned her. Unless Amelia was right. What if He was the only True North?

A Note from the Author

Dear Friends,

Chaney Delaney Rose has been living in my heart for several years now. Her character "spark" was inspired by one of my favorite literary moments—the scene in *Les Miserables* where the priest pretends he gave the stolen silver to Jean Valjean. A similar scene takes place in *The Mischief Thief*, the first story I wrote about my young con artist without a conscience and the minister without a ministry who befriends her.

She was also inspired by one of my favorite TV shows. *Leverage*, which originally aired from 2008 to 2012, is about thieves and grifters who help those in trouble. Their motto is "Sometimes the bad guys make the best good guys."

In this prequel story, Chaney takes the first step toward breaking free from her family's grifting legacy and becoming a "good gal." Her offbeat path will eventually lead her to the only One who can take the broken compasses from our clinging hands and point them to True North—to Jesus Himself as our Lord and Savior.

He redeems our pasts, no matter how unlovely they may be.

Thank you for riding into Hartwell with Chaney and stepping onto the bus with her as she leaves her past behind.

Johnnie

Acknowledgements

This story never would have been written if Stacy Monson and I hadn't visited Red Lodge, Montana, last summer.

Fun fact—that's where we were when the Mosaic Collection authors got together via Zoom to brainstorm ideas for this anthology. From the get-go, we both knew we wanted our *Off the Beaten Path* stories to take place in a fictional version of this great little town.

Where I tasted huckleberries for the first time and had lavender lemonade with a sprig of rosemary at the Hidden Basin.

So a mountain range of thanks to Stacy for this adventure.

Thanks, too, to Deb and Gerrit Elkink for the side trip to Yellowstone. Such a fun day!

As always, my deepest gratitude to my Mosaic sisters who are a bountiful blessing. I'm more grateful than I can say that God brought us together in this indie adventure.

Last but never least, I thank my Heavenly Father for my supportive and fun-loving family: Bethany & Justin Jett; Jeremy, Jed, & Josey Jett; Jill & Jacob Lancour; Kaydi & Presley Lancour; and Nate & Bre Donley. (You're my heart.)

ABOUT THE AUTHOR

Johnnie Alexander, author of over forty works of fiction, writes award-winning stories of enduring love and quiet courage. Her historical and contemporary novels blend compelling characters, enduring romance, and gripping suspense.

A sometime hermit and occasional vagabond who most often kicks off her shoes in Florida, Johnnie cherishes cozy family times and enjoys long road trips. Readers are invited to discover glimpses of grace and timeless truth in her stories.

Connect with her at https://johnnie-alexander.com.

TITLES BY JOHNNIE ALEXANDER

Stories Past and Present.

THE MOSAIC COLLECTION: NOVELS
The Mischief Thief

THE MOSAIC COLLECTION: NOVELLAS
Journey of the Heart (Unseen Valor #1)
Beneath a Rare Blue Moon (Unseen Valor #2)

THE MOSAIC COLLECTION: ANTHOLOGY STORIES
"The Caretaker's Christmas" in *Hope is Born*
"A Stranger Comes to Springlight" in *Before Summer's End*
"Paper Trail" in *Song of Grace*
"Souvenir in My Pocket" in *All Things New*
"Christmas Comes to Springlight" in *A Thrill in the Air*

WORLD WAR II NOVELS
The Cryptographer's Dilemma

Echoes of War Series
Where Treasure Hides
When Memory Whispers (Mosaic)

MISTY WILLOW SERIES
Where She Belongs
When Love Arrives
What Hope Remembers

NOVELLAS
The Healing Promise (Courageous Brides Collection)
Journey of the Heart (Erie Canal Brides Collection)
Match You Like Crazy (Resort to Romance Series)
Blue Moon (Homefront Heroines)
The Thistle Rings (Love's a Mystery in Gnaw Bone, Indiana)
The Potter's Design (Love's a Mystery in Crooksville, Ohio)
Three Dog Knight (Mystery of Cobble Hill Farms Series)
A Will and a Way (Mystery of Cobble Hill Farms Series)
Pride, Prejudice, and Pitfalls (Mystery of Cobble Hill Farms Series)

SHORT STORIES
"Beneath the Christmas Star" (in *A Cup of Christmas Cheer – Tales of Joy and Wonder for the Holidays*)

ANNIE'S FICTION

Novels in the following series:

Victorian Mansion Flower Shop Mysteries

Hearts of Amish Country

Inn at Magnolia Harbor

Sweet Intrigue Mysteries

Love in Lancaster Country

Mysteries of Aspen Falls

Love in Sandcastle Cove

Thank You For Reading

We hope you enjoyed *Off the Beaten Path*, Mosaic's 2026 Summer anthology. If you did, please consider leaving a short review on Amazon, Goodreads, or BookBub. Positive reviews and word-of-mouth recommendations are so valuable and appreciated, as they honor an author and help other readers to find quality Christian fiction to read.

Thank you so much!